CASSEROLE SURPRISE

Barbara,

Life is full
of surprises. Enjoy!

Always,
Lorraine

Other books
By Lorraine M.Harris

Sunday Golf
After Bowling
Casserole Parade
Intuition (co-author, Deborah Seibert)
What Would You Do?

CASSEROLE SURPRISE

A Novel

Lorraine M. Harris
Author of *Casserole Parade*

iUniverse, Inc.
New York Lincoln Shanghai

Casserole Surprise

iUniverse books may be ordered through booksellers or by contacting:

iUniverse
2021 Pine Lake Road, Suite 100
Lincoln, NE 68512
www.iuniverse.com
1-800-Authors (1-800-288-4677)

Because of the dynamic nature of the Internet, any Web addresses or links contained in this book may have changed since publication and may no longer be valid.

This is a work of fiction. All of the characters, names, incidents, organizations, and dialogue in this novel are either the products of the author's imagination or are used fictitiously.

ISBN: 978-0-595-48378-5 (pbk)
ISBN: 978-0-595-60469-2 (ebk)

Printed in the United States of America

Acknowledgements

Thanks are in order for those who continue to support and help me as I worked through my book. God, from Whom all blessings flow; my husband, Lamont and my daughters, Nicole and Natalie who I appreciate for their unconditional love and support. They are my biggest fans.

Mrs. Frank Brennan—Diane, is one of my oldest and dearest friends. She has been in my life for over thirty-five years and has seen me through many trials and tribulations.

Mrs. Leon Burns—Debbie, is a friend I met while working for the Department of Transportation. For years, Debbie listened patiently as I read books to her that I had written. She gave me encouragement and feedback.

To produce an error-free manuscript is close to impossible, even with expert advice. Any errors I've made were of the mind and not of the heart. Yoby Brazo encouraged me to ask Don Whipp for his help. Don did an unbelievable job in providing me with outstanding editorial guidance and feedback. Words cannot express how grateful I am for Don taking the time to provide his expertise during the development of Casserole Surprise.

Thanks to Gloria Frye who is one of my biggest fans. She previewed an unedited copy of Casserole Surprise and provided me with inside from a reader's perspective. I appreciate the time she spent reading Casserole Parade in an effort to make it a better book.

CHAPTER 1

Diane Benson was groggy, confused, and disoriented. She was on her back, motionless and numb. Her body restricted by something or someone. Her shoulders and feet pinned down. She was able to move her head to the left and to the right.

"Where was she?"

The intense light beamed through the windows, causing her to squint. After blinking several times, her eyes adjusted to the sun's brightness. As her eyes darted back and forth, nothing seemed familiar.

She screamed, "Help!" She paused and listened. "Someone, please, help me!"

A sharp-edged object seemed to be cutting deep into her left side. Was it a blade of a knife? Beads of perspiration formed on her forehead and upper lip.

Diane ran her tongue over her lips. Her voice was coarse from her dry throat. Again, she pleaded, "Help! Someone! Please, help me!"

She glimpsed around the room and said, "Focus, Diane. Focus." A slight chuckle escaped her. So much had happened that she had forgotten where she was and why.

The discomforting, piercing throbbing in her side had not disappeared. She changed positions, trying to relax. Diane placed her hand on the sensitive spot that hurt, praying the pain would go away. Taking air in and releasing it, she waited for the sensation to stop. Instead, it began traveling from side to side. To add to her discomfort, a prickly needle-like tingling started in her stomach.

Up until this moment, she thought she had the ability to endure high levels of physical pain, but this was like nothing she ever experienced. Wrenching, she moaned. Slowly, she inhaled several deep breaths and exhaled. Nothing seemed to help.

Tentatively, she swung her legs over the side of the bed and pushed herself to her feet. A wave of lightheadedness and a stabbing pain caused her to double over. She clutched her middle and stood motionless.

Through clenched teeth, she pleaded, "Please God, make the pain go away." She eased back down. Swallowing the lump in her throat she bit her lip and blinked hard. "This was not the time for tears."

The hammering rat-a-tat-tat in her head made her woozy. Diane closed her eyes, trying to focus on something other than the pain. She began the breathing exercises that were taught in the yoga classes she had taken. As her mind drifted into a meditative state, the past several years flashed through her mind.

Recent events of her life resembled a roller coaster. Daily she feared it was going to derail. Fred, her husband of twenty odd years started it all when he announced he no longer wanted to be married.

She stopped and admonished herself. Could she blame Fred for her life changes? You bet she could. She held him responsible for the divorce, her early retirement, and relocation to a Florida retirement community called The Villages.

That had set everything in motion and now she was trapped into a life of lies. All the lies she had told to her children—Freddie and Donna—relatives, friends, and neighbors made her life even more complicated. Most recently, she told everyone that she was on a 21-day cruise. The truth—she was a registered guest of the Hampton Inn and Suites located on County Road 466.

Her friend, Lisa was the one person who knew where and why she was there. Without her help, Diane could not have been able to keep her secret.

Lisa was more than a confidant; she was Diane's connection to the outside world. To ease Diane's burdens, Lisa took charge of every aspect of her life. To add to her misery, Lisa had been caught up in her web of lies by answering questions from relatives and friends, checking on her house, and bringing her food, magazines, and newspapers. Gratitude was the only word she could think of when she thought about Lisa.

As Diane took in a quick breath of air, she noticed the pain had disappeared. She opened her eyes. The real test would be when she tried to stand. "Thank God!" she exclaimed.

She started laughing until her eyes watered. Why didn't it occur to her sooner? How many people could eat two hefty bowls of white navy beans without the body rebelling?

Feeling better, she would shower and dress. She glanced at the clock. Preoccupied with the pain, she had forgotten about her doctor's appointment. She needed to hurry because Lisa would arrive soon.

Stepping out of the shower, Diane grabbed a towel and dried off. She gasped. The sharp razor-like jabs had returned but with the intensity of swift-like punches, one after another. The deep sensation was crippling as she struggled to put her dress over her head.

Diane bit her lip hard, trying to quiet the sobs. She took baby steps to retrieve her cell phone. She punched in the number and listened intently to the ring tone.

After three rings, she grew impatient. "Please answer." Finally, the 911 Operator answered.

"My name is Diane Benson." Diane spoke distinctly and urgently. "This is an emergency. Please send an ambulance to The Hampton Inn and Suites on County Road 466. I'm in Room 202."

"What is the emergency, ma'am?"

The phone went dead.

CHAPTER 2

Lisa Henderson heard the high-pitched sound of the ambulance siren before spotting it in her rear-view mirror. She changed lanes and slowed her speed as the emergency vehicle passed.

As Lisa waited to make the left hand turn into the Hampton Inn, another ambulance sped by. When she made the turn, she saw what might have been one of the ambulances.

Lisa parked her car and got out. Her stomach tensed. The closer she walked to the hotel entry, the more uneasy she became.

Entering the hotel's lobby, Lisa backed out of the way as the paramedics approached her rolling a stretcher. Her hand flew to her mouth. The woman's face that was covered with an oxygen mask and an IV line running from her arm was Diane.

Lisa's eyes clouded over as her heart pounded fiercely. She grabbed the gurney, causing its forward motion to halt.

"Please get out of the way!" The paramedic barked.

Lisa touched Diane's hand and choked on her words as she whispered. "I'm sorry, I was late." Diane did not respond as Lisa walked fast alongside the stretcher.

"Diane, can you hear me?"

No answer. "Is she okay?" Lisa asked the paramedic.

"We have to get her to the hospital."

"Is it okay if I ride with her?" She lied and added, "I'm her sister."

"Okay, but hurry."

Once in the ambulance, the siren blared at full blast but it seemed to be at a standstill. Bumper to bumper traffic slowed their progress. As the ambulance maneuvered from lane to lane, the paramedic driving yelled, "There's an accident on 27/441."

Confused, Lisa asked, "Where are we going?"

"We're going to the Leesburg Hospital."

"Why aren't we going to The Villages Hospital?"

"Doctor's orders."

Lisa watched Diane's anguished eyes. Lisa glanced at her watch; worried lines formed across her forehead. From her estimation, it would take at least fifteen minutes before they would arrive at Leesburg's Hospital.

Diane's fingernails dug into Lisa's hand. Gently, she touched Diane's hand. Sympathetic eyes and a soothing voice, Lisa murmured, "Everything's going to be okay."

Diane opened her mouth. Her response was a loud whimpering groan and a contorted face to match. Her fingernails dug deeper into Lisa's hand.

Lisa shot a fierce angry stare at the paramedic. If only they had gone to The Villages' Hospital, she thought, "Suppose something goes wrong? How would she explain all of this to Diane's children?"

"Oh Lord. Help Diane."

"Wh … Wh … What's wr-wr-wrong?" Diane uttered.

Patting her hand, Lisa said, "Nothing. Nothing's wrong." She did not know what else to say as she heard herself repeating, "Everything's going to be okay."

Closely, Lisa watched the paramedic as he took Diane's blood pressure. The brooding expression and the deep lines across his forehead caused Lisa to bite her lower lip.

Lisa cautioned herself not to jump to conclusions. She straightened her shoulders, willed herself not to cry and to remain calm. But then the paramedic words caused Lisa to tremble.

"Mrs. Benson, can you hear me?"

Diane was non-responsive. Again, he asked, "Mrs. Benson, can you hear me?" Diane's erratic breathing sounded similar to a wheezing asthmatic.

After several minutes, Diane nodded her head.

When the paramedic finished taking Diane's blood pressure, he dialed the hospital. Lisa strained to hear his whispered words. "Have a Code Blue Team ready to meet us."

Lisa's lower lip quivered. Even though she never worked in the health care profession, she watched enough TV medical shows to understand the term, "Code Blue."

She closed her eyes and prayed silently. *"Lord please, protect Diane. Don't let anything happen to her or the baby."*

As Lisa opened her eyes, the ambulance pulled into the hospital emergency entrance. The minute it stopped, the doors flew open and the paramedics lifted the stretcher out and rolled it quickly through the open hospital doors.

CHAPTER 3

❀

The paramedics pushed the stretcher swiftly through the hospital open doors and down the corridor. Lisa was close behind. A tug on her sleeve slowed her quick footsteps.

"Ma'am, you need to stop."

"I can't. I need to …"

A woman glared at Lisa and stood firmly. Her voice as well as her body was imposing.

"Ma'am, you can't go with Mrs. Benson. You need to follow me to the admitting desk. Some papers have to be completed."

"But I need to be with my fr—fr—fr—sister."

The woman persisted, "I understand, but the hospital policy states that specific admission papers must be completed for each patient admitted." Her voice softened. "Mrs. Benson is on her way to an examination room and will be seen by a doctor. I assure you, she's in good hands."

The paperwork could wait, Lisa thought. With a scowl on her face, she followed the military walking woman.

With the paperwork completed, the woman had a volunteer escort Lisa to a waiting room instead of taking her to Diane. Lisa wanted to protest but she figured it was just another hospital policy and she would be wasting her breath voicing her desire to see Diane.

Slowly, Lisa opened the door, and all eyes turned in her direction. When everyone realized Lisa was not hospital staff, they resumed what they were doing.

In the farthest corner of the room was an empty seat. When Lisa sat down, she lost control of all the emotions she had been holding inside. Her body shook as she sobbed softly. She made no attempt to stifle her weeping or to wipe her face.

Although Lisa had not spoken to Diane's attending physician, the bad feeling she had earlier continued to loom over her. When there were no more tears, she blew her nose, stood up and left the room. She wanted privacy when she called the one person she needed and that was her fiancé, Patrick Baylor.

"Hello."

"Pat-t-t …" Lisa's words were mixed with hiccupped sobs. She paused, trying to compose herself.

"Lisa, is that you?"

Sniveling, she murmured, "yes."

"What's wrong?"

"I'm at the Leesburg Hospital."

Patrick's voice was anxious, full of concern, "Are you okay?"

"I'm fine. It's not me. It's Diane."

Patrick interrupted her. "What's wrong?"

"Can you come to the hospital?" Lisa paused for a moment. "I'll explain everything to you then."

"Okay. I should be there in about twenty minutes." Before Patrick hug up talking to Lisa, he asked, "Are you sure you're okay?"

Lisa cleared her throat and managed to say, "Under the circumstances, I'm fine. Just hurry. I really need you."

Before the phone went dead, Patrick asked, "Where should I meet you?"

"What about the main entrance?"

"Okay, I'll see you shortly."

Lisa closed her cell phone. As she was about to put it away, she stopped. She pondered if she should break the promise she had made to Diane.

She dialed the number.

CHAPTER 4

While the phone rang, Lisa took a deep breath and prayed for strength. This was not a call she wanted to make but what choice had Diane left her? As the phone rang, she reminded herself that this was not the time to be disapproving, or to lose her temper.

"Hello. May I please speak to Sam Childers?"

"Yes. This is he."

"Hi. Sam, I'm Lisa Henderson. I don't know if you remember me, but I'm a friend of Diane Benson."

"Yes. I remember you." Sam wanted her to get right to the reason why she was calling. "What can I do for you?"

"Well … this is somewhat awkward but I'm calling about Diane."

"What about her?"

Lisa could not miss the terseness in his voice. She blew out air nosily. "She's in the hospital and …"

Sam interrupted, "I'm sorry but … why are you calling me?"

A flutter in Lisa's stomach cautioned her not to react, remain calm. But she growled as she asked, "whom else should I be calling?"

"I don't know, maybe, her children."

Silence invaded the phone. Lisa grabbed her middle, unable to ignore the strong overpowering feeling. A swirl of emotions bubbled up inside her. She did not know whether to be angry, sad, or frustrated.

Lisa shook her head. She loved Diane like a sister, but these past months resembled a soap opera with all the unexpected day-to-day drama. In addition, Diane's stresses had caused Lisa's blood pressure to be at an all time high. Once again, Diane had put her in a position of having to do what she should have done herself.

"Lisa, are you still there?" Sam's voice was full of annoyance.

"Yes" was all Lisa could utter. While she pondered over what to say, she wondered how much he knew.

"Do you have any idea why Diane might be in the hospital?"

"No. I don't. That's why I'm surprised you're calling me. I mean I haven't seen or talked to Diane in months."

Lisa took a deep breath. "Well … I don't know any other way to say this, but Diane's in the hospital."

"Okay, but again, why call me?"

Lisa knew she couldn't drag this out any longer as she whispered. "She's having a baby." Her voice was a bit louder. "She's having your baby."

Sam blinked, shaking his head. "There must be a mistake." Rather than respond immediately, he thought back to the last time he saw Diane. They had gone to the doctor to discuss an abortion. After that day, he assumed she must have had it and that explained the reason she had refused his calls and the end of their relationship.

"Sam, are you still there?"

"Yes, but … I'm confused and don't know what to say."

"I think I understand and I'm sorry I had to be the one to break the news to you. But right now, I think you need to come to the hospital. If there are any decisions to be made about Diane or the baby, I think you should be here."

"Why is that?" He snapped. As he continued his voice harsh. "Diane has done a pretty good job of making her own decisions. Why include me now?"

Sam waited for an answer. Tension crept up the back of his neck. Before Lisa responded, he was about to say something else but stopped. He couldn't continue to direct his anger at her. It wasn't her fault.

After a long thoughtful moment, Lisa wondered, "Where do I begin?" Carefully, she chose her words. "I know that Diane should have told you about keeping the baby but nothing can change that now. I think she would want you here."

"Then why didn't she call me?"

Frustrated, Lisa no longer had time to argue with Sam. Her voice was angry as she answered him. "Listen, Diane and your baby needs you. Will you come to the hospital?"

Sam ran his fingers through his hair. Nothing Lisa had said convinced him that Diane needed or wanted him at the hospital. He concluded that continuing the conversation with her was not going to give him the answers he wanted.

"I'm sorry Lisa but I think I'll wait until I hear from Diane. Tell her I said, hello and that she has my number."

Lisa stood, shaking her head. Sam had hung up on her.

CHAPTER 5

After Lisa put her cell phone away, she shrugged. "At least I tried." While waiting for the elevator, a woman's commanding voice caused her to turn around.

"Mrs. Henderson. Mrs. Henderson."

Lisa watched as a woman dressed in a blue uniform rushed toward her. She carried a clipboard.

"Mrs. Henderson." The woman extended her hand. "Hello. I'm Dr. Irwin, Diane's doctor. I need to speak to you."

Although Lisa had taken Diane to her doctor appointments, this was the first time she had met her doctor. Diane raved about Dr. Irwin but to Lisa she seemed too young to be a doctor or to be credible or experienced. Lisa hoped Diane's judgment had been right.

The doctor motioned her hand and urged, "Let's step over here." She led Lisa away from the elevator.

Dr. Irwin continued, "Mrs. Henderson, I understand you're Diane's sister?"

"Well … not exactly."

The doctor flipped through the clipboard papers. "Oh, I'm sorry. I guess I was given the wrong information."

Lisa shook her head. Why had she allowed herself to get caught up in Diane's web of make believe? Already, the lies were mounting. She had not expected what she said earlier to have caught up with her so soon.

"She doesn't have a sister. I'm her friend." Quickly, Lisa added, "A close friend. I lied so I could ride in the ambulance."

With a sense of urgency, the doctor continued. "If you're not her next to kin, do you know who I might talk to about Diane's condition?"

"This was such a mess!" Lisa thought.

Before she responded she considered how much she should reveal? She exhaled nosily.

"Well … Diane doesn't have any relatives living in Florida. In addition, she hasn't told many people about … you know … her situation."

"I'm sorry, but I'm not following you."

Lisa raised her hand to stop the doctor. "Please, be patient. It's more complicated than you realize."

Lisa's shoulders slumped, her eyes moist. It was more and more difficult keeping up Diane's charade. She closed her eyes. "Lord, help me. I need all the strength and power you can give me if I'm going to continue with Diane's wishes but yet not betray her."

The doctor had no idea what was going on and she was not sure she wanted to know. She eyed Mrs. Henderson with concern.

"Are you okay?"

Lisa opened her eyes, letting out a heavy sigh. "I'm fine. It's been a long morning and the past several months have been grueling."

From Dr. Irwin's expression, Lisa could tell that she had no idea what she was talking about. She didn't know where or how to explain what was going on with Diane and her problems.

"Dr. Irwin, I'm sorry, what do you need from me?"

"Without violating Florida's law, I can't discuss anything about Diane's medical condition unless you're authorized."

Bewildered, Lisa shrugged. "I don't fully understand the problem." Lisa stopped. Her hand flew to her mouth. "Wait, is something wrong? I mean, nothing happened to Diane, did it?"

CHAPTER 6

Dr. Irwin hated the new law and hospital red tape was just as bad. But she had no choice about what she could and could not discuss about a patient's medical condition.

She tried again. "Mrs. Henderson, I don't want to alarm you but under the circumstances I'm not at liberty to discuss Diane's condition with you."

The doctor was frustrated as she exhaled. "Maybe I'm not making myself clear. Under the new law, I need proof that you have the authority to receive information about Diane's medical condition."

"Oh." Lisa threw up her hands. "You probably think I'm a complete idiot. So much has been going on that …"

Before Mrs. Henderson went off into another explanation that was not relevant to the conversation, the doctor interrupted her.

"Mrs. Henderson, I need to talk to someone who has the power of attorney regarding Diane."

"I'm sorry. I tried telling you a few minutes ago that too much has happened in a short period of time." Lisa's tone was snippy as she added, "I have the authority to discuss Diane's medical as well as to make decisions if or when she's incapacitated."

The doctor tried not to show her annoyance. "Mrs. Henderson, by any chance do you have the documentation with you?"

"Yes, yes. I have them." After rummaging through her purse, Lisa removed several pieces of paper. She smiled and handed them to the doctor.

Dr. Irwin inspected the documents and handed them back to Lisa. She wasted no time explaining. "Diane's water broke before she arrived at the hospital. She's having contractions."

The doctor paused, giving Lisa an opportunity to ask questions. When Lisa did not, she proceeded.

"Diane's vitals are stable. She's doing well and the baby's heart beat is strong."

The tears Lisa had been holding back cascaded down her face. She thanked God for answering her prayers.

She asked, "Will Diane deliver the baby any time soon?"

"At the rate of her contractions, I would say no. When I examined her, she had just begun to dilate."

The doctor glanced at Lisa. "Do you have any other questions? I hate to rush but I need to go."

Reluctantly, Lisa asked, "I'm no doctor but on the way to the hospital, Diane seemed non-responsive and her breathing was shallow. Is that normal?"

Dr. Irwin hedged. "I'm not sure what you're referring to."

"Well, on the way to the hospital, the paramedic called for a Code Blue Team to meet the ambulance?"

Dr. Irwin grimaced. "It's not that unusual for the paramedics to request a Code Blue Team. It's a precaution. As I stated earlier, Diane and the baby are doing fine. I really need to go."

Through pursed lips Lisa said, "Thanks for answering my questions." Despite Dr. Irwin's assurances, Lisa was not convinced everything was fine with Diane. As the doctor turned to leave, Lisa blurted out, "Can I see her?" Dr. Irwin might be saying that Diane is fine but she wanted to see for herself.

"Yes, but keep in mind, she might be a little groggy but that's normal considering she's having contractions. There's nothing to be alarmed about."

"Thanks, Dr. Irwin." As an afterthought, Lisa added, "For everything." The doctor gave Lisa a slight smile, nodded her head, and walked away.

CHAPTER 7

Impatiently, Lisa punched the elevator button. When the elevator's doors opened, she exited and saw Patrick pacing back and forth. She ran to him, throwing her arms around him. After several moments, Lisa pulled away from the embrace and looked up at him with teary eyes. Instead of explaining what was going on, she grabbed his hand and rushed toward the elevator.

Once the doors closed, Patrick could not miss Lisa's drained, worried expression. He opened his mouth several times to ask the burning questions that were running through his mind but he didn't. Instead, he rode with Lisa, listening to the humming of the moving elevator. When it stopped, Lisa bolted through the open doors. Hurriedly, she walked to the nurse's station.

"Excuse me. What room is Diane Benson in?"

"She's in Room 324A, down the hall on the right hand side."

"Thank you."

Lisa rushed down the corridor, Patrick directly behind her. When they reached Diane's room, neither one of them said anything but Patrick understood he would not be going into the room.

Quietly, Lisa entered. Several nurses stood near Diane's bed. When they noticed Lisa, they acknowledged her, stopped what they were doing and eased out of the room.

Hesitantly, Lisa approached the bed. Although Diane was hooked up to several monitors and an IV, her appearance was angelic and peaceful. Lisa picked up her hand.

"Hey girl. I'm sorry I was late."

Lisa paused and thought she should not waste time and got right to the point. "You're in the hospital and I've talked to your doctor." She hesitated and continued, "You probably know but the doctor said you're in labor."

Lisa thought, "I wish she would open her eyes." As if Diane had read her mind, her eyes fluttered open.

In a soft, drowsy voice, Diane said, "Hi."

Lisa twisted her head slightly away from Diane and cleared her throat. Tears threatened to spill from her eyes. She turned back to Diane.

Hey girl was the only thing Lisa uttered as other words lodged in her throat. Finally, she let out a nervous laugh and said, "Do you always have to do everything with so much drama?"

A slight smile crossed Diane's lips. Lisa frowned as she watched Diane's contorted face. As Lisa opened her mouth to ask Diane what was wrong, the monitors connected to her began to buzz, beep, and alarm.

Lisa wasn't sure what triggered the monitor's activities as she ran out the room, screaming. "Help! Quick, someone help!"

Patrick rushed to Lisa. "What's wrong?"

"I don't know."

A nurse appeared. "What's wrong?"

"I don't know." Lisa's trembling voice explained, "Mrs. Benson, something's wrong. The machines started making noises and …"

The nurse rushed pass Lisa and Patrick and entered into the room. Patrick and Lisa followed her. The machines were blinking and Diane's breathing was uneven. Before the nurse finished checking Diane's vitals, she called for assistance.

Patrick squeezed Lisa's hand as they watched.

Without warning, a swarm of nurses entered the room. A minute later a code blue broadcast could be heard over the P.A., followed by a medical crash team running into the room.

Patrick and Lisa watched as the hospital personnel worked on Diane until a nurse turned around and spotted them. She ushered them out of the room.

CHAPTER 8

❀

Outside Diane's room, Patrick urged, "Lisa why don't we sit and wait over here?"

Lisa followed as Patrick directed her to a chair. While they waited for news about Diane, Lisa explained to Patrick what happened on their way to the hospital.

"I also called Sam but he refused to come to the hospital."

"Why?"

"Because he didn't know Diane had decided to have the baby?"

Patrick eyes bulged. "Are you serious? Why didn't she tell him?"

"I guess she didn't know whether she was going to keep the baby and when she decided I guess she didn't know how to tell him."

Lisa shook her head. "To be honest, I don't really know. When I tried to talk to her about the pregnancy and Sam she wouldn't discuss either one. We might be friends but I knew not to push the issue. Besides it was more important to me that Diane knew I would be there for her. She had enough to cope with."

"Well, how did Sam react when you told him about Diane having the baby?"

"He expressed shock, confusion, and anger. Can you blame him?"

Patrick shook his head. "If it were me, I'm not sure how I would react."

"I know it's a mess. If something happens to her I'm not sure what I'll tell her children."

Patrick put his arm around Lisa and drew her close to him. "I don't know how you've been able to keep all the secrets." He stopped and kissed the top of her head. "You didn't even tell me."

Lisa's voice was low and uttered, "I know and I'm sorry but I promised Diane."

"Do you think you should call Sam again?"

Before Lisa could answer, she pulled away from Sam's embrace as she watched Dr. Irwin approach them. "Mrs. Henderson, may I speak to you."

Lisa stood up, followed the doctor and asked, "How's Diane?"

"She's holding her own but I need to deliver the baby."

"Why? What happened? Earlier, you said Diane and the baby were doing fine and she would not deliver any time soon."

"I know but things changed and I need to perform an emergency C-section." The doctor paused. "I'm going to be straight with you. Diane is unconscious. With further testing, I believe she may be in a coma."

Lisa's hand flew to her mouth. Her knees began to buckle.

"Mrs. Henderson, are you okay?"

Weakly, she responded, "What happened?"

"At the moment, I have no answers. The only thing I do know is that the baby needs to be delivered. I need you to sign the form giving me permission."

"Is the baby going to be okay?"

"Yes, I believe so."

"What about Diane? Will delivering the baby help her come out of the coma?"

"At this point, I think we need to concentrate on one thing at a time. Right now, I need to deliver the baby but I can't do it without your consent."

"Before I make a decision I want to be sure I understand what you've told me. So, let me repeat what I think I heard. You need to perform a C-section to deliver the baby. By doing this, the baby will probably be fine. You think Diane might be in a coma but you're not sure. Delivering the baby may or may not change Diane's current condition." Lisa waited for Dr. Irwin's confirmation.

"That's right." Dr. Irwin gave Lisa a form. "You might want to read it but the bottom line is that you are giving me permission to deliver the baby."

Drained, Lisa asked, "Where do I sign?"

CHAPTER 9

Once Lisa signed the form and before Dr. Irwin left, she asked, "Can I see Diane before you deliver the baby?"

Lisa did not care that Diane was unconsciousness she wanted to tell her what was going on.

"Yes, but you'll have to make it quick."

"Okay."

Lisa slipped into the room and eased up to the bed. Diane appeared as if she was sleeping. She picked up her hand.

"Diane, I don't have much time. I don't know if you can hear me or not but I signed papers giving Dr. Irwin permission to deliver the baby. According to her explanation, this is best for you and the baby."

Lisa started to go into greater detail but changed her mind. "Listen, everything's going to be okay. You and the baby are in God's hands."

She kissed the top of her head and walked out of the room.

After Lisa walked out of the room, she rejoined Patrick. She was tired and would love to go home, get in bed and pull the blanket over her head.

"How's Diane?"

Lisa heaved a heavy sigh. "She might be in a coma. Dr. Irwin doesn't know." Lisa paused and swiped at a falling tear. "The doctor can't wait. She's going to deliver the baby now."

Patrick gathered Lisa in his arms. He eased his grip and said firmly but in a soft tone, "You need to call Sam."

Lisa nodded, pulled out her cell phone and dialed Sam's number. She waited, hoping he would answer.

"Hello, Sam. It's Lisa."

"Hello. What's up?"

"It's Diane."

"What did she have?"

"Excuse me?"

"Did she have a girl or a boy?"

"That's not why I'm calling." She paused as the words caught in her throat. "I think you need to come to the hospital."

"Why? What's going on?"

"I'd rather not tell you over the phone."

"Well, I don't want to be rude but I'm not coming to the hospital just because she had the baby. She needs to call me."

Although Patrick could only hear one side of the conversation, he reached over and tried to take the phone from Lisa. She leaned away from him, waved her hand, and mouthed the words so Sam could not hear her. "It's okay."

"Uh … It's complicated. As I told you earlier, Diane is having your baby but …" Lisa stopped and cleared her throat. "Something has happened and the doctor is performing an emergency C-Section to deliver the baby."

Before Sam could interrupt, Lisa rushed on. "If the doctor doesn't deliver the baby … and Diane, well …" Lisa couldn't finish the sentence.

Sam ran his hand over his face. "Where are you?"

"At the Leesburg Hospital."

"I'll be there as soon as I can."

Before Sam hung up, Lisa said, "I'll meet you in the hospital main lobby entrance."

CHAPTER 10

Patrick suggested they go to the cafeteria and get something to drink while they wait for Sam to arrive. At first Lisa protested but relented after Patrick convinced her that there was nothing she could do. He wanted to comfort her but didn't know how.

"Why don't you sit while I get you a cup of hot tea?" Lisa chose a chair near a window and sat down. She closed her eyes and prayed.

Sam touched her gently. She opened her eyes and looked up.

"Here, drink this."

Lisa reached for the hot drink. As much as she didn't want it, she found it soothing after she took the first sip. She prayed that Patrick would not talk. The last thing she wanted was to engage in idle conversation. Her mind was too occupied with Diane, the baby and what she would have to tell her children if something happened to her.

When she and Patrick finished their drinks, they walked to the lobby.

Sam drove to the hospital in less than time than he had estimated. He was in the hospital's lobby, waiting for Lisa. He wondered where she was. He thought she would have been in the lobby, waiting for his arrival. He approached the information desk once and started to inquire about Diane but changed his mind and took a seat.

Sam closed his eyes and thought about Diane. From the time she delivered that mouth-watering casserole to his door, his life had been filled with unexpected surprises. He smiled and considered what a "Casserole Surprise" that had been.

After the death of his wife, he never expected to find someone to love again but he did and he fell hard. As much as he knew Diane loved him, it had been difficult coping with her insecurities, especially with her lack of trust regarding men but he understood.

Diane's ex-husband, Fred, divorced her after twenty some years of marriage. It was difficult for him to understand how Fred had treated her. As for the divorce, Sam knew only bits and pieces. Diane never shared the entire story. The more Sam had gotten to know Diane he knew that the divorce had left its lasting effects.

Shortly after the divorce, Fred remarried and he and his wife had a baby. Fortunately for Diane, her company offered an early retirement and she was able to relocate to Florida and start over again.

❋ ❋ ❋

Patrick and Lisa spotted Sam. He was sitting in a chair, near the entrance. As they approached him, he did not notice them.

Lisa touched his shoulder. "Sam."

Slowly, he turned around and stood up.

"How's Diane?"

Before Lisa answered him, Patrick took charge. He extended his hand to Sam. "Hi. I'm Patrick Baylor, Lisa's fiancé.

He urged, "Rather than talk here, why don't we go to the waiting room? That way you'll have some privacy and it will be easier for the hospital staff to locate Lisa if she's needed."

While waiting for the elevator, Patrick purchased three cups of hot coffee from the nearby vending machine. Once inside the waiting room, they found three empty seats in the back corner.

CHAPTER 11

Lisa sipped the hot coffee before beginning. "Sam, first of all, I'm sorry I had to be the one to tell you about Diane and the baby. I thought you knew."

"I'm sorry too. I had no idea. But since Diane made this decision by herself and did not include me ..."

He stopped and reminded himself that Lisa was not the enemy. He continued, "That was why I wasn't interested in coming to the hospital. I believe it was Diane's place to tell me that she had kept the baby."

Patrick watched Lisa's body tense as she listened to Sam. The last thing he wanted was Lisa losing her temper. He touched her hand and gave it a gentle squeeze. She glanced at him.

"I know Diane didn't tell you about having the baby but under the circumstances, I thought you would want to be here. After all, it is your baby."

Sam did not like Lisa's tone. To suppress his anger, he lowered his voice and tried to explain. "You're probably right about me needing to be here, but Diane was the one who excluded me when she made the decision to keep the baby."

"You're probably right and I can't begin to understand how you must be feeling but you have to realize Diane has been through a lot. Right now, all she needs is your support and understanding ..."

Sam chided, "Oh, I haven't been supportive and understanding? Don't make me the bad guy."

Lisa said nothing as Sam continued, his voice was harsh. "I know she's been through a lot and I haven't made things any easier for her either but that doesn't excuse her for not telling me she was keeping the baby."

Lisa threw up her hands. She was fed up with Sam's finger pointing and trying to place blame.

"Look, there's no need in discussing what Diane did or didn't do. The reason why I asked you to come to the hospital is that Diane and your baby may be fighting for their lives."

"What?" Sam scowled. "You said the baby was being delivered."

"What I said was that an emergency C-section was being performed to deliver the baby. It's being done as we speak. But that isn't the only problem. Diane appears to be in a coma."

Sam's voice grew loud. "Oh, my God! Why didn't you tell sooner?"

"I suggest you calm down," Patrick stated.

Lisa watched the two men as she continued. "Despite Diane's unconsciousness, the contractions increased and the doctor wanted to avoid other possible complications. That's why the doctor is doing an emergency C-section."

Lisa took a long sip of the coffee. She watched Sam as he digested the information she just shared. His face had lost its color. In addition, his eyes were full of water.

In a low murmur, Sam asked, "Will Diane stay in the coma once the baby is born?"

"The doctor doesn't know. However, she thinks Diane would have a better chance of survival by delivering the baby.

"Have you contacted Diane's children?"

Lisa sucked in her lower lip. She glanced at Patrick and then at Sam. "I guess I should, but under the circumstances I don't know if this is the time."

"If not now, when? I think you should call them."

Patrick noticed the outline of Lisa's clenched jaw. He knew she was trying to be patient as well as controlling her temper.

Patrick offered, "Why don't we wait until the baby is born? At that time, Lisa can talk to the doctor and make a better, decision."

CHAPTER 12

Diane was anxious. Was she dreaming? If so, why couldn't she wake up? It was difficult to explain but she knew her body was being non-responsive.

As much as she tried, she could not recognize what was happening around her. The sounds were indistinguishable. Off and on, she thought she heard voices but then they would drift away before she could tell who was talking. Other times, she thought an array of individuals was asking her questions, but if they were, why wasn't she answering them?

The unknown was annoying and frustrating. She could not differentiate between what was going on and what wasn't. Whatever was going on, it was happening without her.

She remembered the ambulance ride to the hospital but somewhere between the transport and now, she was having difficulty with reality. Rather than brood over what she couldn't control, she decided to be productive.

"Think." Diane begged herself to recall the last thing that happened.

She was in the hotel room, there was pain and she had called 911 because her water broke. All her symptoms told her she was in labor. Either before or during the ambulance ride, she thought she had seen and spoken to Lisa. The vagueness began after she arrived at the hospital.

"Okay Diane." She admonished herself. "Stay focused. What else can you recall?"

As she attempted to call forth the memories from her archives, a sharp sting caused uneasiness in her lower back.

She concluded that she must still be in labor. Would it be possible to deliver a baby and not be aware of it? Wouldn't she have to be alert and responsive for that?

When the uncomfortable feeling eased, Diane began thinking about her situation. Being 48 years old, she had been anxious about the baby's birth. She was grateful when she found a female doctor who had been sympathetic and understanding.

In addition, the doctor had taken all kinds of prenatal precautions. At times Diane thought all the tests were unnecessary. The most important test was the amniocentesis. When she received the results, it made her feel more confident about the baby. The test indicated that the baby had no abnormalities.

She thought about her other two pregnancies. When she compared the two, they were so different. She had not worried about her health or gaining weight. But this pregnancy, she took exceptional care to follow the doctor's precise orders to ensure a healthy baby. Despite her prudence, her intuition told her that something had gone wrong. Whatever was going on, she had to be positive, especially for the baby.

Diane wished Lisa were with her. But maybe she was and she didn't know it. At this point, she wasn't sure of anything. If Lisa was not with her, where was she?

Throughout her pregnancy her biggest concern was, being alone. That decision was one she made and at times regretted not telling Sam. After all, he had a right to know she was having the baby.

Although the pregnancy presented problems she never imagined, she had fantasized about what it would have been like to have a life with Sam and their child. When she confided in Lisa, she made her swear she would not tell Sam but now, she hoped Lisa had broken that promise and had called Sam.

If Lisa did call him, she could only imagine how he reacted. He would be disappointed, hurt, and angry, but in the end perhaps he could learn to forgive her, especially after the baby was born. Another decision she had not bothered to discuss with Sam.

CHAPTER 13

As much as Donna did not want to be concerned about her mother, she could not shake the feeling that something was wrong. When she talked to her brother, Freddie, he told her to quit worrying. In his baritone voice, he kept reminding her, "Mom might be our mother, but she is also a grown woman."

She disagreed. It wasn't like her mother not to return her calls. In addition, she called her mother's best friend, Lisa and left several messages but she had not heard from her either. She would try again.

"Hello. Lisa."

"Hello."

"Lisa, this is Donna."

"Donna who?"

Donna wanted to scream. How many Donnas do you know? Sweetness dripped from Donna's voice as she responded. "I'm Diane Benson's daughter, Donna."

"Oh, yes. Yes. I'm sorry. How are you doing?"

"I'm fine but I'm worried about mom."

Lisa began speaking in a slow and even tempo, trying hard to keep the nervousness out of her voice. "Your mother, what's happened to her?"

Donna rolled her eyes, trying to hide the annoyance in her tone. "That's what I'm trying to find out. That's why I'm calling. I've called and left her numerous messages but she hasn't called me back."

Lisa let out a nervous laugh. "Of course she hasn't returned your calls. She's on a cruise."

Donna yelled, "A cruise! You've got to be kidding me."

"Uh … no. She went on a 21-day cruise." Lisa added, "If I remember correctly, she left some time last week."

Donna shook her head. Now, she knew something was wrong. It took her several minutes before she could respond.

"Lisa, listen to me. My mother has never been on a cruise." Donna was adamant, "There's no way mom would go on a cruise without telling me or Freddie. I can't believe she would do that."

Donna could almost predict Lisa's answer but she asked again. "Are you sure she said she was going on a cruise?"

"Yes, that's what she told me." Lisa was trying not to volunteer too much information. That way, she wouldn't have to tell too many lies.

"By any chance, do you know the cruise ship she's on?"

"I-I-I …" Lisa was stuttering. She didn't know how to answer her. She blinked hard. Lisa thought, "Now, the lies begin."

"Lisa."

"I'm still here. It might have been Carnival but then maybe it was Holland America. This mind doesn't work like it used to. I can't remember. I'm sure I wrote it down. If you like, I'll look for it and I can call you tomorrow with the information."

"You're telling me that mom went on a 21-day cruise and didn't give you any information?"

"I didn't say that." Lisa was indignant. "I said I couldn't remember."

Donna was frustrated. She changed subjects. "Lisa, did mom tell you about me?"

"What do you mean?"

"About me not being able to have a baby?"

Lisa hesitated. She was glad Donna had changed subjects but why was she asking about this? "I think she might have mentioned it. Why?"

"Well, she acted really strange when I told her I couldn't have a baby. I know she was saddened by my news but there was something else but I wasn't able to put my finger on it."

"Well, you know your mother. She hates to see her children suffer in anyway. Not to mention, she likes to help in any way when you have a problem. You might be grown but to her, you'll always be her baby. I guess that's what it means to be a mom. Wait until you're a …" Lisa stopped before she said, mother.

"It's okay. I'm still trying to cope with not being able to have a baby but with mom's help, she convinced Gary and me to consider other options."

"See what I mean? If your mother can fix it, she will."

Donna returned to the original reason she called. "Do you know exactly when mom will return?"

"Yes, it's 21-days from last week." Lisa knew Donna probably thought she was an idiot but how could she tell a lie and make it sound convincing?

Donna was annoyed. "Lisa, exactly when did she leave?"

"Last Thursday."

CHAPTER 14

When Donna hung up the phone, she shook her head. She could not believe the conversation she just had with Lisa. Sometimes she wondered if she wanted to grow old. From what she could tell, there would be lots of forgetfulness, lack of concentration, and confusion.

Her thoughts went to her mom's friend, Arlene and her dementia problems. She hoped the same was not beginning to happen to Lisa. When she talked to her mom, she would mention the perplexing conversation she had with Lisa.

She thought long and hard before calling Freddie. The last conversation they had about their mother, he was not in the least bit worried. Maybe when she shared with him that their mother was on a 21-day cruise his reaction would be different.

Despite her misgivings, she called her brother.

"I think it's great, she's on a cruise."

"But you don't find it strange that Lisa didn't go with her? Usually, they're glued at the hip."

"Maybe Lisa doesn't like to cruise."

Donna shook her head. "I don't think that's it. You don't think it's strange that Lisa couldn't even tell me what cruise she was on or when she left or would return. As a result, I'm thinking about going to Florida."

"For what?"

"To find out what's going on. Something isn't right."

"Listen to yourself. Mom is a grown woman. She has adult children and about to have a grandchild. She's entitled to have some privacy and secrets. Maybe, she has a boyfriend and that's why Lisa didn't want to tell you about her trip."

"Not mom. There's no way, she's dating."

"Why would you say that?" Freddie added, "Mom is an attractive, vibrant, mature woman. Why wouldn't she want to date?"

"You know … because of dad."

"What do you mean?"

"I think she still has feelings for him. He might have moved on but mom will love dad forever."

"Don't be so sure." Freddie pursed his lips. He couldn't believe his sister. He continued, "If she's on a cruise, I think it's great."

He pumped his fist in the air. "Go mom." He continued, "If she's doing something that she doesn't want us to know, that's okay too. After everything she's been through, she's entitled to a life."

Donna stuck her tongue out at the phone. She was sorry she had called Freddie. Everything he said was right but she didn't want it to be true. When she thought about her mom being with another man, she wanted to gag.

"Come on Doddie. Quit pouting."

Donna smiled. Freddie hadn't called her that since they were kids. Maybe she was acting like a child. The life she once knew was gone. Nothing would ever be the same. She needed to accept the fact that her parents were never going to get back together. Obviously, everyone had accepted that fact but her.

"I'm not pouting, smarty pants. I was thinking about all the changes our family has gone through."

"I know. It's been hard for everyone. Change is hard. Let's talk about something else. How's the adoption process coming along?"

"Slow but we're encouraged as well as discouraged."

"What do you mean?"

"We thought we had a baby. When we arrived at the hospital, the young woman had changed her mind. I reacted like a woman whose child had been kidnapped. Freddie, I was so close and in a blink of an eye, the baby was snatched right out of my arms. After I recovered, I received a call from the lawyer who said there's another woman who wants to give her baby up for adoption. We could be receiving a call any day."

CHAPTER 15

Diane's mind drifted in and out. Nothing was clear. It was like she was driving through the fog. She had not been able to interpret what was going on. She knew she had the ability to communicate but she could not explain why her mouth was not working.

Thoughts of her life came forth. In general, it was supposed to get better with age, but her experiences had been nothing but heartache, disenchantment, and isolation.

When it came to being a parent, she and Fred had failed. At least they had provided a safe, loving environment while their son and daughter were growing up. As for their children's adult lives, she and Fred seemed to have caused them disappointment, hurt, and sadness.

Flashbacks of how it all started invaded Diane's mind.

A typical Florida sunny day was how Diane's day started. As she glanced through her day planner, the phone rang.

"Hey, good looking."

Fred's voice startled Diane. She was not used to him calling her at the office unless a problem occurred regarding the children that he was unable to handle. Worried lines formed across her forehead.

"I was wondering if you could come home early. I'm planning a special night."

Surprise lit up Diane's face. His gesture thrilled her. Their busy work schedule was causing their relationship to suffer, but she had been afraid to discuss it with him. She did not know what had changed but they acted more like room-mates than husband and wife.

On occasion, both of them voiced the need to spend more time together, but it never happened. That's why his call made her excited when she considered the possibility of them rekindling the romance back into their marriage.

"I'm free. There's nothing on my calendar that should prevent me from coming home on time. In fact, I might be able to leave early."

At the end of the day, those words haunted Diane, as she glanced at her watch. She called Fred. As usual, she was going to be late.

At seven-thirty, Diane rushed through the door and staggered backwards. Her mouth dropped open and her eyes widened.

The sight was incredible. Hundreds of lit candles adorned the foyer. She entered into the living room where more candles and yellow roses, her favorite, lined the room. The aroma from the roses filled her nose, making her light headed, almost as if being intoxicated.

She raised her eyes upward and said a quick prayer. "Lord, thank you for my wonderful, adoring husband. After tonight I will pay more attention to what is important in life."

That meant she would have to cut back her work hours. She would have to stop working at home to complete unfinished projects. And, she would have to be firm about not traveling two-to-three weeks out of the month.

The memory flashback halted. A sharp twinge struck Diane hard in the back. The contraction was hard. She wanted it to stop. As if her body listened to her wishes, the pain eased from her back but traveled to her stomach.

With her first pregnancies, her contractions caused her to curse, scream out to God, and ask for pain medicine. If she was doing that now, she was not aware of it.

From past memory, she knew the contraction would not last long. She had to ride it out and she did. The pain disappeared.

Her mind drifted back to when she entered the house and was trying to locate Fred. She remembered how aloof he was when she tried to hug and kiss him.

As the evening progressed, Diane was disappointed because it had not been like she had imagined. When they were eating, their conversation was artificial, the laughter limited and neither one of them sounded genuine.

The ambiance was romantic but something had been missing. She remembered how she attempted to put a little spark into the evening. She felt amorous and couldn't wait to shower him with kisses, hugs, and anything else he wanted to do.

She batted her eyelashes and winked at Fred. "Why don't we skip dessert? Or we can take the dessert to the bedroom."

CHAPTER 16

Diane tried to hide her disappointment. Instead of agreeing to Diane's seductive suggestions, Fred had something else in mind.

"I think we better have a seat in the living room."

Diane followed Fred's instructions and sat on the sofa. He sat in a chair facing her. Diane watched as he kept his eyes lowered and swirled the red wine in the glass. When Fred's words broke the room's stillness, she remembered how attentive she sat similar to a disobedient child, waiting to be disciplined.

"I don't really know where to start." He ran his fingers through his hair. "I will always love you. After all, we will always have a connection because you're the mother of my children." Pausing, he cleared his throat.

"I could say a lot of standard rhetoric about how many wonderful years we've shared together or that you have been a caring and loving wife and mother, but I'm not going to insult your intelligence. Plus, I don't want to prolong …" He stopped, running his fingers through his hair.

"I guess what I'm trying to tell you, is that we deserve some happiness. Life is short and we're not getting any younger."

She said nothing as she tried to figure out what he was referring to, especially since he started out with "*I*" and then switched to "*we.*"

He ran his hand over his face and exhaled nosily. "I guess I need to come right out and say it. I want a divorce."

Did she hear him correctly? She hoped he was going to elaborate.

Instead of an explanation, he started asking her questions. "Are you happy? Do you see us growing old together? Do you think our marriage has changed?"

Since he seemed to be the person whose happiness was in jeopardy, why was he asking her about her happiness? Since she was not responding, he tried a different approach.

"When I talked to Donna and Freddie, they agreed that they had noticed a change in our relationship."

Diane interrupted him, her voice booming. "What? You discussed our relationship with the children? How could you? This isn't about them. This is about us—our marriage."

She continued at a high-pitched level. "Or were you trying to get them to validate why you want a divorce? Answer me."

"Diane, please calm down. I was hoping we could be adults about this and have a civil conversation."

She did not care what he wanted or that she was yelling. She was not hiding her anger. She was mad as a toddler throwing a temper tantrum.

"You have a lot of nerve. You arranged for this wonderful dinner only to tell me that you want a divorce. You want to throw twenty plus years away and you don't even have the decency to talk about it? But yet, you talked to the children?"

Fred exhaled. "That's not the way it is. You're turning this around. I'm trying to talk to you now."

"That's what you call this? Since you've already said you want a divorce, you've already made up your mind. There's nothing else to discuss."

"If that's the way you see it, then fine. However, I need to tell you something else." When Fred tried to speak, the words stuck in his throat.

Diane waited. She urged, "What else do you have to tell me?"

"I've been seeing someone."

"So, you had no intention of trying to save our marriage. When things got difficult, you found someone else!"

"That's not how it happened. You traveled so much and ..."

She broke in and shrieked, "So, now it's my fault. You were the one who encouraged me to have a career and go after the next promotion, even if it meant traveling."

He threw up his hands in defense. "Listen, you need to know that I've been seeing someone from church."

"What?"

Before she could react any further, he rushed on. "It's Joanne."

"You mean the woman who sings in the church choir? Is this the same woman who constantly offered to help out when I had to take business trips?"

He lowered his head and murmured, "Yes."
Diane reached over and slapped his face hard.

CHAPTER 17

After Fred told her about the affair and his desire for a divorce, Diane thought things could not get any worse. When the phone rang, Diane hesitated. She did not want to talk to anyone.

"Mommy, how are you doing?"

Sniffing, Diane cleared her throat. Crying was her constant emotion, like a leaking faucet that could not be fixed. The only considerate thing Fred had done was to have their final dinner on a Friday. The entire weekend gave her the chance to drown in her misery.

"I'm as fine as I can be. How are you doing, sweetie?"

"I guess, okay,"

"I mean how are you feeling about me and Daddy getting a divorce?"

"How do you think I feel? No child ever wants his or her parents to divorce, no matter how old the child might be." Diane's daughter's voice sounded annoyed, laced with anger.

"I'm sorry honey. I … I mean you and your brother Freddie are grown and married … I thought the divorce wouldn't affect you that much."

"Why, mother? I might be grown and married, but your divorce does impact my life. What happens on holidays? I don't even want to think about grandchildren. The only saving grace is that I am married."

"Well, it's going to be different, that's for sure. I hope you don't let this interfere with how you feel about your father."

"Look, what happened between you and daddy is your business. I can understand you being upset about the divorce and all … but Freddie and I don't want to be in the middle."

"You and your brother aren't in the middle of anything. And I certainly don't want you two taking sides. As you said, this divorce has nothing to do with the two of you. Your father and I still love you very much."

"Mother, I know you and daddy love me and Freddie but there's something you don't understand...." Donna paused.

"It's just that I don't want you to be upset with us. What you don't know is that we knew about daddy's affair with Joanne." Diane's mouth flew open and she lost control.

"How did you find out?" She shouted even louder. "Who told you?"

Diane was fuming and she felt betrayed. Her own children knew but yet they didn't confide in her.

Diane demanded an answer. "Well, are you going to tell me?"

"Mommy, I don't think ... I mean what difference does it make?"

"Because, I think I have a right to know."

"Don't blame me. I didn't do anything."

"Oh yes, you did. You could have told me."

Donna did not reply. It would only make matters worse. It was better not to discuss this any longer.

"Donna. Are you still there?"

"Yes mother." Donna was sorry she had told her mother but she wanted her to know before she heard it from someone else.

"Now, you're sulking," Diane said.

"I'm not sulking. I just don't know what you want me to say. I'm sorry I didn't tell you. I didn't think it was my place to say your husband was having an affair."

"You're my daughter. That's all the more reason why you should have told me. If the tables had been turned and I found out your husband was running around, I would tell you."

"Mom ... it's not the same. I'm your daughter and...."

Her mother cut her off. "That's no excuse. Let me ask you this, does everyone know about your father's adulterous behavior?"

"How would I know?"

"Well, you know more than I do. After all, I was the wife and I was the last to find out."

"Mom, I don't want to continue this conversation. You're too ..."

"I'm too what? Angry—you're right, but I'm more than angry—I'm hurt, disappointed and I've been betrayed."

CHAPTER 18

Diane slammed the phone down and starting sobbing until she could no longer produce tears. When she calmed down, she thought about calling her daughter back to apologize but changed her mind. Instead, she called her son.

"Hello."

Diane had hoped her son would answer the phone, but instead she heard her daughter-in-law's voice.

"Hi, Diane."

"Hi, Angie. Is Freddie home?"

"Yes. But, how are you doing?"

"Fine." Diane was terse. She did not intend to be rude to Angie, but she was not in the mood for idle chit-chat.

"May I please speak to my son?"

"Hi, mom." The minute Diane heard her son's voice she ripped into him.

"Why didn't you tell me about your father? Did you think you were helping me by not telling me?"

"Calm down mom."

"I am calm. If you don't believe me, call your sister when we finish our conversation. When I talked to her I wasn't calm."

"I'm sorry, and I don't know what I can say to make it better."

As much as Diane tried to be calm, she had difficulty containing her temper. Her hurt was too new. She was feeling nothing but humiliation and betrayal.

"Mom, I'm sorry about the divorce."

"At this point, who cares about the divorce? Why didn't you tell me about your father having an affair?"

"Look, you and daddy have placed me and Donna in an awkward position. We're your...."

"Your daddy and I—excuse me. I haven't done anything. I'm the innocent one. Your dad was the one who made it uncomfortable for you and your sister when you found out about his affair."

Freddie did not dare share with his mother that it was their father who told them about the affair. His reason was that he did not want a church member telling them about it. Every Sunday, Freddie feared that someone would say something to his mother about the affair. No one ever did.

"I'm sorry. You're right about dad, but now you're causing Donna and me to feel guilty because we didn't tell you. Mom, can't you understand it wasn't our place to tell you."

"That's where we don't see eye-to-eye. If I knew Angie was playing around, I would tell you."

Diane was tired. She was wasting her time talking to Freddie. Despite what her children told her, she could see they had already taken sides. She would have expected it from Donna. She had always been a daddy's girl. But Freddie—that was a different story. She thought they had a special mother and son bond, but obviously she had been wrong.

"Look, I have to go."

"Mom, wait. We need to talk about this."

"What is there to talk about? You, your sister, our friends, the entire church, and probably all the neighbors knew about your father and his affair. I feel like a fool and you and Donna helped me to feel that way."

"Mom, please. Mom!" It was too late. She had hung up.

Frustrated and not wanting to talk to anyone else, she picked up her favorite comforter, curled up on the sofa, and turned on the television. Stopping on the TV listing channel, Diane scrolled down the ledger. She wanted to see a movie where the woman was causing havoc on a man's life. She was in luck.

A movie titled, "The Burning Bed" was playing. According to the description, it was about a woman who was being physically abused by her husband. When the wife couldn't take any more beatings, she burned the bed while her husband was asleep.

CHAPTER 19

Diane received excellent advice from friends and family. They said that with every yesterday, there was a tomorrow and tears shed at night would be gone in the morning.

But, the holidays were fast approaching, and she did not know how she was going to cope. The holidays would be more painful because she and Fred married on New Year's Eve.

She remembered how her mother tried—no pleaded with her—not to marry on a holiday, but she would not listen. She recalled the words she had told her mother, *"But a party will always be given to celebrate our blessed event."*

Her mother died several years ago. At least she did not have to listen to her mother say, "I told you so."

How did she know she would ever regret her decision when to marry? If she had a magic wand she would change two things. She would change the date of her wedding and eliminate this year's holidays and all the festivities.

Going to work was the only comfort she had, but with the holidays, work had become her enemy.

Everyone was in the *"holiday spirit."* People she did not even know wanted to discuss their holiday plans. The topic of everyone's conversation was about last minute shopping, toys they had not been able to find, addressing Christmas cards, and all the party invitations they had received. With every discussion, Diane feared that her emotions would erupt and the result would be her crying or screaming.

Since she was still trying to forgive Donna and Freddie, she refused their invitations and would be alone for the holidays. Despite her ill feelings, she had bought them gifts. Since she had no plans to see them, she would leave the gifts outside their homes, call, and tell them where they could find them.

Reading her office e-mail, she groaned, *"Oh no. The office holiday party notice."*

She had completely forgotten. Although she had declined all party invitations, she had to attend this particular event. Being a manager, it was one of those mandatory activities that you were expected to attend. Diane called it, silent pressure.

The only excuses accepted for not attending was that you were dead, hospitalized, or religious beliefs.

She thought, *"Why couldn't I be a Jehovah Witness or Jewish?"*

It had seemed like yesterday that Diane had read the e-mail about the office party. With a blink of an eye, the party date had arrived.

She did not bother buying something new to wear. She figured the dress from last year was one of those basic, black, forgettable dresses. Even if someone remembered it, she didn't care.

Purposely, she would arrive thirty minutes after the party started. She could slip in without being seen. In addition, most people wouldn't notice or remember if Fred was with her.

After saying her *"hellos"* and making small talk to all the necessary higher ups, she ordered a glass of wine. Without anyone noticing, she escaped to a corner in the back of the room.

Diane was happy to sip her wine away from the laughter, chatter, and dancing. After about an hour, she would depart like she arrived, without anyone paying attention to her.

That would be the extent of her holiday commitments.

As Diane took a sip of wine, she spotted a woman approaching her. She had no escape mechanism.

CHAPTER 20

The memory of Diane meeting Lisa drifted away. The bits and pieces of people and events clouded her mind. Some of it made sense while other parts were vague.

Something else was going on but she was not sure what. Nothing was clear, only confusion. As much as she tried, thoughts of Lisa were gone.

Until now, everything had been darkness. Off in a distance was a light, a bright light. Why was she seeing it? What did it mean?

In the waiting room, Lisa was anxious. The old saying of, *"no news is good news,"* was not helping her. She wanted news, anything.

When Lisa closed her eyes, she thought about when she first met Diane. She smiled and shook her head as she recalled that night.

Lisa saw Diane sitting in the corner of the room, alone. When she first spotted Diane's brooding expression she thought, "This woman wants to be at the party about as much as I do."

Lisa approached the woman, not knowing what to expect.

"Hi. I'm Lisa Henderson. I work in the Equal Employment Opportunity Department."

Diane did not acknowledge the introduction. She thought that perhaps her rude behavior would discourage the woman and she would go away. Instead, the average height, middle aged, olive-skinned woman continued to stand near Diane's chair.

Since the woman was not leaving, Diane responded through clenched teeth, "Hi, I'm Diane Benson. I work in Human Resources."

"Do you mind if I sit down?"

Diane threw up her hand and made a gesture. "Help yourself. It's a free country."

Lisa sat down but from the woman's glaring look, she could tell that was the last thing she wanted her to do.

Lisa asked, "Are you here with anyone?"

Diane's bottom lip began to quiver, and before she knew it, tears cascaded down her face like a waterfall. She tried controlling her sobs as her body shook. It was not just the holidays it was everything. Too much had happened to her in such a short period of time.

Fumbling in her purse, Diane could not find a tissue. Lisa offered her one. Through sniffles, Diane mumbled a thank you.

"I'm sorry if I said something to upset you. Maybe I should leave."

Lisa stood up and instead of Diane welcoming her exit, she pleaded for her to stay. Blowing her nose, Diane composed herself.

Through gritted teeth, she blurted out, "Several weeks ago, my husband asked me for a divorce."

"I'm sorry," Lisa said, trying not to show her surprise.

"You have nothing to be sorry about," Diane snapped.

"My husband is the one who should be sorry. On New Year's Eve, we would have celebrated our 25th wedding anniversary."

Diane paused. Her voice was low and full of hostility. "But, he has chosen to bring the New Year in with his new-found love."

As Diane glanced at the woman, she said nothing. Diane did not deserve the kindness she was receiving. She was grateful that this woman listened to her rant and rave about her problems.

"Do you know the three worse things about him asking me for a divorce?" Diane wasn't expecting an answer.

"First, he was having an affair with one of the church choir members. Secondly, my grown, married children knew about it. And lastly—I, the wife, was, the last one to find out."

Wide eyed, Lisa was speechless. How could she comfort this woman? "I'm really sorry."

"Would you stop saying that? You have nothing to be sorry about. It wasn't your fault." The woman was now beginning to annoy Diane. She didn't need her apologies.

"My husband is a cheat and he broke his vows before man and God. You know the old saying, "there's no fool, like an old fool." And that would be me, an old fool."

"You're not a fool. It could have been worse. My motto is: "*something good always comes out of something bad.*" The minute Lisa shared her outlook on life she knew she had made a mistake.

Diane rolled her eyes in disbelief and lashed out. "Oh I get it. The bad is the affair my husband had. The good is that I don't have to worry about being married to the SOB because he's divorcing me."

"You might not understand it now but I guarantee there will be some good to come out of all of this. I mean …"

Diane interrupted her. "Aren't you little Miss Sunshine?" Diane pursed her lips and continued her tirade.

"I notice you're wearing a wedding ring. Where's your husband?" Diane held up her hand before Lisa could respond.

"I know, don't tell me. You were dumped too."

Diane cocked her head to the side and waited for Lisa to answer her. Their eyes locked as Lisa shook her head.

She stood up and gave Diane a long stare through watery eyes. "My husband died. I'm here alone."

CHAPTER 21

Lisa laughed as she thought about she and Diane's first encounter, it was rocky. However, over the next several months, they became friends.

In a strange way, they formed a friendship that was similar to a support group. At their first dinner out together, it was as if both of them needed to have burdens lifted from their shoulders. They shared some of their deepest concerns, fears, and desires.

Continuously, Diane told Lisa how she needed a change. Baltimore, Maryland was not big enough for her and ex-husband, Fred, to live.

After twenty plus years, Diane sold the house she had shared with her husband and children. She bought another house in a totally different section of the city and found a new church. Despite her efforts, she constantly ran into Fred and his wife.

Diane grew weary of her situation. She stayed in a state of melancholy. Everything seemed to revolve around her ex-husband and his wife. No matter how hard she tried not to be a part of their life, she was drawn into it.

Lisa worried about Diane's mental state. Every time Diane thought she was starting over and had accepted the divorce, something seemed to throw her off balance, like the time her daughter innocently called her.

"Mom, I'm sorry. I thought you knew daddy and Joanne were expecting a baby."

Diane was taken back. She did not intend to release her anger on her daughter, but she did. When Diane finished her loud outburst, it was not until she asked Diane a question she realized her daughter had hung up on her.

Every time Diane shared what seemed like bad news, Lisa continued to be the eternal optimist and gave her constant words to be hopeful and encouraged.

"Look, something will work out for you. Be patient."

"You keep saying that, but every time I start to believe what you're saying, something else happens. The news of Fred's wife having a baby was enough to push me over the edge."

"I know, but trust me. Things are going to happen for you. Give it time."

"Well it had better happen soon because I'm not sure how much more I can take."

❦   ❦   ❦

Diane received the most unbelievable "good" news just when she was about to give up. She could not wait to talk to Lisa. When Diane dialed her number she was disappointed when she got her answering machine.

"Hi, Lisa. This is Diane. Call me as soon as possible, it's urgent!"

When Lisa checked her messages, she heard the urgency in Diane's voice. She thought, *"Please God, make this good news. I know you never give us more than we can manage, but I'm not sure how much more Diane can handle. Amen."*

When Lisa called Diane, she could not miss the excitement in her voice.

"I hate to admit it but you were right," Diane exclaimed. "I just needed to be patient. My life is finally turning around."

Diane was doing all the talking, Lisa had not been able to ask a question or make a comment.

"The power company is offering early retirements for anyone with twenty-five years of service."

"That's great but ..." Lisa did not want to sound discouraging but someone had to be level headed.

"What about health benefits?"

"No problem. I'll receive a full pension with health benefits." Diane gushed. "I've already completed my paper work. You're the first to know."

She giggled and added, "And the most exciting news is that I'm moving to Florida."

"Slow down. You're retiring and moving to Florida."

"Fred and I own a home in a retirement community called The Villages. I'm going to see if he'll let me buy him out."

Diane smirked, "Just a few years ago, we were planning our retirement. Now, his priority is college tuition. So, I doubt if he'll want the house."

"This is good news but tell me about this retirement community."

"Well, it might sound kind of hokey but it's an active retirement community. There is every type of recreation imaginable and you know how much I love golf? Well, it's free, sort of. I'll have to pay a minimal trail fee on the Executive Golf Courses and I can golf at a discount on the Championship Courses if I pay for a membership. There's a monthly amenities fee for things like maintenance and recreational clubs but no cost to belong to the country clubs. There's nightly entertainment at two town squares, restaurants galore, and two movie theaters."

Excitedly, Diane continued, "Oh, and if for some reason, you can no longer drive your car, you can use a golf cart as your means of transportation. Anyway, you'll have to visit me."

"As soon as you're settled and I receive an invitation, you know I'll be there."

Lisa did not share her concerns with Diane but she worried her decision was impulsive. Instead, she congratulated her.

Someone bumped Lisa's chair. She opened her eyes and stretched her legs. She interrupted Patrick and Sam's conversation.

"I'll be right back. I'm going to the restroom."

CHAPTER 22

Being in a dream like state, Diane's memories were coming and going without them making sense. As much as she wanted to be in control of what and how she recalled things, she could not.

She thought she had been reminiscing about Lisa but if she had, it was gone. Her mind was such a blur.

If something happened to her … poor Lisa … she would be left with the responsibility of telling her children. How did she make such a mess of everything?

She saw her children's faces as she recalled when she told them about her move to Florida.

Diane saw no reason why Donna and Freddie would not be supportive of her relocation plans. Since the divorce, this was the first time she visualized a life in the future. She called her daughter first.

"You're moving where?"

"To Florida. This should not be a surprise. Remember, that's where your father and I were going to …"

Diane paused in mid-sentence. Her children knew their retirement plans was to live somewhere warm. They had been looking for the right location for years.

"I know you and daddy …" Donna stopped and then hurried on. "Florida had been a place that you and …"

At times Donna found difficulty talking to her mother about anything that involved her father. Her mother did not want them to mention his name.

"Is it the same place that you and…."

"Yes. It's the same place where your dad and I bought property." Diane tried hard but her words came out bitter. "That's when we were making retirement plans together."

Donna refused to enter into that conversation with her mother and changed subjects. "Do you think daddy will agree to give you the property?"

"Oh, I don't expect him to give me the property. I want to buy him out. Besides I'm sure he will need the money for his new baby's college fund." Again Donna didn't take the bait as she concentrated on her mother's plans.

"How soon do you want to move?"

"As soon as I settle the property issue with your dad and sell the house."

"Does Freddie know?"

"No. I called you first. When you think about it—it's what I need. When the power company offered an early retirement with full pension and health benefits, I thought I had won the lottery."

"Are you old enough to live in a retirement community?"

"Yes. This community has already met the Florida state law requiring residents to be at least 55 years old."

Donna was curious. "Do you think you'll enjoy living with people old enough to be your parent or in some cases your grandparent?"

Diane let out a laugh. "Say what you mean. Will I like living with a bunch of old people?"

"You said it, not me."

"It's not like that. You'll see when you visit me. Besides, age is just a number. At least you won't have to worry about me in my old age. That was one reason why we …" Diane stopped.

That was the exact reason why she wanted to leave Baltimore. Even though she was single, everything was still in terms of *"we"* or *"they."* For her, those words were no longer in her vocabulary. She needed to start thinking in terms of *"I"* and *"me."*

"I need to call your brother. Take care." Diane hung up and immediately dialed her son's number.

"Hello."

"Hi, Freddie."

Immediately, Freddie cringed. He used to enjoy talking and visiting with his mother but since the divorce she had been anything but pleasant.

"Are you busy?"

"Not really. Why? What's up?"

"I'm moving to Florida." Diane waited for a reaction. He said nothing.

"Do you remember the property your father and I bought in Florida? Well I'm going to move there.

"Do you think that's a good idea? What about your job?"

"Oh, I'm sorry. I forgot to mention that the power company is offering an early retirement to anyone with twenty-five years of service. I'll receive a monthly pension with health benefits. I'll be living on a fixed income but financially I shouldn't have a problem. Besides, with the sale of the house, I should receive a substantial profit."

"It sounds like you've given this a lot of thought. How soon are you thinking about moving?"

"I move as soon as I sell the house. After I settle things with your father, I'll make a few trips to Florida and move shortly after that."

"Mom, I'm happy for you. If there's anything I can do to help, let me know. I love you."

"I love you to."

For the first time in months Diane believed she could truly put the past behind her and begin to live in the present.

CHAPTER 23

Feeling a pang of guilt, Diane prayed that either Freddie or Donna would tell their father about her intentions. It did not happen.

Two weeks passed before she found the courage to phone him. Diane sat, staring at the phone. Taking a deep breath, she dialed his telephone number.

With her eyes closed, she prayed Joanne did not answer the phone. After the third ring, she was prepared to leave a message. She practiced what she was going to say when she heard Fred's voice.

"Hello."

"Hi, Fred."

"Diane."

"Yes. Are you busy?"

"I just returned from my morning run. What's up?"

"I'm not going to take up much of your time. So, I'll get right to the point. Remember the Florida house?"

Defensiveness was in Fred's voice. "Yeah, what about it?"

"Well, I would love to relocate. Since we already own a house in Florida, I'm hoping I can buy it from you. I mean this way I wouldn't have to start from scratch."

"Are you going to work down there?"

"No. The power company is offering an early retirement with full pension and health benefits to anyone with twenty-five years of service."

"That's great news for you."

"Yeah, I'm really happy about it. So, what do you think about me buying you out?"

"I'm thinking."

He lied. He did not want to seem too anxious. Joanne would be thrilled to hear Diane was going to relocate. Maybe now Diane could get on with her life and the same with them.

"Listen, I'm not going to need a retirement home any time soon." He was trying to make a light comment until he heard Diane say under her breath.

"You're telling me. The only thing you'll be thinking about is diapers and college tuition."

Fred took a deep breath and counted to ten. He did not want to lose focus as to why Diane called. As he responded, he hoped his voice sounded friendly and sincere.

"What I was trying to say is that you can have the property."

"Oh I couldn't. You've invested as much as I did. I want to be fair." She could not resist. "I'm sure you'll need the extra money with the baby coming."

He heard the delight in her comment, but again he was not going to play a game of hide and seek and get caught. The last thing he wanted was to give her the satisfaction of thinking that she had pushed his button.

"I wouldn't have offered if I didn't want you to have it. You deserve a fresh start."

Diane thought, "*So that was it.*"

Fred would be happy to see her leave Baltimore. With her out of the city, his life and marriage to Joanne would be easier.

Diane felt the temperature rising up her neck. She inhaled and exhaled. She had to control her temper. This was what they both wanted. The sooner the property issue was settled, the quicker she would be able to leave everything behind her.

CHAPTER 24

The house sold in a month and she was on her way to Florida. Diane's past made it difficult for her to accept her good fortune. Everything had gone as planned but nothing prevented her from worrying that something would go wrong.

Nothing happened. Within thirty days, Diane moved to Florida. Rather than move into the designer house she and Fred had bought, she sold it and bought a colony villa style home. She did not need a big house or yard. It met her every need, especially the yard—it required minimal care. The one feature she loved was the little white picket fences in front of each house.

Neighbors were friendly as Diane settled into her new home. She could not remember a time when she was as at peace. Two weeks after she moved in, she met her neighbors, Kellie Olson and Arlene Woodson. To get acquainted with each other, they went to breakfast at the Glenview Country Club. They talked about their move to The Villages. Diane shared her story first.

"There isn't much to tell. I'm one of those statistics of an older woman dumped by her middle-aged husband who wanted a younger model. He found his replacement in the church choir. They married and are having a baby. Together, we have a daughter and son who are married." Diane took a sip of her coffee.

"I needed a change, and thank God my company offered an early retirement and I didn't hesitate to take it."

Arlene was curious. "Can I ask you a personal question?" She asked before Diane replied. "Are you old enough to live here?"

Diane laughed. "Thank you for the compliment, I think." Without revealing her age, she said, "The Villages had to meet a Florida state requirement of 80 percent of the residents be 55 or older. They met the rule, and as a result I can live here."

Arlene nodded her head as if she understood. If she had any other questions, she did not ask as she began telling her story.

"I'm married. My husband's name is Harold. We have a daughter who lives in California. Harold and I saw an ad for The Villages in the AARP magazine. We sent for the videotape and after we viewed it and visited, Harold and I agreed that the video did not capture the true essence of the community or the lifestyle. Within three days we bought a house."

"What about you Kellie?"

"Well, my life is kind of complicated. I'm married and I moved from Ohio. My husband, Roger, doesn't live with me. He's in the Regal Care Assisted Living Complex. It's less than two miles from The Villages."

"That doesn't sound complicated to me."

"Well, I'm married but I consider myself single." Diane tried not to react.

"My husband had a series of strokes and I could not care for him that's why I placed him in an assisted living home. Since he will never recover, I believe owe it to myself to live my life."

"Oh." Diane hoped her face was emotionless.

"Daily, I visit Roger. Usually, I go in the morning and again in the evening. Occasionally, I even spend the night. I don't think there's a single person who can say that I neglect him." Kellie halted and looked at Diane.

Diane said nothing. She wondered why Kellie defended how she cared for her husband. She did not know her well enough to have an opinion about what she was or was not doing for her sick husband.

Quickly, the three bonded, but each woman had their own interests. Arlene and her husband were inseparable and most of the time they did things together. As Kellie stated, she was not available to socialize until she made her evening visit to her husband.

Diane appreciated her new friends but wasted no time establishing her own social calendar. Primarily, she filled her days golfing. Despite everyone's individual busy schedules, they met once a week for lunch, a fashion show, or a "Chick Flick." They belonged to a book club that met once a month at the bookstore, All Booked Up.

CHAPTER 25

As Diane settled into her new life, she had not expected the constant sound of sirens. Morning, afternoon, and night the blaring noise continued to catch her off guard, causing her to pray, wonder, and take notice.

In addition, she had not been prepared for the number of deaths. The fact was brought to her attention when she golfed or played cards. Someone would be missing and when she inquired about them, her question was answered with sad eyes. Nothing else had to be said, she knew, the person had died.

That part of living in a retirement community was difficult. It was not that she was that much younger, but in comparison to some of her friends and neighbors, she was closer to their children or grandchildren's ages. When she thought about people dying, she never imagined the impact it would have on her.

"Hello Diane. It's Kellie. Can you drive me to The Villages' Hospital?"

"Sure. I'll meet you out front."

As Diane backed out of the garage, she saw Kellie crossing the street. When she got inside the car, Diane asked, "What's wrong?"

"It's Arlene. She mumbled something about Harold but after that I couldn't understand a single word she said."

When they arrived at the hospital, they located Arlene. Crying uncontrollably, she did not see Diane and Kellie approach her.

Diane stood beside Arlene's chair and softly said, "Arlene. Arlene."

Looking up and seeing her friends, she started screaming. Diane put her arms around her and Kellie followed suit. After several minutes of embracing Arlene, providing her with soothing words she needed to hear, she blew her nose, cleared her throat and began.

"Harold's gone." Sniffing, she said, "He died on me. He promised he would never leave me."

"What happened?"

"We were having dinner at the Nancy Lopez Country Club. We were talking and without warning he said he didn't feel well." She dabbed at her falling tears.

"It happened so fast. One minute he was talking and the next thing I knew he had fallen out of the chair. Someone called the paramedics, but when they arrived, it was too late. Harold was dead."

"Arlene, I'm sorry," Diane said.

Kellie inquired, "What can we do? Have you called your daughter?"

"No. I haven't called Missy because I need to be in control before I talk to her."

"Do you want one of us to call her?"

"No. I have to do it. It's just that I need a little more time. Having you two here makes me feel better."

Kellie left Diane with Arlene and returned carrying three hot beverages. She handed a cup to Arlene.

"Here, drink this. You'll feel better. After we finish our drinks, we'll leave and take you home, so you can rest. There's no need in worrying about the things you have to do. Tomorrow you'll have plenty of time to make telephone calls and arrangements."

Without protesting, Arlene took her time and drank her hot tea. Before they finished their drinks, Diane checked at the nurse's station to see what paper work needed to be completed. With nothing else to be done, they left.

Once they were at Arlene's house, she called her daughter. Surprisingly, she was calm and provided comfort to her. Missy made arrangements for a red eye flight, and would arrive in the morning.

Diane and Kellie spent the night at Arlene's house. In the morning, Arlene felt better. Diane went to the airport and picked up Missy. Kellie called the nursing home to tell them she would be late visiting Roger because of a family emergency.

❀   ❀   ❀

After the funeral and Missy went back to California, Diane and Kellie cared for Arlene. They forced her to do all the necessary daily functions—get up daily, wash, dress, and eat. Either Diane or Kellie cooked her meals or they ate at a restaurant to ensure she ate three meals a day. They urged her to take one day at a time.

Arlene went along with whatever Diane and Kellie told her to do. After several months, Diane suggested. "I think you should join my church's grief support group. I think you'll find it helpful."

Arlene was reluctant to go to the meeting but after much encouragement from Diane, she relented. The people were caring and Arlene realized she was not alone.

With Diane, Kellie and the support group, Arlene discovered she could go on living. She did as the group suggested, take one day at a time.

Soon after, Arlene began to socialize. In addition, she found new interests she enjoyed as a single woman.

CHAPTER 26

The light had grown brighter. Diane's body seemed to be drawn towards it. As she floated closer to the glow, she felt warmth along with an angelic peace that came over her.

She was worn-out and found it easier to let the nothingness and emptiness take control. Rather than fight to conjure up memories, she relaxed and began to let her mind bring forth whatever was present.

When Lisa returned to the waiting room, she carried drinks. She handed Patrick and Sam a can of soda. A man had taken her seat. She opened her mouth to tell him but she changed her mind. She spotted an empty seat at the other end of the room. Lisa thought about her circumstances and how she moved to Florida.

It had been several years since the death of her husband. She continued to work, not for the money but to have something to do. That was why everyone was surprised when she announced her retirement plans. Until that day, she never mentioned it to anyone, especially her staff.

Within two weeks of retiring, Lisa made good on her promise to visit Diane. Several times, Diane invited Lisa to The Villages, but she had always declined.

Diane could not understand or she had forgotten what it was like to be employed and be on vacation. The old days were gone. In today's climate a manager could not avoid the constant communication with the office thanks to cell phones, blackberries, and lap top computers. When she visited Diane, she wanted to be free of all office responsibilities.

Lisa knew Diane had been disappointed each time she invited her to visit and she declined. After awhile, Diane quit asking her. Lisa knew she would have to broach the subject. During their weekly telephone call, Lisa did just that.

"Hi, Diane. How are things going?"

"Great. What's up with you?"

"Well, I thought I would visit you. That is if the invitation is still open?"

"When are you coming?"

"Well, since I've retired, I can come any time that's convenient for you."

"You did what?"

"You heard me. I retired."

"Congratulations. Get off the phone and make your reservations. Let me know when you finalize your plans."

❧   ❧   ❧

When Lisa saw Diane, her eyes widened and her mouth flew open. She almost did not recognize her.

Diane's transformation was more than a haircut with blond highlights and the loss of fifteen pounds. What surprised Lisa were Diane's genuine smile, her perkiness and the fact that her new life was agreeing with her.

"You look absolutely fantastic." Lisa wasn't thinking when she said, "I wish Fred could see you."

Diane did not seem to mind as she put her hand on her hip and twirled around and struck a model pose.

"Do you think he'll notice the new me when I go back to Maryland and attend church service?"

"Are you kidding me? He might not recognize you. Retirement life in Florida is what you needed to start over."

They hugged. "I'm glad you came to visit."

"Me too. While I'm here, I'm going to think seriously about relocating to The Villages."

"Girl, what is there to think about?"

"I don't know. Outside of you, I don't know anyone else and at my age change is not easy. Not to mention all my family lives in Maryland."

"Come on Lisa. If I can make a change why can't you?"

"You're almost ten years younger than me and … I don't know Diane."

"Well, you're here for a week and you can decide. I'm not going to put any pressure on you. The only thing I want you to do is to keep an open mind."

During the week, Lisa rode the trolley and toured The Villages. She visited several different pools, took a few free exercise classes, played tennis, and tried the various restaurant and country club cuisines. Lisa could understand why Diane loved living in The Villages. Lisa hated when the week ended.

When Diane drove Lisa to the airport, she blurted out with excitement, "I bought a lot."

"You did what? When were you going to tell me?"

"I was going to tell you, but I started getting scared. It's a little overwhelming when I stop to think about it. I have to sell my house, tell my sisters, and make decisions about building a house. Every time I think about it, I start to have second thoughts."

"First of all, congratulations. Secondly, it will all work out and lastly, I'll help as much as possible."

"Selling my house will be easy in comparison to telling my sisters. They are not going to be happy."

"So what? This is not about your sisters. It's about you. Remember what my fears were like when I had to tell Donna and Freddie. This is your life and being the strong, independent woman I know you are, you can face your sisters."

CHAPTER 27

Returning to Maryland, Lisa was ecstatic. What had she been thinking about when she purchased the Florida property? At the time, it felt right and now there was no need questioning her decision. Her first priority was to sale the house.

After Lisa put the house on the market, she called her sisters. When they arrived, they were shocked seeing a *"For Sale"* sign in the front yard.

Before Lisa's sisters could bombard her with their questions, she took control of the luncheon.

"Girls, let's eat and then we can discuss everything, especially your questions about the *"For Sale"* sign. Although her sisters tried to ask Lisa questions, she refused to answer them until they finished lunch.

Lisa suggested, "Let's go into the living room and sit down. Now, what do you want to know?"

Alicia, Lisa's oldest sister's lips curled as she snarled, "What are you doing?"

Lisa was calm. "I'm selling my house and moving to Florida."

"Who do you know in Florida?"

"Diane Benson. You met her."

"Oh, you mean the crazy woman. The husband dumped her for a younger, prettier model."

"Alicia, don't be cruel. She's my friend."

Alicia shrugged, "If you say so. What's the diversity make-up of this retirement community?"

"I don't know and I don't care. What's important is why I'm moving there. The lifestyle is unbelievable. I can be an active senior without putting a strain on my fixed income. Besides, as a single woman, I was comfortable going to dinner, the movies and other places. I don't have children and let's face it you all have your own life. How often do we see each other?"

Lisa answered her own question. "We get together maybe once or twice a month."

Rachel dismissed what Lisa said and exclaimed, "I have an idea. Why don't we move in together? It could be fun and we would have each other as we age." Rachel's husband died after battling cancer. Lisa's husband, Paul died when a drunk driver drove down the wrong side of the street and hit his car head on.

"I have a better idea. Why don't you move to Florida with me?"

"I ... what would Francine say?"

"Your daughter has her own life. I doubt if she'd care."

"You might be right about Francine, but Lisa, I don't think I could live away from my family and friends." Her statement irritated Lisa.

"You would make new friends. Besides we would have each other. Don't make up your mind until you visit and take a look." Lisa smiled. "To help you understand where and why I'm moving, I have a videotape of the community."

They viewed it, but they did not see what Lisa saw, nor did they have the same understanding of the lifestyle. For several hours, they debated the merits of her moving. Before they left, Lisa thanked them.

"I appreciate your concern but I've made up my mind." She murmured, "I've already bought a lot and I'm having a house built. All I want is your support."

Within three months, Lisa sold her house and moved to The Villages. The only change was that she sold her lot and rather than build, she bought a previously owned house. As if it was divine intervention, Lisa found a house on Diane's street.

Settling into The Villages was easier than Lisa had expected. With Lisa's outgoing personality, she made friends easily. Her days were filled with exercise, learning new card games and taking a variety of lessons such as yoga, line dancing, and painting.

Lisa also began to date. However, it was not easy finding single men. To assist her, she turned to the usual dating methods, such as the Internet, a dating service and the newspaper ads. She also joined the First Methodist Church single's group. Lisa was more than disappointed in the dates which were less than satisfactory.

Being frustrated with her dating results, one morning an idea came to her while reading the newspaper obituaries. She started attending funeral services of deceased married women who left behind a husband.

After a reasonable time period, she delivered the grieving widower a casserole. That usually ended with her getting an invitation to dinner. She was lucky enough to find Patrick Baylor. They started dating and after months of dating, he asked Lisa to be his wife. She accepted.

CHAPTER 28

"This is a different type of pain," Diane thought. She didn't know what or who was causing her to be uncomfortable. An unusual sensation caused Diane to wish whatever was going on, that it would stop. The feeling gave her the impression that her body was being invaded.

She was tired and as much as she tried she could not communicate. Whatever was going on, she wanted it to end soon.

Lisa was restless. She could not understand what was taking so long. She told Patrick she was going for a walk.

"Don't go too far, just in case the doctor needs you."

"I won't leave this floor."

As Lisa walked around the corridor, she prayed that Diane and the baby would be okay. When she returned to the room, she opened the door and was about to enter when she hear her name being called. She turned around.

"Mrs. Henderson …" It was Diane's doctor.

"I would like to talk to you before you go inside."

As Lisa started to close the door, Patrick and Sam spoke in unison. "Wait, Lisa. Can we come?"

Lisa looked in their direction and then at the doctor who was waiting. The doctor shook her head. Lisa put up her index finger and shut the door.

In disgust, Lisa thought, privacy rules. In the old days, the doctor or nurse would come into the waiting room and share the good news of a baby's birth for everyone to hear. Today's climate had changed all of that.

Outside the waiting room, the doctor offered Lisa a chair. From the doctor's tone, Lisa did not ask questions, instead she waited. The doctor's brooding expression caused her to wonder if something went wrong.

"Mrs. Henderson, I don't know how to tell you this but ..."

"Please, just tell me. I need to know what's going on."

"The babies are doing great."

"Did you say, babies?"

"Yes. Diane surprised me as well as the delivery team. She gave birth to twin boys. They're doing fine. You can see them if you want."

"How's Diane?"

"Unfortunately, there has been no change. She is definitely in a coma and that's the good news. She made it through the delivery without any problems. We're monitoring her, and shortly she'll be moved into the intensive care unit for further testing."

"Can I visit her?"

"Uh ... Usually, the hospital prefers that only the next of kin be allowed in ICU, but under the circumstances I'll make an exception to the rule."

"You can visit her. In fact, hearing your voice might help her."

"What about the babies' father? He's here, in the waiting room. Can he see her too?"

"Yes. I'll leave permission at the nurse's station that will give the two of you visitation privileges."

The doctor said nothing else and left Lisa sitting. After the news sunk in, she went to the waiting room door and waved to Patrick and Sam. They stood up and rushed through the open door.

When they joined her, Sam waited to hear about Diane and the baby.

"Why don't we sit over here?"

Sam wanted to say something but he changed his mind. He hated drama. He wanted to hear that Diane and the baby were okay.

"Congratulations. You're the father of twin boys."

CHAPTER 29

Sam's eyes bulged as he shook his head. Did he hear right? The news of the twin boys stunned him into silence.

Lisa waited for Sam to react. She wanted some sort of emotion to erupt, even if it was anger. Although Lisa did not want to judge, she was disappointed in his lack of response.

Patrick broke the deafening quiet. "Sam. Are you okay?"

"Um … I'm sorry. I don't do well with the unexpected. How are the babies?"

"According to the doctor, they're both healthy. They weigh more than anyone expected. One weighs five pounds and the other weighs five and half pounds. If you want, we can see them?"

"Yes. I would like to see them."

He was so taken back that he had forgotten to ask about Diane. "How's Diane? Did she come out of the coma?"

"I'm afraid not, but the doctor said she's holding her own. Although there's been no change in her condition, she's been placed in ICU. According to hospital rules, only family can visit ICU patients, but the doctor made an exception for us."

At the nursery window, Lisa, Patrick, and Sam stared in wonderment.

Lisa thought how birth was such a miracle. Everyone believed their babies are adorable, but these boys were beautiful. Words could not describe their handsome, man-like features. They each had a head full of dark hair, were wrinkle free, and identical in appearance.

Lisa still could not believe Diane gave birth to twins. When Diane was pregnant she did not appear large but then again how could anyone tell? The minute Diane began gaining weight she started wearing a fat suit to disguise her pregnancy. It worked because most of her friends and neighbors thought she was gaining weight but did not find it that unusual since everyone complained about putting on weight since moving to The Villages.

When Lisa turned towards Sam, she watched his pensive facial expression and wet cheeks. When he saw Lisa studying him, he swiped at this face with the back of his hand. He forced a smile when they made eye contact.

"Sam, I'm going to visit Diane. I want to tell her about the twins."

He coughed, cleared his throat and stammered. "Uh … Uh … would you mind terribly if I told her about the boys?"

Lisa did not answer right away. She did mind but she relented. "As the father, I guess you should be the one to tell her. But I would like to see her."

When they arrived at the ICU desk, Sam and Lisa were given instructions. Sam went in first.

He eased into the room and sat down in the chair beside the bed. He picked up Diane's hand and held it. The tears came quicker than he expected. A lump formed in his throat when he tried to speak. He squared his shoulders and sniffed.

"Hi darling. Even though you're in a … what I'm trying to say is that you did good. I know you were expecting a baby girl or boy but instead we have twin boys. They are as beautiful as their mother."

Sam peered at Diane and waited, as if she was going to respond. He continued, "Diane, please wake up. Our sons need their mother." He whispered, "And I need you."

He wished Diane would blink her eyes, grunt, or move her fingers. He wanted some assurance that she was aware of what he was saying. But the only sounds in the room came from the monitoring machines.

"What I'm about to say, I should have said the minute you told me about the pregnancy. I love you Diane, but I was having difficulty with all the life changes. My wife died, I met you, moved, and then you told me you were pregnant. I did not know how to react, so I left everything up to you. I was wrong to do that. I'm sorry."

CHAPTER 30

Sam and Lisa could only visit ten minutes at a time. Sam's time had gone by too fast. As much as he wanted to stay, he left the room.

Lisa entered the room and did not waste time talking to Diane. Her appearance had not changed from when she saw her before she delivered the boys. Her face was aglow and she appeared to be sleeping.

"Girl, you did it this time. Your babies are gorgeous." Slyly, Lisa said, "They have Sam's handsome face. He could have spit them out but I keep saying they're the exact image of their beautiful mother."

Lisa turned serious and chewed on her lip before saying, "Diane, I haven't called Freddie or Donna. If you don't wake up soon, I'm going to have to make a decision. They should know what's going on. If something happens to you …" Lisa did not finish what she was going to say in fear that by saying it aloud it would somehow make it true.

Ten minutes was up. Lisa had to leave. She wanted to stay with her friend and assure her that everything was in God's hands and he would not let anything happen to her. When Lisa left the room, tears rolled down her face.

Patrick worried about Lisa. She needed to take care of herself. "You need to rest and eat something." Lisa started to protest but she knew Patrick was right.

"We can come back later or wait until tomorrow. The hospital has your number and I'm sure they'll call if there's a change."

"Lisa, I'm not leaving," Sam was firm. "I'm going to stay as long as the hospital will permit. I know I can't be in the room with Diane but I'll be here. If there's any change, I'll call you. Listen to Patrick and get some rest."

Lisa gave Sam a hug. At first he flinched but then returned the affection. When Lisa tried to pull away, he held on.

Patrick interrupted their embrace. "Sam, you need to eat too. Let me get you something. Then Lisa and I will leave."

Before Sam could protest, Patrick walked off. When he was no longer in hearing distance, Lisa went straight to her concern.

"Sam, since the babies are not under weight and have no health issues, the hospital may want to release the boys especially since we don't know how long Diane will be in a coma. Have you considered what you might do?"

"What do you mean?"

"If the boys are released from the hospital, are you going to take them?"

"Oh. Uh ... I haven't given it any thought. I'm still trying to get used to being a father of two and now you're asking me if I can take care of them until Diane gets better."

Lisa cocked her head to the side and wanted to add but didn't. "You need to consider what you're going to do if Diane doesn't make it."

Sam ran his hand over his face. He sat motionless and numb. In a low voice, he groaned. "I'm not prepared to take care of one baby, let alone two. If I don't take the boys what do you think will happen to them?"

"I'm not really sure. I guess the hospital will call social services and place the boys in foster care until Diane comes out of the coma or ..."

Sam turned his head. He did not want Lisa to see his tears. He cleared his throat and asked, "Are there any other options?"

"I don't know."

CHAPTER 31

Lisa was worried about Diane's condition. At first her appearance had a beautiful radiance, but as the days passed, her cheekbones were more prominent, her skin pasty, and her hair dull. Overall she appeared frail.

If Diane's doctor had been in to see her then Lisa had missed her. She had questions and she wanted some answers. She walked to the nurse's station.

"Dr. Irwin should be in around ten o'clock. I'll page her for you." After the page could be heard over the P.A. system, Dr. Irwin appeared.

Hello Mrs. Henderson. It's nice to see you again. How are you?"

"I'm fine, but I'm concerned about Diane. Her condition doesn't seem to be improving."

"You haven't seen her new doctor?"

"New doctor, what do you mean?"

"I've turned her case over to her primary doctor. This isn't my specialty. I'm an OB-GYN. Since she's had her babies, I'm no longer qualified to treat her. I suggest you contact Dr. Myers."

"Thank you," Lisa said through clenched teeth. She held back her anger and managed not to take it out on Dr. Irwin. She knew Dr. Irwin was right, but why didn't the doctor tell her sooner. Did anyone care?

Lisa called Diane's new doctor. He said he would discuss Diane's condition with her when he made rounds.

❦   ❦   ❦

"Mrs. Henderson, I'm pleased to meet you."

"I'm Dr. Myers. Again, I'm sorry I did not speak to you when I was assigned Diane's case."

Lisa waited for an explanation but he provided none as he continued. "Diane has been examined by a neurosurgeon. He gave her a battery of tests."

Dr. Myers paused. Lisa thought from his expression he was searching for the right words.

"Diane did not respond to any of the tests. She may be brain-dead."

"What? How can you be sure?"

Dr. Myers did not mince his words. "The medical profession sees this all the time. Coma patients are difficult to predict. When you have someone, like Diane, who has been unresponsive to stimulation and commands, there's little hope. Generally, the tests do not lie."

"But, it hasn't been that long and you're giving up on her."

"Mrs. Henderson, it's not that we're giving up on Diane but if she doesn't improve within two weeks, she may die or go into a vegetated state."

Lisa could not believe what she was hearing. She wanted to scream at the matter-of-fact, non-feeling doctor—"You don't know Diane. She's a fighter. Diane was going to come out of the coma."

Before leaving, the doctor added, "At some point, you may want to consider taking her off life support."

Lisa should have asked more questions but numbness consumed her body. The information the doctor told her was not what she had expected.

She was not looking forward to telling Sam. Like her, he refused to accept the doctor's conclusions. He wanted and asked Lisa to order a second opinion. The results were the same.

CHAPTER 32

Each day Lisa waited and prayed nothing else would go wrong. To her dismay she received a telephone call from social services. An appointment was made for her to meet with the social worker.

"Mrs. Henderson, I understand but there is no reason for the boys to remain in the hospital."

"I'm begging you. Please wait. This is an unusual situation. Isn't there anything you can do?"

"I'll tell you what. It's my understanding that Mrs. Benson will be transferred to a nursing home sometime next week. The boys can remain in the hospital until then."

"Thank you. You have no idea how happy you've made me."

After Lisa's meeting with the social worker, she talked to Sam. Unfortunately, he had not changed his mind.

"I don't want to discuss this. I have no answers. I'm not equipped to take care of two infants."

"What if I babysit the boys while you work?" Lisa paused and rushed on. "I mean I'll help you as much as possible. I know we could care for them."

"I appreciate your offer but I can't do it. Besides, I know Diane's coming out of the coma."

Lisa wanted to scream, "You haven't heard one word of what I've said. Your boys are close to being placed in a foster home."

Lisa was running out of time. She was going to try one last option. She broached the social worker.

"I would like to become the boys' legal guardian. What would I have to do?"

The social worker took her time in answering Lisa. "Mrs. Henderson, the process for becoming the boys' guardian is similar to those that want to adopt." She shook her head.

"Let's be realistic. I mean no disrespect but considering your age, you live in a retirement community and you're on a fixed income. I doubt you'll receive guardianship approval."

The social worker must have been reading Lisa's mind as she continued, "Mrs. Henderson, I doubt you would even be approved to be a foster parent."

Lisa left the meeting downhearted. She was at the point that she needed to start making some hard decisions. She would have to call Diane's children. She had six days before she would have to make a decision. That was when Diane was to be transferred to a nursing home.

Why was Sam being so indifferent with regard to the boys? Every time she talked to him, she wanted to shake some sense into him. She was not sure why he was reluctant to take responsibility. With each conversation, she began to dislike Sam to the point she began to avoid him. When they did talk, the dialogue was unfriendly and strained.

Before the strain developed into an unhealthy confrontation, Lisa and Sam worked out a visiting schedule. Lisa sat with Diane, starting at nine o'clock until Sam arrived at noon and left between one and one-thirty. Lisa returned and stayed until he returned around six o'clock.

❦   ❦   ❦

Lisa failed to notice the dentist appointment that was scribbled on her wall calendar. She would be late going to the hospital. She thought about calling Sam, but changed her mind.

As she sat in the dentist office, she grew impatient. The dentist was late, which meant all the appointments were delayed.

By the time she left the office, it was almost noon. She hoped she would arrive at the hospital before Sam. The last thing she wanted was to explain why she missed the morning schedule and why she did not call him.

After breaking the speed limit, Lisa arrived at the hospital. She rushed to Diane's room. When she opened the door, she covered her mouth so her scream could not be heard.

The beat of Lisa's heart was loud, her burning throat was dry, and her eyes began to water.

As calmly as possible, she turned around and proceeded to the nurse's station. Before she could reach the station, Sam walked off the elevator.

CHAPTER 33

As Lisa approached Sam, she avoided making eye contact with him. She gulped and swallowed the lump in her throat.

"You're early aren't you?"

"Not really, what's going on?"

"Well … I …" She paused as she stammered out an explanation. "I was late and when I arrived, Diane …"

Sam brushed pass Lisa. She grabbed his arm with force. He turned around.

"What's happened?"

"Diane isn't in her room. I was on my way to the nurse's station." Sam glared at Lisa. She ignored the look and proceeded to the nurse's station.

"Excuse me."

A nurse put the file folder down and glanced up at Lisa. "May I help you?"

"Yes. My name is Lisa Henderson." She paused, realizing she had been holding her breath. "I'm …"

Sam stood beside her. She motioned her hand toward him. "We're here to visit Diane Benson, but she's not in her room."

"I'm sorry. Someone was supposed to call you. I guess you didn't get the message." Lisa shook their head.

The nurse grimaced and murmured, "We needed the bed. Since Mrs. Benson was no longer in any immediate danger, the doctor ordered her to be moved out of ICU."

Before Lisa exploded, Sam had both hands on the desk and leaned close to the nurse's face. His tone was firm as he spoke through tightened teeth. "Who ordered this?"

"As I stated, Mrs. Benson's doctor ordered the move. I'm sorry sir. If you have any additional questions, you should discuss them with the doctor."

Lisa placed her hand on Sam's arm and said, "Fine. What floor has she been moved to?"

"Fifth floor, she's in room 524."

Lisa and Sam walked down the corridor in silence. Lisa knew he was angry for a number of reasons but it wasn't anyone's fault. They knew it was a matter of days before Diane would be relocated to a nursing home. Decisions had to be made, and neither one of them wanted to make them.

When they walked off the elevator and looked for Diane's room, Lisa thought how different it was. In the ICU unit, nurses guarded every entry and were attentive to patients. On this floor, people were coming and going as they pleased and there were fewer nurses.

Sam entered Diane's room, Lisa followed. All the monitors had been removed except for the IV and a heart monitor.

Lisa's knees buckled when she saw Diane. She blinked, trying hard not to cry. A drastic change had occurred in Diane's overall appearance. Her skin was rough, pale and it had an ashy hue. Her hair lacked luster.

Lisa thought overall, Diane appeared lifeless and resembled … she couldn't finish her thought. How could this have happened so fast? Was Diane giving up?

Although Sam's reaction was not as noticeable as Lisa's, he was stunned. Despite the two empty chairs, Lisa remained standing as Sam slumped into one.

The room was quiet except for one humming machine. Lisa could not wait to leave. She needed air. She was glad it was Sam's time to visit. She needed time to regain her composure.

Sam picked up Diane's hand. Before leaving, Lisa touched his shoulder. "I'll be back. Take your time."

When Lisa walked out of the room, Sam pressed his lips against Diane's hand. He cleared his throat.

"Diane, you have to wake up. Please don't die. We're running out of time. I don't know what to do? I'm confused. I know I signed adoption papers before we met with the doctor about you having an abortion. Since you kept the baby was it your intention to have the baby adopted?"

Sam had so many questions. If Diane was going to give the babies up for adoption, whom was he supposed to contact? From Lisa's questions and persistence about him taking the boys, she obviously was not aware of Diane's adoption plans.

Thirty minutes later Lisa returned to the room. She eased inside. Sam did not acknowledge her.

She whispered, "Sam, are you going back to work?"

He placed Diane's hand on the bed and kissed her on the forehead.

Sam left Diane's bedside. As he walked by Lisa, he forced himself to smile as they made eye contact. Neither said anything.

CHAPTER 34

Diane's jigsaw puzzled mind was not coming together as fast as she had liked. It was as if pieces were missing and that was why she could not complete the picture. In addition, as much as she tried to open her eyes and to communicate, all attempts had failed. She hoped to unlock the mystery as she continued to scroll through her memory bank.

Fred's affair, the divorce, and heartache had left Diane bitter, angry, and a distrust of all men. After her experience with Fred, she vowed never to be vulnerable again. Dating was something she had no interest in.

Lisa, Arlene, and Kellie respected Diane's viewpoint about relationships; therefore, they seldom discussed topics involving dating, marriage, or divorce.

On one of their girls'-night out, Kellie decided to broach the forbidden subject. Kellie did not care if she ruffled Diane's feathers.

Kellie knew the answer but asked anyway. "Diane, have you dated anyone since your divorce?"

"No, I haven't and I have no plans to." Bitterness dripped from Diane's response. "Besides, after Fred, why would I trust another man?"

"Because you're young, beautiful, and you shouldn't deprive yourself of male companionship. If women stopped doing things every time they had a bad experience, they wouldn't do much of anything. I mean who hasn't been hurt?"

"That may be true, but I'm not ready for that kind of heartache again. The hurt is too fresh and at times my heart still feels the puncture wounds. Besides, I'll never be able to forget the painful event that changed my life forever."

Kellie shifted her attention. "What about you Arlene?"

"I don't think I could go out with another man since ..." Arlene's voice trailed off.

Diane was annoyed. She was not sure why they were having this discussion. She glanced at Arlene and without either of them saying it they both knew what the other was thinking. *"Why was Kellie interested in dating? After all, she was married and Roger was very much alive."*

"I can't believe you two. You're both attractive women who have lots of years to live. You can't tell me you've decided never to have male companionship again? Come on ladies." She looked at them through narrowed eyes.

"You need to take a page out of Lisa's book. Nothing in her past has caused her not to date."

"What do you mean?" Arlene asked.

"She hasn't allowed her husband's death or her relocation to a different state prevent her from dating. If you haven't noticed, she dates quite often."

"Oh I've seen her go out, but I've only seen her with one man." Arlene had to admit that, she was curious. "Have you asked her about her dates, Diane?"

Defensively, Diane replied, "No I haven't and I don't plan to ask her. It's none of my business. Besides, since I'm not interested in dating, why would I care that she's dating?"

Kellie responded. "Please. Inquiring minds want to know. I can't believe neither of you is the least bit interested."

Arlene shrugged. "As I said earlier, I'm curious. Maybe I would like to know how she's finding men to date, especially living in The Villages. But, I'm not necessarily interested in dating."

As an afterthought, Arlene added, "Until you brought the subject up, I really had not given dating too much thought. If the situation presented itself, maybe I would keep an open mind."

"Why don't we ask Lisa?" Kellie suggested.

CHAPTER 35

Within days of the discussion, the women confronted Lisa. She was less than willing to talk about her dating.

The women were curious. Kellie pressured her. "We want to know your secret in finding single men to date."

Lisa avoided answering Kellie. Instead, she asked them a question. "Have you tried a dating service, the want ads, or the Internet?"

"Come on Lisa, those methods don't work. Tell us your secret."

"For one thing, I'm only dating one man and his name is Patrick Baylor."

"That might be true, but before you settled on one man, you were dating lots of other men. What's your secret?"

A thought occurred to Arlene. "Are these men married and that's why you won't tell us how you find them?"

Lisa sat wide-eyed. "Oh, my goodness ... no."

The women kept hammering Lisa until she relented. "I find the men in the newspaper obituaries."

They stared at Lisa as if she had said she was dating the dead. They made funny comments until they laughed. Raising her hand, Lisa quieted them and defended her answer.

"You asked and I told you." Lisa crossed her arms across her chest. "I know it's hard to believe, but that's what I do. I read the daily obituaries." The women realized Lisa was serious.

Diane was intrigued. "How does it work?"

"I read the local area daily newspaper obituaries. I review the women who have died and left behind living spouses. I attend the funeral service, do some research on the couple, and take the grieving widower a homemade casserole. The casserole delivery works better when the man doesn't cook."

"And this works?"

"Yes." Lisa raised her right hand. "I swear, Girl Scouts Honor."

Kellie was leery. "This is not new." She shook her head. "Other women have delivered casseroles and from what I understand, they didn't have much success. Not to mention, I've laughed at the casserole parade brigade. To me they seemed a little desperate." Diane and Arlene nodded their heads in agreement.

Kellie continued, "If you don't want to share your secret with your friends, we understand."

"Kellie, I'm telling you the truth. That's my secret." Lisa made a tent with her hands and tried explaining again.

"I think the reason why my method works is because I have a jump start on the other women. By the time they realize the man's wife has died, I've already delivered the casserole and in most cases have been on several dates."

Lisa waited for the women to comment. "Since you don't believe me, why don't you try it?" She cocked her head to the side and said, "Then, let me know if it works."

Kellie was anxious to try it. "Will you explain your method to us?"

Diane and Arlene had reservations, not only about the method, but also about dating. They were not convinced that dating was in their best interest.

Finally, Kellie wore them down and they agreed to try Lisa's method. After receiving Lisa's instructions, the women were pleasantly surprised at the results. Each woman had identified a man to date, and they were pleased.

CHAPTER 36

Every time Diane thought she was making progress, it was like her mind would shut down. In addition, her head was woozy from the bright light. Her body was growing closer and closer to it.

Every day, Sam sat with Diane. Some days, he read to her while other times, he just talked to her.

"Diane, please wake up. We need you. If you don't come back to us, the boys might be placed in foster care." He waited there was no response.

"Do you remember the day you showed up on my doorstep?"

Sam would never forget the day she came, carrying a casserole. She appeared nervous when he opened the front door.

"Hi. May I help you?"

"Hi." Diane extended her hand and introduced herself. "I'm Diane Benson."

Smiling broadly, he could not help notice how attractive she was. Her voice was like music to his ears.

"I'm looking for Sam Childers."

"That's me."

"I heard about your wife and I wanted to offer my condolences."

An awkward moment stood between them until Sam asked, "What is that heavenly smell? I'm sorry, but the aroma is distracting me."

Shyly, she said, "Oh, the casserole. I thought maybe you might want to eat something home cooked."

"I appreciate your thoughtfulness. Please come in."

"No, I couldn't do that. I don't want to intrude. She pushed the dish toward him, but he refused to take it."

Opening the door wider, he insisted, "Please, come in." Diane did not lodge any more protests as she walked inside.

It wasn't until Diane entered inside the house that he noticed the house's décor. His late wife had been the decorator. It was done in bamboo and wicker, open and airy. Large palm trees and other green plants had been placed throughout the room. He remembered how they had argued over the tall, palm trees indoors but it was her intent to bring Florida's outdoor scenery indoors.

While eating the casserole, Sam hoped he had not overwhelmed Diane by talking so much about his late wife, Wendie. This was the first time he had ever shared his feelings about her death. He explained how a drunk driver had killed her as she crossed the street.

After Sam discussed his wife, they both shared other information about their lives. They were both from Maryland and still had family living there. They also discovered they had similar interests—golfing, tennis, and hiking.

After Diane helped him clean up the kitchen, she said, "I've over stayed my welcome. I really need to go."

"Do you have to?" He asked.

"Yes. I do."

"Listen, why don't you let me take you to dinner tomorrow night?"

"I don't know." It took her several minutes to accept his invitation.

"Okay, I'll go, but on one condition."

"What is that?"

"You pay for your dinner and I'll pay for mine."

CHAPTER 37

Sam thought his first date with Diane was magical. Sam hated clichéd statements but it was, as if he had known Diane his entire life.

When they were not seeing each other, they spent hours on the phone talking about everything and anything. Within weeks, Sam realized his feelings shifted from a light romance to something deeper and more meaningful.

Their conversations were interesting and lively, the laughter effortless, and their kisses electrifying. They enjoyed each others' company more than either of them had expected.

Sam brought Diane pleasure, but he believed Diane guarded her feelings. He was sure he reminded her of the hurt he could cause. He might be different from her ex-husband, Fred, but they both put their pants on one leg at a time.

He continued to reminisce about Diane.

Glancing at his watch, Sam admonished himself because he had fifteen minutes before picking Diane up. He sped in an effort not to be late.

Opening the door, he smiled. When he stepped in, he gathered her into his arms. Their kiss was long and deep. She put her arms around his neck and their bodies began to mold together similar to a sculpture. Up and down her neck, he planted kisses.

"Mmm. You taste good enough to forget about dinner." Diane threw back her head and giggled

Diane's body responded to Sam's touch and she seemed agreeable but he was not confident she was ready to take their foreplay to the next level. They had discussed sex and she had been clear about it.

"When I make love to a man, it will be what I want and when I'm ready." As a result, he had not pushed the issue.

Without warning, Diane pulled away. "We better leave if we want to catch the seven o'clock movie."

Sam had gotten confused as Diane's mood changed so abrupt. "Did I do or say something wrong?"

"No, but I'm just not sure we should … you know."

Taking her hand and brushing a kiss across her lips, Sam said, "I understand and I don't want to do anything you're not ready for."

Sam took a deep breath. They stood gazing into each other's eyes. Again, without warning, Diane laid her lips on his. Nervously, they pulled apart and a slight laugh escaped her.

He covered her lips again. After that, everything faded into a vague memory of pulling at each other's clothes, hands touching each other's sensitive areas and then nakedness on the bed.

Sam planted kisses along her neck and slowly worked his way down her body and up again. She responded naturally without persuasion.

Panic covered her face and Sam understood her concern. He reached over on the bedside table and pulled a condom out of his wallet.

After Diane and Sam made love, it was as if that moment cemented their relationship.

After several months, Sam knew he wanted more. When he broached the subject, either Diane started talking about something else or they ended up in the bed. As much as he enjoyed making love to Diane, he wanted more than a casual fling. He wanted a future with her.

CHAPTER 38

One evening Sam took a risk. He wanted Diane to understand his intentions. He decided to be clear.

"I'm selling the house and moving. I need a new start and I can't do it in this house. I'm no longer comfortable living here, especially when we're together. It's as if I'm cheating on Wendie."

"Where are you moving to?"

"I'm not sure, but I've been looking for an apartment in Leesburg."

He noticed the tension in Diane's face disappeared. She was probably thinking about the conversation they had about him leaving the state of Florida. He could tell his decision made her happy.

He found the apartment he wanted in Leesburg but was afraid it would be taken because the house was taking longer to sell than he expected. When the house sold, he declined Diane's offer to help him move. It wasn't until he was settled that he called her.

"Hi, Diane. This is Sam."

"Hi." Hearing his voice, Diane's body temperature began to rise.

"Remember I told you I was moving. Well, I'm settled and wanted to give you my new address and telephone number."

"Okay, but I wished you had let me help you."

"I'm sorry, but this was something I had to do on my own. It was like a ritual for me—saying good-bye to the old and hello to the new."

"I think I understand more than you know."

Diane never told Sam the entire reason for her divorce. That was a part of her life she did not care to share with him. Sometimes baggage was best left unclaimed.

"I couldn't have done this if I hadn't met you."

"You give me too much credit."

"No I don't. Why don't you come over for dinner?"

"You've been keeping a secret from me. I didn't know you could cook."

"I can't, but if you're excited about my cooking skills wait until you see what else I can do." His smooth baritone voice sounded sultry and enticing.

"You're a tease."

"No, I'm not. Wait until you see how thorough I can be when marinating and seasoning."

"Maybe you'll have an opportunity to show me later."

"Oh I will be more than happy to show you."

"What about dessert?"

"Do we need dessert? You're sweet enough that if you put your finger in my mouth it would satisfy my sweet tooth."

Diane blushed. With every word he uttered, her body warmed flushed with heat. Quickly, she put the conversation back on track.

"What time do you want me come to dinner and can I bring something?"

"Six o'clock and just bring your gorgeous self."

"Okay."

Hanging up the phone, Sam smiled. She was so sexy and she made him feel alive. At times, she expressed how she felt too old to be sexy. He did everything to assure her that she was more desirable than he could explain.

Sometimes when Sam thought about Diane, he was embarrassed. He wondered if she had the fantasies he had about their sex life. At times, all she had to do was to brush against him or gaze at him and his thoughts went from his head to his pants.

CHAPTER 39

From ear to ear, Sam grinned. He was anxious about seeing Diane. He no longer wanted to wait he needed to talk to her, even though it was risky.

After Wendie's death he questioned why he should live. Losing the love of his life had been the most difficult experience he had ever encountered.

He never told Diane but other women had delivered him casseroles but when she showed up on his doorstep he knew it was the turning point in his life.

As much as he had loved and missed his wife, he slowly came to grips with how death was a part of life. Moving on with his life did not mean he would stop loving Wendie. In addition, he would always cherish her memory. Sam also knew she would want him to get on with his life, even if that meant loving another woman.

When he first met Diane, he had to admit he was probably trying to fill the void Wendie had left behind. The last thing he wanted was a relationship, but as he spent more time with Diane, he realized how lonely he had been.

His friends and relatives were not happy with his decision. They warned him about getting involved with a woman so soon. His sister was the most vocal.

"Sam, you're trying to replace Wendie. This is not healthy. Why don't you give yourself more time?"

As close as he was to his sister, she did not understand. Diane and Wendie were different. Wendie was petite and small. She enjoyed indoor activities—reading, sewing, and soap operas.

Diane was average height and a size ten or twelve. She was energetic and preferred physical activities such as golfing, bowling, hiking, and tennis.

The only similarity—both women were twelve years older than him. Unlike Wendie, Diane wasn't comfortable dating a younger man.

He believed Diane's uneasiness was because of her two grown children whom she seldom talked about. Not to mention, he was sure she had not told them about him.

The reason was probably because of Diane's insecurities. To help her feel more secure, he decided to take the guesswork out of their relationship.

The ringing doorbell interrupted his thoughts. Glancing around the room, he was pleased with the flowers and lit candles.

Opening the door, he stood with a big, goofy grin. His face turned crimson as he admiringly surveyed Diane.

"Hi, Sam. Is something wrong?"

"No."

Grabbing her hand, he pulled her into the apartment. Unable to contain himself, he kissed her deeply.

Diane responded. He could feel her heart pounding against his chest. Their kisses left him wanting more. When their lips separated, Diane pulled slightly away.

"We better stop if we're going to eat dinner." Diane could not hide the natural redness in her face.

"I agree with you, but you're so delectable that I could forgo dinner." Sam tried to kiss Diane again, but she dodged him playfully. Besides Sam's natural fragrance, the most wonderful aroma filled Diane's nostrils.

"What is that delicious smell?"

"It's my mother's secret chicken casserole dish. It's an easy recipe to make, but I promised, I would never give the recipe to anyone."

Dinner was exceptional, but Sam knew it had nothing to do with the food. He could not remember the last time he felt so alive, even when he was married.

They cleared the table, put the dishes in the dishwasher, and put away the leftovers. Sam couldn't wait any longer as he pulled Diane into his arms.

Easing his embrace, Sam gazed into Diane's eyes. "I know we just met, and my wife hasn't been dead that long, but I'm falling in love with you."

CHAPTER 40

Telling Diane that he loved her was the hardest thing Sam had ever done. Rather than rush her, he let her digest what he had said. He had no idea what she might have been thinking.

He watched her, not knowing how she might respond.

Diane tried to put things into perspective as she thought—not another unexpected surprise. A lump formed in her throat. Hearing Sam's response paralyzed her vocal cords.

Diane had not been prepared to hear the "L" word. When she first met Sam, she referred to him as her *"boy toy"* and did not want any emotional attachment to him. And now he was confessing his love for her.

How could she respond? Diane did not want to be hurt again, but why shouldn't she take a risk? Life was short and she was not getting any younger.

When Diane was about to respond, her eyes caught a glimpse of a framed photo sitting on a nearby table. In all the times she had been to Sam's house, she had never noticed it. She needed to take a closer look at it. Could it be? Her stomach was queasy and her head was spinning.

A nervous laugh escaped from Sam. "Diane. Did I shock you that much? Diane."

She shook her head. "Uh … no. It's just that you surprised … I wasn't expecting you to say that."

As much as she wanted to tell him that she had similar feelings, she could not. The unanswered questions she had regarding the photo would impact any type of relationship they might have.

"I want you to get used to hearing those words. I'll say it again. I'm falling in love with you."

Again, he waited. Diane's legs were wobbly. Gently, she pulled away from his embrace.

"Sam, let's sit down."

They sat on the sofa. Lovingly, she looked at him through misty eyes. "You're a wonderful man, but I think it's too soon for you to know what you feel."

Running his fingers through his hair, he was frustrated and disappointed. He wished people would stop telling him what was in his heart. He was not a teenager with a crush or a rebound from a bad breakup or even a death.

"Diane, please listen to me. It might be too soon to discuss my feelings, but I know what it means to be in love. Maybe I should have waited, but I thought you felt …" He did not finish his sentence.

"I didn't mean to question your sincerity. How can you be sure? I'm not sure what I feel is love. I enjoy being with you and …"

He prevented her from saying another word as he gathered her in his arms. His kisses were tender and sensual. Without Diane protesting, he laid her back on the sofa.

He covered her mouth with intensity and a hunger she recognized. Diane's body followed Sam's rhythmic moves as if they were on the dance floor, bumping and grinding to a slow song.

Diane's mind was enthralled by Sam's foreplay. Sam was the drug and she was the addict. Her body desired, ached, and craved him, similar to an alcoholic needing the next drink.

Their body temperatures were similar to a sweltering, summer day. She knew it was a matter of minutes before they would be swept into a world of ecstasy.

Before they reached a pleasurable level of satisfaction, Diane's whispered, "Sam, you need …"

CHAPTER 41

Under different circumstances, Sam would not mind time moving fast but when he visited Diane, he wanted it to slow down. In addition, it was a matter of days before Diane was to be moved from the hospital and he had made no decisions regarding their sons.

In addition, he knew Lisa was not pleased with his indecisiveness. If only Diane would wake up. All his problems would be resolved. He prayed every day but his prayers had gone unanswered.

"I have to go my sweet. I'll see you later."

Lisa spotted Sam leaving Diane's room. They were acting like children after a fight, avoiding each other. To Lisa, it was plain and simple Sam needed to take responsibility. If not, his boys could end up in foster care.

When Lisa entered Diane's room, Lisa thought she looked better. Her complexion was pale but there was a little color on her cheeks.

"Hey, girl. How are you doing today?" Lisa brushed her hair and changed her gown. When she finished, she sat in the nearby chair and started talking to her.

"Do you remember when you were sick and didn't know why?" Lisa chuckled as she talked about it.

Diane had no sense of time. It might have been hours or days but it had been awhile since she had recalled any memories. Just as she pondered about it, she began thinking about Lisa.

Lisa had called Diane. They had not talked in several weeks.

"Hey girl, what have you been up to? I don't know about you, but I've been enjoying the time I spend with Patrick. Has Sam been keeping you busy?"

Diane grinned. Lisa had asked her several questions, but had not given her time to answer. When Lisa paused Diane jumped in quickly.

"I was wondering how you've been doing? I've missed you, Arlene, and Kellie. I hope that having men in our lives won't stop us from doing our girls'-night out."

Something in Diane's voice caused Lisa to pause. She wondered what was going on.

"Are you okay?"

"To be honest, I don't know." In a weak voice, Diane continued, "For the first time in a long time I'm happy, but yet I've been depressed, queasy, and moody. To be truthful, I can't describe how I've been feeling."

Lisa chuckled. "Have you had a visit from your little red-headed cousin?"

Diane started laughing. "No. I haven't had my monthly."

"Well, maybe, you're menopausal."

"Do you think I could be? I mean until now, it never entered my mind." She stopped and smiled. "I guess I am at that age, aren't I?"

"You should make a doctor's appointment. When I had similar symptoms, my doctor gave me a simple blood test to determine what menopausal stage I was in."

"Are you taking replacement hormones?"

"No. My doctor and I were at the beginning stages of menopause at the same time. She discussed the pros and cons about taking hormones. She decided not to take them and I figured if my doctor wasn't going to use them, why should I? Based on the doctor's recommendations, I took the natural remedy route."

Diane wanted to know. "Did it work?"

"Well, there's nothing to support the theory that natural remedies work, but I took black cohosh, vitamins, and drank green tea. I'm at the end of menopause, and I have to say I coped fairly well. As for my private summers, I have learned to ride them out."

"What in the world are you talking about?"

"You know—hot flashes. All women talk about their hot flashes in different terms, such as private summers, power surges, or heat waves. For some reason, I liked the phrase "*private summers*" and use it when referring to hot flashes."

"Are they the worse of menopause?"

"Everyone's different. For me, I would rather have the hot flashes than the mood swings. There are days when all I have to do is think, see, hear, or smell and I become weepy. In addition, I never know what will set me off emotionally."

"Boy does that sound familiar. At the drop of a hat, I've been crying about everything and anything. What about queasiness?"

"Not only queasiness, but lost of appetite, weight gain, bloating, insomnia—you name it and I experienced it. But, let me stop. I don't want to paint a grim picture of menopause. As I said earlier, every woman is different, but yet every woman is alike. Think of menopause as you did when you first started your period."

CHAPTER 42

After they talked, Lisa could hear the relief in Diane's voice. Lisa was happy she was able to ease Diane's mind. She no longer had to worry and imagine that she had some incurable disease. Lisa was 98 percent sure Diane's symptoms were nothing more than the beginning stages of menopause.

Getting the confirmation from the doctor would be the best medical news Diane could possibly receive. Diane told Lisa that she enjoyed not having her monthly—the one positive menopausal benefit. Diane promised to call Lisa after her doctor's appointment.

"Mrs. Benson, I'm sorry I've kept you waiting, but I had a telephone call I had to take." Silence hung in the air as the doctor thumbed through Diane's medical folder.

"From my exam, I think you're doing fine. However, I do want you to come in tomorrow for some additional blood work."

"Why? What's wrong?"

"There's nothing to be alarmed about. I might be premature, but I'm almost positive that your problem is because you're pregnant."

"What are you talking about?"

"When I examined you, I would say you might be about four weeks. That's why I want...."

"Dr. Irwin, I'm forty-eight years old. How could this have happened?"

"You don't know?" Dr. Irwin smiled.

"No. I'm serious. I thought I was beyond childbearing age. I mean aren't I too old to have...."

Diane stopped. Several things occurred to her. She was divorced, retired and had two grown married children. She started laughing until she cried.

"Mrs. Benson, are you okay?"

"Yes." She cleared her throat. "It's ... never mind." Diane started to tell the doctor about her current situation, but she changed her mind. She did not think the doctor would think what she was going through would be that funny.

"Once we receive the blood work results, we'll discuss prenatal care and other precautions we'll take during your pregnancy. On your way out, remember to schedule an appointment. Have a great afternoon."

When Diane got in her car, she was not convinced she was pregnant. She did not care what the doctor said. Medical mistakes happen, more often than doctors were willing to admit.

Not realizing it, Diane had driven to Walgreen's and had parked her car. She got out and walked inside the drug store.

She bought a home pregnancy kit and could not wait to take the test. After the results, she would have a good laugh.

Opening the kit, she read the directions, twice. She did not want to make a mistake. The test took fifteen minutes.

She followed the directions and set the timer. Fifteen minutes was going to seem like an hour as she put the toilet lid down and sat on it. She closed her eyes and thought about the saying, *"A watched pot never boils."*

When the buzzer went off, it startled her. Before she picked up the kit, she took a deep breath.

Closely, she stared at the results. She refused to panic. "How reliable can a home kit be?"

CHAPTER 43

Something was weird. Diane was happy to recall her visit to the doctor but it was as if Lisa was telling her about it. After all, Lisa knew every detail and could repeat the incident verbatim. Was she hearing Lisa's voice or was her mind so jumbled that she didn't know what the difference between a dream and reality was?

Lisa hoped that telling Diane about her doctor visit and how she found out she was pregnant and not menopausal might help her come out of the coma. Sam walked up behind Lisa. She jumped when she noticed him. She had no idea how long he had been standing there.

It was Sam's time to visit. She stood up, leaned over and kissed Diane on the cheek.

Sam felt a tinge of guilt when Lisa turned away from Diane and passed by him. He had heard Lisa recalling the time when Diane received word from the doctor that she was pregnant. That was the first time he had heard any of the story.

Sam spoke to Diane and sat down. Hearing Lisa it reminded him of what it was like when he learned about the pregnancy.

Several days had passed and Sam had no idea why he had not heard from Diane. The last time they were together, he thought she was different. He could not explain it.

She had said she was going to the doctor. He knew from being married to an older woman that she was probably at the beginning stages of menopause.

Calling several times a day was not cool, but he wanted—no needed—to talk to her. Menopause was not a death sentence. It was just another phase of a woman's life. Since Diane had not called him, he had not been able to sleep or eat. He was distracted and could not work. He called in sick.

Although he was not sick, he had taken catnaps off and on all day and had little or no energy. Going to the kitchen, he thought he would fix a bowl of soup. As he opened the refrigerator, the phone rang.

"Hello." He was sure his heart skipped a beat.

"Hi, sweet.…" He stopped. "Hi, Diane."

"I need to see you." Her voice was terse.

That is what he wanted to hear. He did not know what to say next. He wanted her to come to his apartment, but he did not want to push her.

"Why don't I come over there?"

"Okay. I'll see you later. Take care and I …" He didn't say it. The phone went dead.

Ever since Diane's telephone call, all he had done was think about what she had to tell him. He tried to be positive, but the sound of her voice had made him uneasy.

When Diane rang the doorbell, her hand shook. Her heart boomed against her chest. Her hands were clammy. Before she could push the doorbell again, Sam opened the door. He looked handsome as ever and he smelled delicious enough to eat.

"Hi, Diane. Come in."

For a second, they stood awkwardly. Finally, Sam offered her a seat. They sat on the sofa, at opposite ends. To Sam, Diane appeared tired and her eyes were brimmed with water, similar to a waterfall ready to spill over.

Wringing her hands in her lap, she sat avoiding eye contact. Sniffing, she pulled a tissue from her purse to wipe her nose. She closed her eyes for a moment and counted to ten.

When she opened them, she spotted an open envelope on the coffee table. A picture was hanging half way out of it.

She grabbed her middle. It felt like someone had punched her in the stomach, hard enough to make her double over.

He asked with concern. "Are you okay Diane?"

Her response was barely above a whisper. Sam leaned closer to her in an effort to understand what she was saying.

She cleared her throat. As she began to speak, her voice cracked.

He had no idea what she was mumbling. He thought, *"What was with all the drama. She was a bit too old for this."*

He was about to say something, but watched as she picked up the envelope and took the photo out. She stared at the picture.

"How do you know the woman in the picture?"

CHAPTER 44

Sam took the picture from her and pointed. "That's my sister." He continued and pointed to the man. "And that's her husband and baby boy."

He watched Diane, her breathing was even. Her chest was rising and falling. Her face was contorted and he thought she was going into cardiac arrest.

Before he could say anything, she jumped up and ran to the bathroom. Before the door went shut, he listened as she lost the contents of her stomach.

His concern made him knock on the door. "Diane, are you okay?"

She did not answer. He knocked again. "Diane." Sam tried the doorknob. She had locked it.

"Diane. Answer me. Are you okay?"

She responded. "I'm okay. Please, give me a minute."

He heard running water. The door opened. Diane's tear-streaked face was drained of color, eyes swollen and red. Sam stared at her and wondered what was going on?

No explanation was given as he heard. "I need to go. Do you mind? I'm sick."

"I can see you're sick. What's wrong? Do you think you might have eaten something that made you sick?" She did not respond as he continued, "Or does this have anything to do with your doctor's appointment?"

"I don't know what's wrong. And no, this doesn't have anything to do with my doctor visit."

"Before you go, how do you know my sister?"

Sam was afraid of what her answer might be. When he heard that her last name was Benson, he wanted to ask her, but never did.

"Oh, I don't know your sister. Why?"

"Because when you picked up the picture, never mind. I assumed you knew her?"

"I don't know. Uh … she looked familiar, like someone I used to work with."

"Yeah, but when I told you that the woman in the picture was my sister, you seemed to …"

Diane held up her hand. "When I saw the picture, my stomach began to churn and I had to throw up. It had nothing to do with the picture."

She was rambling. From Sam's facial expression, she could tell he did not believe her. Before he had time to question her further, she continued.

"I'm sorry, but I really need to go."

She reached for her purse and was about to leave when Sam grabbed her hand. He turned her around and embraced her.

He wanted her to feel safe. Regardless of what may come, he wanted to say that it would be okay. He also wanted to kiss her, but he did not. Slowly, he let his hug ease. He released her.

"I have an idea. Why don't I take you home?" Before she could answer, he hurried on. "You could pick your car up tomorrow?"

"Oh Sam, that's so sweet, but I'm not that sick. I can drive home."

"Are you sure?"

She nodded her head. "I'll call you as soon as I get home."

CHAPTER 45

❀

The phone rang as Lisa rushed out the door. She was running late. She hesitated and thought about not answering it. She needed to get to the hospital.

"Hello." Lisa could not believe the voice she was hearing. It couldn't be. She sat down, her knees shaking.

"Kellie, is that you?"

"Yes, and hello to you. I know it's been a long time. How are you?"

"I'm fine."

To be honest, Lisa never expected to hear from Kellie again. After Roger's death, Kellie sent a letter to her, Diane, and Arlene giving a vague reason for her quick departure. Lisa wondered why she was really calling.

"Listen, I don't have much time but I was calling about Diane."

"What about her?"

"I know she didn't select any other option besides having the baby. So, don't lie. Has she had the baby yet?"

"How did you know she decided to have the baby?"

"Come on Lisa. We're talking about Diane. When you called us over to her house and she told us she was pregnant and we started talking about options, I knew then. Diane might have been listening to the options but she had already decided to keep the baby."

"Yeah, you're right."

"Well, tell me the details. Did she have the baby yet?"

"You're not going to believe it. She had not one but two babies—twin boys."

"What? You're right. I don't believe it. How are they doing?"

"The boys are healthy and weighed in at five pounds and five and a half pounds."

"What did Diane name them?"

Lisa exhaled. "Are you sitting down?"

"Why? What's wrong?"

"It's Diane. While she delivered healthy baby boys, she's having some problems."

As always, Kellie was short on patience. "Would you please hurry up and spit out the details." Kellie's voice was harsh. "In fact, that should have been the first thing you told me when I asked about her."

Lisa's voice matched Kellie's. "Listen, if you knew Diane kept the baby, then you should have called before now."

Kellie snorted, "You always were protective of Diane."

Lisa pursed her lips and through clenched teeth said, "Let's not argue."

"You're right and I'm sorry. Tell me about Diane."

"She's in a coma and the doctor can't explain why or if or when she'll come out of it."

Kellie's voice had a catch in it. "Is she still in the hospital?"

"Yes but within a few days, she's going to be transferred to a nursing home."

"What about the babies?"

"They're in the hospital."

Kellie shook her head. "When I called I had no idea I was going to hear all of this. How did Arlene take the news?"

Lisa's hand flew to her mouth. "Oh, my God. Do you believe I haven't called her? She doesn't know anything about Diane."

"You mean you didn't tell Arlene that Diane was having the baby?" Before Lisa responded, under Kellie's breath she said, "This is so typical of you and Diane. You always liked keeping secrets."

Lisa was about to lose her temper but remained calm. "It wasn't my secret to keep. This was about Diane. You were gone and Arlene has good and bad days. I was the only friend Diane could confide in."

Kellie didn't respond to what Lisa had said. Instead, she asked, "What's going to happen to the boys if Diane doesn't come out of the coma?"

"I'm not sure. The hospital agreed to keep the boys until Diane is transferred to a nursing home. I tried to get guardianship but the social worker said the process was long and considering the circumstances, I probably wouldn't get the approval."

Kellie did not know if she should ask but she did. "What about Sam?"

Lisa sniffed, "That's another story. As Diane would have it, he didn't know she was having the baby. I had to tell him and it's been a mess."

"You're telling me. What about Diane's children? Have you asked one of them to take the babies?"

Lisa's voice was barely above a whisper when she responded. "I haven't told Donna and Freddie."

"You're kidding. Their mother could die. What are you waiting for?"

"I guess a miracle."

After Lisa's response, Kellie changed subjects and asked about Patrick, when they were getting married, and about other mutual friends. Before they hung up, Lisa thought Kellie would ask about visiting Diane or at least tell her how she could get in touch with her, but she didn't.

CHAPTER 46

The telephone call from Kellie made Lisa feel guilty about not telling Arlene about Diane. When Lisa returned home from the hospital, she made the call.

"Hi, Missy. How are you? This is Lisa."

"I'm doing fine. How are you? Mom will be glad to hear from you."

"How is she?"

"Today, it's a good day. Let me get her."

Lisa yelled. "No, wait. I need to discuss something with you before I talk to Arlene. It's delicate and I want to know if you think she could handle it?"

"What is it?"

A loud gush of air escaped from Lisa's mouth. She thought, "I'll probably have a heart attack before Diane comes out of the coma."

"Our friend Diane had a baby. I should say she had twin boys."

Missy let out a giggle. "What?" Then she added, "So it's true."

"What do you mean?"

"One day when I thought mom was rambling, she told me Diane was pregnant. I thought she was confused. I mean Diane is what, fifty years old?"

Lisa did not bother to respond to Missy's comment. "When Diane told us about the pregnancy she had not made up her mind about what she was going to do. I'm surprised Arlene concluded that Diane was having the baby."

"Maybe someone told her."

"I don't see how. Do you have minute?"

"Sure."

"I would like to start from the beginning. Diane had experienced unexplained bouts of crying, queasiness, and insomnia. I had similar symptoms

- 108 -

when I started menopause. I thought Diane was going through the same thing. She went to the doctor only to discover she was pregnant."

Missy interrupted Lisa. "Before you go any further, how old is Diane?"

Lisa didn't know why Diane's age was important but she answered. "She's forty-eight."

"Okay, go on."

"When Diane told me she was pregnant I did not hesitate and I called Kellie and Arlene over to her house. When they arrived, Diane shared her news with them. We discussed options with her but that was it."

"Wait, I'm confused. If Diane didn't tell you all, then, how did mom know?"

"I think we all knew. Diane is pretty transparent when it comes to certain moral issues. I think that's how we all concluded she would have the baby."

"Whew. You women are something else. I had no idea that when I moved to The Villages this was not the typical retirement community. I have tons of other questions but it's none of my business. As for my mom, I think she'll be okay when you tell her. After all, she already knows."

Lisa thought about telling Missy about Diane being in a coma but she changed her mind. She had already told her enough for one day.

When Lisa told Arlene about Diane having the twin boys, she was delighted.

Arlene gushed, "I can't wait to see them. Will you pick me up and take me to the hospital?"

Lisa avoided answering Arlene. She waited to see if Arlene would insist on her picking her up to visit Diane at the hospital. Instead, Arlene began talking about when she was pregnant and had Missy.

CHAPTER 47

Sam was distracted at work. The only thing on his mind was Diane, the coma, and what to do about the boys. He was all alone, no one to discuss his concerns.

He did not consider himself a religious person but he thought about talking to someone in the ministry. He had seen a priest at the hospital and thought about asking him but he wasn't sure. After all, he was not affiliated with any particular church and he did not know the protocol about such things.

After work Sam went to the hospital. Usually, he was upbeat and could not wait to see Diane but today he was feeling anxious, depressed, and an unexplained hopelessness. After all, he had no answers and if there was a God, why hadn't he answered his prayers?

Before going to Diane's room, he went to the hospital's chapel. He entered and sat in the back, not to disturb the man who was sitting up front. Sam did not know what else to pray for and maybe that was the problem or perhaps he did not know how to pray.

His eyes were closed but they flew open. Something startled him. The man who had been sitting up front was approaching him. When the man was about to pass Sam, he hesitated.

"Hello." The man extended his hand and they shook. "My name is Justin Williams. Forgive me if I'm intruding but I sense you need to talk to someone. I'm a minister."

Sam peered up at the man as tears began streaming down his face. He could not believe it, God had not answered his prayers but he had sent a representative.

"Do you have a minute?"

"I sure do. I was about to make my daily visit to a church member but he died earlier today. I came to the chapel to pray for him and his family."

"I'm sorry."

Justin shrugged. "Do you want to stay here in the chapel or do you want to get something to drink?"

"Do you mind if we stay here?"

"No problem." Sam slid down and Justin joined him on the pew.

Sam put his head in his hands. Now that he had someone to talk to, he did not know where to start. Justin patted him on the back.

"It's okay."

Sam sat up, blew his nose and began. "First I want to say I don't go to a church on a regular basis but I was raised by a religious mother. From her, I know God answers prayers. I also learned from my mother that all things are possible to anyone who believes in God and is obedient."

Justin smiled. "You may not go to church on a regular basis but from what you've said, you're probably further ahead in your walk in faith than many church goers."

Sam did not know how to respond. He wanted to unburden his heart but again was not sure if that was the right thing to do.

"Sam, I don't know what you're going through but I think you are probably feeling alone and abandoned. No matter what the difficulty might be, you need to understand that God has not forsaken you."

Justin's words made Sam sob. As much as he wanted to spill his burdens, his words stuck in his throat.

They sat in silence. Sam could tell Justin was waiting for him to explain what was going on but as much as he tried, he could not find the words.

"Sam, I'm sorry but I need to go. Here's my card. If you ever need someone to talk to, I'm here."

Somewhere, Sam was able to utter, "Before you go, will you pray for me."

"I would love to."

Justin sat for a few minutes. He was hoping this man would tell him what was going on in his life but he didn't. Justin believed prayers were better answered when the problem was clearly stated. As much as Justin would have liked to ask Sam more specific information, he decided not to. After all, God knew what was in Sam's heart.

"*Heavenly Father, we give you all the praise and honor. We thank you for Sam who knows who You are. No matter what problems he might be facing let him know that Jesus has overcome them for him. Lord, bless Sam and let him know that You will meet his needs and take all hopelessness away. Give him strength. Thank You Lord, that in Sam's distress he can call on You. And when he cries out to You, Lord, hear his voice and answer his prayers. Amen.*"

CHAPTER 48

When Justin left, Sam sat for a few more minutes. As he entered Diane's room, Lisa glanced up.

"Hi, Sam. How are you doing?"

"I'm okay. What about you?"

"I'm doing as well as can be expected. I want you to know I'll probably give Diane's children a call by the end of the week."

Sam did not know what to say. He had urged Lisa to call them and when she had refused he never broached the subject again.

"That's probably a good idea."

He waited to see if Lisa was going to mention the boys and ask if he had decided to take them. To his surprise, she said nothing as she stood up.

"Well, it's been a long day and I need to go." When Lisa passed him, she put her hand on his arm and said, "Take care. I'll see you tomorrow."

Sam was thankful he met Justin Williams. He had made him feel better than he had in days.

"Diane, how are you doing today? You're looking better. I hope you can hear me. I met the most wonderful minister today. He made me feel as if Lisa and my prayers will be answered. I do not have to tell you that we're running out of time. Next week, you'll be released to a nursing home."

Sam paused. He did not want to burden Diane. He did not want her to be disappointed that he still had not made up his mind about taking the boys. He felt inadequate. He wanted to be a responsible father but could he do it?

Sam was relieved he had brought a book with him. Instead of talking to Diane, he would read to her. Something drew him to the Bible sitting on the table next to Diane's bed. He picked it up and began reading from the Book of Psalms.

❦   ❦   ❦

Diane's mind continued to rewind the events of her life since she still did not know what day it was or whether she was still in labor or what. When she decided to keep the baby, she had to admit she had not fathomed all the problems associated with her decision.

The first foremost problem was her living situation. She was living in a retirement community where children were not permitted unless they were visiting and that time was limited. Then there was the problem of being on a fixed income.

Every time she thought about her situation, she came up with more problems, but no solutions. She could not remember a time in her life when things were so complicated.

And Sam, his reaction had been on the same level as a teenage boy. Since she had told him about the pregnancy and the visit to the doctor's office, she had not heard from him. Whatever decisions she made, it appeared as though she was on her own.

While she sat drowning in her tears and getting more depressed by the minute, the phone rang. She was tempted not to answer it, but changed her mind.

"Hello."

"Hi, mother."

"Hi, sweetheart. How are you doing?"

"Okay."

Diane was not going to drag out their conversation before she asked her daughter about her doctor's visit. She knew Donna probably did not want to talk about it, but she did.

"What did the doctor say?"

"The doctor said my chances of having a baby are slim."

"What does that mean?"

Donna snapped. "I might get pregnant, but it doesn't seem likely. My uterus is situated in an unusual position causing difficulty for me to conceive. There is nothing that can fix it."

"But, there is a possibility."

"Yeah, but the odds are slim."

"What about adoption?"

"What about it? I've been told that I can't have children and you're talking about adoption. Look I have to go."

"Wait, Donna. I'm saying you have options. There are so many children that want, no, need parents. Don't let this little bump in the road stop your dream of being a mother."

Donna did not continue the conversation. She changed gears. "I guess you heard about Freddie's good news?"

"Yes, I've talked to him and he told me about he and Angie expecting. I didn't ask him, but when is the baby due?"

"I'm not sure."

"Were you surprised about them having a baby?"

"Yes and no. To be honest, I think Angie was fearful because of some sort of family heredity medical problem that could be passed on if she and Freddie had a baby. I think what helped her was when Daddy and Joanne had a healthy baby."

"What are you talking about?"

"I'm sorry. I don't know the complete story, but it seems that Joanne's family has some sort of inherited medical problem. The entire time of her pregnancy she worried, but the baby's fine. I think that gave Angie hope."

Diane could not believe what Donna was saying. When she hung up the phone, she patted her stomach.

Was her baby in danger?

CHAPTER 49

After talking to Donna, Diane called Lisa. She knew Lisa was waiting to hear how Sam took the news about the pregnancy.

"Hey Lisa. Are you busy?"

"Not really. Why?"

"Why don't you come over?"

"Give me a few minutes."

When Diane opened the door, Lisa was taken back. Diane appeared unhealthy as her clothes hung off her body.

"Hey girl. What's up?"

"Come on in and please don't try to cheer me up."

"Why not? The sun is shining and as the saying goes—it's a beautiful day in The Villages."

"Lisa, please. You have no idea what I'm going through. My problems keep mounting which means I have decisions to make. I'm not sleeping and I can barely eat and when I do, it comes right back up."

"You need to take one day at a time and things will turn around."

Diane pursed her lips. "You think so."

"Talk to me. What's going on?"

"Well, let me bring you up to date. The latest is that my daughter can't have children—I'm sorry that's not true—her chances are slim to none."

"Okay, but she has options."

"I agree, but she doesn't want to adopt. Besides, there's nothing like having a baby of your own."

Diane knew her words had been insensitive. Lisa had tried for years to have a baby and it never happened. She considered apologizing, but decided she would probably make things worse.

"What else is going on? What did Sam say about the pregnancy?"

"Please, one thing at a time. When I told Sam, his reaction was how did an old woman, like me, get pregnant?"

Lisa tried to stifle her laugh. "He didn't say that and you know it."

"No he didn't say it like that, but that's what he meant."

"Did you discuss your options?"

"No. I was too upset and couldn't talk to him. We're meeting tonight because I'm running out of time if I'm ..." Diane didn't finish her thought.

Lisa stood up and gave her a hug. Lisa held her until she broke away from the embrace and started shaking her head.

"I'm not finished. I didn't tell you the worse of the news yet. Sam is Joanne's brother."

Lisa held up her hand. "Wait a minute. You mean your Fred's wife—your ex-husband's wife is your boyfriend's sister?"

"Yes."

"Are you kidding me?"

"No. I'm serious. That was the reason why I didn't tell Sam initially about the pregnancy. When I was at his apartment I saw a picture of Fred, Joanne, and the baby. I wasn't sure until I asked him and he confirmed my worst fears."

"Do you think Sam knows the connection?"

"How would he?"

"Well, your last name is Benson and so is his sister's."

Diane had not thought about it until Lisa brought it to her attention. "If he knows why hasn't he said anything?"

"I don't know. Maybe he was too shocked, like you."

"Maybe, but I would think he would say something."

Lisa thought about an old saying and it definitely applied to Diane, "If it wasn't for bad luck, she wouldn't have any luck at all." If Lisa did not witness Diane's life, it would be hard to believe.

"I don't think I can continue to deal with all of the unexpected surprises ... oh." Diane started laughing, followed by sobs.

"What is it?"

Diane's crying caused her to hiccup. As hard as she tried, she could not stop them.

"Take a deep breath. No, drink some water."

The hiccups eased. She blew her nose. "I'm sorry, but you won't believe the latest bit of unexpected news. Sam and his sister come from a family that has some sort of heredity genetic disease."

CHAPTER 50

The day had been exhausting and it was getting late. Sam did not require much sleep but today was different, his eyes were heavy and he was having difficulty concentrating. He needed rest.

The highlight of the day was meeting Justin Williams. He would be forever grateful for his kindness. In the future, he would call him and see if he had a church. If he did, Sam vowed to visit it.

"Well, sweetheart it's time for me to leave. I'll see you tomorrow. Have sweet dreams."

Sam thought he would have slept well but instead he tossed and turned. He credited the sleeplessness to having to decide what to do about his children. Within his heart, he knew what he should do but his mind told him he was not capable.

Maybe, he could give it a try and if it did not work, he could consider other options, such as foster care or adoption. He did not know how that would work. He was in the dark with the arrangements Diane had made because he had already signed adoption papers.

Rather than continue to toss and turn, Sam got up. He wandered to the kitchen and turned the coffee pot on. As he waited for the coffee to brew, his thoughts flashed back to when he and Diane discussed options regarding the pregnancy.

Despite Sam's response to the pregnancy, he had waited for Diane to discuss the options with him. When the days passed without hearing from her, Sam made the call.

He did not know for sure but when he called, he thought he heard surprise in her voice. She invited him to her house.

Waiting for seven o'clock was like time had stopped. When he rang the doorbell, he thought she had changed her mind about the meeting. He was about to leave when the door opened. From her appearance, she looked as if she had been sleeping.

"Hi, Sam. Come in."

They gazed at each other, each having their own thoughts. Diane was thinking how Sam was the only man she knew who could wear a polo shirt and khakis and look like a magazine model.

While Sam thought pregnant women were supposed to have a special aura about them. Instead of a glow, Diane's face was gaunt and her body was thin.

"Are you taking care of yourself?"

"As much as I can." She peered down at her slacks. She smoothed her hair and straightened her wrinkled clothes. "Thanks for asking. I was napping when you arrived."

He inspected her. She gave an explanation as if to address her appearance, but he was not convinced that was the reason for her haggard look.

"Sam, I can't begin to understand how you feel just like you can't possibly know what I've been going through, but one thing for certain, we're having a baby."

"I know and I apologize for my behavior. It's just that I had been worried about your health and pregnancy was the last thing I expected to hear."

"Me too."

"Have you made up your mind as to what you want to do?"

"Not really. We … I have options which include adoption, keeping the baby, or abortion."

"How do you really feel about having an abortion?"

"If the doctor told me that my life was threatened in some way then I would consider it, but abortion wasn't an option I was considering."

"I see. What about adoption?"

"What about it?"

"Would you consider it?"

"I might. Would you?"

"Yes, I would. But I have to ask, Diane, do you want to keep this baby …"

Diane words were filled with anger. "It isn't *"this"* baby—it's our baby."

Sam ran his fingers through his hair. Diane could tell he was frustrated, but she wanted to make it clear that this was his baby as well as hers.

"Look, I'm going to be honest with you. I've never wanted children. That was one of the reasons why I dated older women. Most of them no longer wanted or desired children. I guess I should have had a vasectomy."

Diane glared at him and jeered, "Better yet, we shouldn't have had unprotected sex."

Silence filled the room similar to smoke, thick and suffocating. Words escaped Sam as he watched Diane's eyes fill with water and her facial expression full of disgust. Diane did not have to say it he saw the disappointment. She was probably thinking she had just learned to trust another man and she had been blindsided again.

What he could not share with Diane was the real reason he never wanted children.

CHAPTER 51

Lisa was being pressured. Donna had called numerous times. She wanted information about her mother. Although Lisa vowed to call Donna and Freddie by the end of the week, she was not prepared to talk to either one of them until she was ready.

Every time Donna called, Lisa had been vague about Diane's whereabouts. Each call had been increasingly difficult to continue the lies.

As Lisa was about to go to the hospital, the phone rang. When she picked up the phone, she cringed.

"Lisa, something's wrong. If you don't tell me, I'm booking the next flight to Florida. That way I can find out for myself."

"Donna I don't know what you want from me. Your mother is on a cruise. She didn't give me a lot of details."

"But I don't understand. This is not like mom."

"I know but ..."

Donna persisted, "Either you tell me or I'll be on the next plane."

Lisa did not know what she could say to prevent Donna from coming to Florida. She had to come up with something as droplets of sweat cascaded down the side of her face.

"If that's what you want to do. Then, come to Florida but you won't find your mother here. It will be a waste of your time."

"I don't believe that. I think you're hiding something from me. I can feel it. Something isn't right."

Lisa's breathing was heavy. "Fine, I shouldn't be the one telling you this but you leave me no choice. Has your mother mentioned anything to you about her social life?"

"Like what?"

"That she's dating?"

Donna wanted answers and now that she might get them, she did not want to hear what Lisa had to say.

"No, mom never mentioned she was dating. Why?"

"Well, I think that's why she didn't tell you about the cruise."

"What do you mean?"

"You know … she went on the cruise with a man."

"Are you sure?" Donna didn't hide the surprise in her voice. "I can't believe mom's been dating and she never bothered to tell me."

Lisa was treading lightly. She did not know how far to take this but she thought she would go with the flow.

"I think your mom didn't know how to tell you. I also believe your mother thought you and Freddie have been through enough. She didn't want to add one more element of surprise to your life."

"You might be right Lisa. I mean when Freddie suggested that mom might be dating I was not happy."

Lisa was curious. "Why not?" In Diane's defense, Lisa added, "Your dad remarried."

"I know." Donna pouted and sighed. "I probably have a fifth grade attitude but I thought if mom began dating other men that would close the door forever of any chances of her getting back with my dad." Donna paused.

Lisa was not sure but she thought Donna might be crying. She shook her head. Until now she always thought divorce was something that affected younger children. Talking to Donna, Lisa realized that divorce had an impact on children at any age.

"It's hard for me to accept the fact that mom would have feelings for another man, other than my dad."

Since Lisa never had children she was not sure how comforting her words would be. "I'm sure it's hard on both you and Freddie but I believe your parents will always love each other but differently."

"You think so?"

"Of course, they have an everlasting bond—you and Freddie."

"I never thought about it like that. Lisa, I'm sorry I've been such a brat about mom. I owe you an apology because I thought you had been lying to me. I had this nagging feeling that you were covering up something.

Lisa wiped her forehead with the back of her hand and exhaled. At least she had told half the truth. She was no different than a mother bear protecting her cubs.

CHAPTER 52

Since Diane decided to keep the baby, it had changed Lisa emotionally and physically. When she looked in the mirror, she swore she had aged ten years. The lies and deceit were taking a toll on her. She needed Diane to come out of the coma.

At the hospital, Lisa took her usual seat beside Diane's bed. Without warning, tears rolled down her face.

Through sobs, Lisa pleaded. "Diane, please wake up. Everything is such a mess. I have to tell Donna and Freddie soon. They have a right to know. The only reason why I've waited so long to tell them is because I thought you would have come out of the coma by now."

Lisa had been waiting for days for some kind of a sign but day after day, she showed no improvement.

"I talked to Donna yesterday and I told her about you dating. As usual, I was vague with details."

Lisa blew her nose and continued. "Donna was not pleased with you dating but after our talk I think she'll be okay with it."

Lisa was not up to talking to Diane today. She was losing faith. Would she ever come out of the coma?

Every day, she spent time in the nursery. The babies needed to see a face other than the hospital personnel. The nurses allowed her to hold and feed the boys. She wanted them to know they were loved and not alone. Lisa knew Sam was doing the same which surprised her. The way he refused to take the boys, Lisa assumed he wouldn't bother with the boys but that had not been the case.

"Oh. I forgot to mention Donna and Gary were called to the hospital to adopt a newborn baby."

Lisa stopped. She looked closer. For a moment, she thought Diane's hand moved and her breathing seemed different. Before Lisa called the nurse, she watched with keen eyes, but it must have been an involuntary reflex.

Lisa relaxed back in the chair and continued, "Where was I? Oh, yes. The adoption did not happen because the teenager changed her mind."

Lisa shook her head and hissed, "It was hard for me to believe that someone would be that cruel. Either you want to give the baby up for adoption or you don't. No one should be allowed to change their mind in mid-stream. According to Donna, the law provides the mother with a grace period that permits her to change her mind. I don't care what the law permits, it's not fair. I admire Donna and Gary because I don't think I could take the stress and disappointments of the adoption process."

The door opened and a nurse entered. After she took Diane's vitals, she left.

Usually Lisa did not share things that might upset Diane but she needed to know what was going on.

"Donna said that this was the second time they had been given hope just to have it taken away. The worse part for Donna was that she wanted and needed you. That was why she was trying so hard to find you. And I had to tell her you were on a cruise. Now, I may have to tell her that you're in a coma and may not come out of it or worse."

Lisa murmured, "Donna said she could never remember a time in her life when she felt so alone. Gary, Freddie and Angie supported her but it wasn't the same."

Lisa chuckled. "It's probably not funny but Donna said at one point she wanted to strangle Fred's wife because she called her, offering some wisdom. What caused Donna to explode was when she said and I quote, "This was probably a blessing in disguise. God has a way of not giving you what you want but what you need. This was not the baby for you and you should be thankful.""

CHAPTER 53

Just like the light had been bright, now it was growing dim. In addition, it was no longer calling Diane. She was not sure what caused the change but she could tell the difference. What did it all mean? Was it a sign of some sort? Diane had no answers.

In addition, Diane was positive she heard Lisa's voice and she had been telling her about Donna and Gary and their adoption woes. She thought she was moving her arms but if she was, no one had noticed.

Whatever state she was in, she had to come out of it. Donna and Gary could not adopt a baby as she recalled the last actions she had taken to guarantee an adoption for them.

Mr. Wade, the attorney that was recommended to Diane would not be available for at least a month. She could not wait that long.

"I have to see Mr. Wade as soon as possible. Could I see him after hours?"

"I'm sorry Mrs. Benson, but …"

Firmly, Diane explained. "This is a matter of life and death. I'm about to deliver my baby any day now which means I need to see Mr. Wade as soon as possible."

Mr. Wade's secretary put Diane on hold. When she returned, she scheduled Diane for an appointment during Mr. Wade's lunch hour.

"Mrs. Benson, it's nice to meet you. Please have a seat. I hope you don't mind if I eat my lunch?"

"Mr. Wade, I don't mind. I'm glad you were willing to meet with me on such a short notice. I know you're a busy man and I think you would agree that it was better now than later."

Diane let out a nervous laugh. Mr. Wade did not join her in what she thought was humor.

Diane did not miss Mr. Wade staring at her. She could care less. With the fat body suit, it was hard to tell how far along she was in her pregnancy.

"I understand that you can arrange adoptions."

"My law practice handles various areas of the law, but my specialty is adoptions."

"Good. I have some questions about adoption. How do I go about arranging one? How can I protect my identity? My last question is whether or not I need the father's consent?"

"Let's take one question at a time. Is there any reason why you don't want the couple to know who you are?"

"Yes. The couple is my daughter and son-in-law."

"I see."

He glanced over his eyeglasses with a raised eyebrow. Without saying anything, he wrote something on the legal pad in front of him. He stopped and asked, "Do you know the lawyer your daughter and son-in-law are using to handle their adoption?"

"Yes, her name is Kathy Battle. She practices in the State of Maryland."

"I'll be in contact with her. Now, what about the father? Will he give up his parental rights?"

"Yes. What do I need from him?"

"The father will be required to sign consent papers that state he is giving up his parental rights. Before that happens, I would have to meet with the father to make sure he understands what he is signing."

"Does he need to know who is adopting our baby?"

"No. I will handle it as a closed adoption, meaning the records will be sealed."

"Is there anything else I need to know?"

"The only thing I need is for the papers to be signed before you go into labor."

CHAPTER 54

Diane heard noises. It was a voice? But it was faint? It reminded her of an echo. Why was she having difficulty making out the difference between sounds and words spoken?

The voice sounded low, baritone—was it a male speaking? Could it be Sam? Was he talking to her? The words were not clear. Or, was her imagination playing a trick on her? She paid close attention, trying to make sense of the jumbled sounds of what she thought were words.

Her eyelids were heavy. As she tried to open them, it felt like a weight was holding them down. Several times she blinked her eyelashes. She was squinting through tiny slits. When she finally opened her eyes, a blast of light caused her to shut them.

Sam sat up. Diane's eyes fluttered. Sam leaned closer, watching for another flicker of what he thought he had seen. Was it his imagination? Or had he seen Diane open her eyes?

"There. There she goes again." Excitedly, he pressed, released, pressed and released the nurse's call button.

The nurse's face frowned when she bolted through the room's door. With hands on her hips and a firm voice, she glared. "Mr. Childers, what seems to be the problem?"

"Diane's eyes fluttered ... I mean her eyes blinked ... I can't quite explain what I saw, but I know she moved. I think she's coming out of the coma."

"Mr. Childers, sometimes patients in comas have involuntary movements and that is what you might have observed."

"No. It was more than that. She opened and closed her eyes."

"Mr. Childers, please step back and let me take a closer look." As the nurse approached Diane's bedside and leaned toward her, she jumped.

Diane's movement startled her. She regained her composure, straightened her shoulders and spoke.

"Mrs. Benson. Can you hear me?" Diane did not respond, but her eyes were in a constant blinking motion.

Anxious, Sam asked, "Is she out of the coma?"

The nurse did not answer him. "Mr. Childers, I'll be right back. I need to page the doctor."

The nurse left the room and Sam took out his cell phone. As he dialed Lisa's number, he hoped she was home.

"Hello."

"Lisa, this is Sam." The words stuck in his throat. "Diane's out of the coma."

"Oh my God." Lisa's hand flew to her mouth, as water filled her eyes. She looked upward and said, "Thank you Jesus."

Sam chose his words with care as he explained. "I called you the minute I was sure she was awake. The nurse is paging the doctor now. I don't know ..." His voice drifted off.

"Sam Childers, you listen to me. Diane is going to be fine. I'm on my way."

Sam hung up the phone and picked up Diane's hand. He kissed it. His face wet as he whispered, "Thank you God for answering our prayers."

The page for the doctor could be heard over the P.A. system. When the nurse returned, she ushered Sam out of the room and into the corridor. Sam saw the doctor rushing down the hall. He went straight into Diane's room.

Sam's nerves were on edge as he paced back and forth. Finally, he sat in a chair near Diane's room. As he thought about his prayers being answered, he wept.

❦   ❦   ❦

Despite Lisa's faith and prayers, at times she doubted whether Diane would come out of the coma. That was no longer a worry. Although she assured Sam that Diane would be fine, she shared his concern about Diane's health.

Lisa arrived at the hospital and spotted Sam. When their eyes met, Sam ran to Lisa and grabbed her. He held her in a tight hug.

As he eased his embrace, Lisa was full of questions. "Has the doctor arrived? Has anyone told you anything?"

"The doctor is examining her now."

"How long have you been waiting?"

Sam glanced at his watch. "It's been about thirty minutes since the doctor arrived." Sam paused and was about to say something when he emerged from Diane's room.

CHAPTER 55

Lisa did not like the doctor's expression as he approached them. Lisa glanced at Sam but his eyes were focused on the doctor.

"Mrs. Henderson." He motioned her to join him. Lisa did not budge.

"I know the law. You know Mr. Childers, please, tell us about Diane." He nodded. His speech was slow and deliberate.

"I know you want Diane to come out of the coma and with her eyes opening; it probably appeared as if …"

Sam interrupted. "What are you trying to say?"

"Mr. Childers, it's not uncommon for people in comas to open their eyes. I don't want to tell you anything else until the neurosurgeon examines her."

Lisa was confused. "I don't understand. This is the first time Diane has made any movement but yet she's still in a coma?"

The doctor nodded his head. "It's possible. I'm sorry."

"When will the neurosurgeon be here?" Sam asked.

"I called him and he'll be here tomorrow morning around ten o'clock. Do you have any other questions?"

Lisa and Sam did not know what to say or what to ask. Their faces were frowning and their eyes were filled with sadness as they watched the doctor walk away.

Sam put his head in his hands. Lisa patted his back. She did not know how to comfort him. She was sure Sam was thinking about the decision he had to make about the boys. And, she was deciding when to call Diane's children. She would wait until tomorrow after the neurosurgeon examines Diane.

"Sam, I'm tired and I'm going home. I'll see you in the morning."

"Thanks, Lisa for everything."

Lisa smiled at him and left.

❦   ❦   ❦

When Lisa arrived home she had to call Patrick. They were supposed to have dinner but when Sam called she had to cancel. It was not until she talked to him earlier that she noticed Patrick was less than understanding when she said she could not make their dinner date.

His response was not what she expected. "You and Sam need to accept Diane's fate. She's in a coma and probably won't come out of it. In addition, if Diane comes out of it, she'll probably be a vegetable."

Lisa was disappointed with him but she understood his position. Many people did not believe that coma patients would survive. Like Sam, she was not giving up on Diane. She did not care what the doctor said.

"Hello, Patrick."

"Hi, Lisa." She noticed the chill in his hello but she ignored it.

"How's Diane?"

"Well, it's not the news Sam and I had hoped for. The doctor said it was not unusual for someone in a coma to open their eyes but until the neurosurgeon examines her, we won't know for sure."

Patrick was blunt. "Is Diane out of the coma or not?"

"It's not that simple."

"In other words, you're going to continue the hospital visits? What about her children? When are you going to call them?"

"Patrick, what's wrong?"

"What's wrong?" He exhaled nosily. "Lisa, when do you think we're going to regain our life?"

"When Diane gets better. She has no one but me."

Patrick's words were harsh. "She has Sam."

"You know their relationship is complicated." Lisa blinked away the tears. "I have to be there for her. I thought you understood?"

Patrick ran his fingers through his hair. "I understand but reality is that you need to make some decisions and it doesn't seem as though you are."

Lisa sniffed and swiped at the falling tears. This was the time she needed Patrick's support and he was letting her down. Why was he acting like this?

"I'm sorry you feel this way. Diane is my friend. In fact, I knew her before I met you. I'm not sure what's going on with you but I'm not going to abandon her."

"Fine, there's nothing else to discuss."
Lisa held the phone but Patrick was gone.

CHAPTER 56

The next morning, Lisa and Sam arrived at the hospital early. They met in the cafeteria and had a cup of coffee. Neither of them had much to say. When it was nine forty-five, Sam suggested they go to Diane's room. The doctors had not arrived yet. The nurse-in-charge said that they could go in and see Diane.

When they entered, Lisa walked over to her bed. "Good morning, girl-friend. I'm glad to see you're with us."

Diane did not respond but to Lisa she seemed aware of what she was saying. As Sam spoke to her, the door opened. Dr. Myers and another man walked in.

"Good morning. This is Dr. Johnson."

In unison, Lisa and Sam greeted the doctor.

The doctor approached the bed and asked Lisa and Sam to step back. Before he did anything he looked at Sam and Lisa.

"I understand she opened her eyes and had some kind of movement?" He withdrew a flashlight from his white coat pocket. He wasn't expecting much from the examination.

Before he began, Diane spoke, "What-what-what-did-did-did—I—I—I—have?"

The words startled the doctor. He started to ask Diane a question when she blurted out, "Where—where—where—is—is—is—my—my—my—baby—baby?"

Lisa and Sam moved closer to the bed. Tears were flowing down both their faces. They continued to watch.

The doctor answered, "You had the baby and …" He paused. Too much too soon could agitate her.

"The baby is fine." In an effort to avoid answering any more questions about the baby, he asked, "Do you know where you are?"

"In-in-in—the—the—hospital?"

"That's right." The doctor asked her several other questions and she gave the correct answers.

The doctor patted Diane's hand and said, "I want you to rest and I'll be right back."

The doctor turned to Lisa and Sam and motioned them to follow. When they were outside Diane's room, he did not hesitate.

"Well, I would be lying if I said I wasn't surprised. The only conclusion I can come up with is that whatever prayers were lifted up for her have been answered. Miracles do happen and I would say in this case, this is not the standard coma results."

Sam interrupted the doctor. "Is she as aware as she appears?" Sam wanted to ask another question but he was afraid to voice it. "Is there a possibility she might relapse?"

"Diane does seem aware of her surroundings but I need to conduct other tests to determine whether she's lost any of her physical or mental abilities."

"Like what? Lisa asked.

"I don't want to speculate. Rather than discuss what is or isn't, I want to conduct the tests, and then we can discuss the best treatment for her."

Again, Lisa and Sam were disappointed. To them, Diane was making a full recovery but no doctor wanted to agree with their assessment.

"When will you be conducting the tests?" Sam asked.

"Tomorrow morning."

Lisa chimed in. "When will you have the test results?"

"Some of the tests will provide me with immediate results while others will take several days."

Sam was anxious. "May we see her?"

"Yes, but don't tell her too much. I don't want to upset her."

Lisa asked, "So, we shouldn't tell her about the twin boys?"

"That's correct. Be as general as possible. There will be plenty of time to tell her about the twins. In addition, she's been through a lot and she needs rest. Please, don't stay but a few minutes."

In unison, Lisa and Sam said, "Thank you doctor."

Lisa urged, "Go ahead Sam. You can see Diane first. I'll wait."

"No, I want you to come with me." Sam took Lisa's hand and they walked into the room together.

Lisa and Sam approached Diane's bed as if they were walking on eggshells. As they stood by the bed, Diane looked at them. She was grateful that Sam was with Lisa. The silent joy that was in the air put smiles across everyone's faces.

Lisa dabbed at her eyes. She opened her mouth to say something, but her emotions prevented her from speaking.

Finally Lisa found the strength to break the quietness. "How are you feeling?"

Diane's words were slow and soft, "I'm—I'm—I'm—o—o—okay."

Sam ran his fingers over Diane's hand. "You gave us a scare. We've been worried sick about you."

"I'm—I'm—I'm—I'm—sorry."

From Diane's pensive expression, Lisa thought she was tiring. "We better let you rest."

"N-n-no, d-d-don't—g-g-go"

Before Lisa or Sam could respond, the door opened. A nurse came in.

"I'm sorry but the doctor left strict instructions. Mrs. Benson needs her rest. You're going to have to leave. You can come back in the morning."

Lisa gave Diane a kiss on her cheek and squeezed her hand. "I'll be back in the morning. I love you."

Sam lingered for a few minutes as Lisa walked out the room. He opened his mouth but the words hung in his throat. He leaned over and kissed her forehead.

Although Diane had been out of the coma for several days, it was taking her longer than she expected to be fully aware of everything. According to the doctor, she was experiencing some long term memory loss. This was based on questions she was asked about her early childhood.

Every day, Lisa told her things to help her remember. The earliest thing she could remember was when she and Fred married. Everything else was a blur even when she was shown pictures.

At times Diane was confused. It was not only her memory but when she tried to speak, her mind and mouth seemed to be disconnected.

Since being out of the coma, Diane could tell Lisa, Sam and the hospital staff were guarded when she asked questions about the baby. They were hiding something despite their denials.

She decided to confront Sam. "I know you're not telling me everything that happened while I was in a coma. Is it about Donna or Freddie?"

"No."

"Then, what's wrong? Is it the baby? I have a right to know."

Sam exhaled and broke down. "You had twin boys."

Diane inhaled and exhaled and went limp. He ran from the room and got a nurse.

"Is she okay?"

"Yes, she only fainted."

CHAPTER 57

One morning when Diane opened her eyes, she woke rejuvenated. Her mind was as clear as a clean window but when she tried to stand, her body betrayed her. The nurse had to help her out of the bed and assist her while showering.

Although her recovery continued to surprise the doctors, the test continued. As a result, her days were busy with therapists, x-rays and giving blood. By the time she returned from the various tests, either Lisa or Sam was there, making a fuss over her.

Despite everything that was going on, she had not forgotten what she had to do regarding the babies. Before the day became hectic, she made a telephone call.

It was early. Diane prayed Mr. Wade was in his office. She waited. On the fourth ring, his secretary answered.

"Hello. May I speak to Mr. Wade?"

"Yes. May I ask who is calling?"

"Diane Benson."

"Good morning, Mrs. Benson."

"I don't have much time. I'm in the hospital and I had my baby." She let out a nervous laugh. "Actually, I had twins—two little boys."

"How are you and the babies doing?"

Diane hesitated. She wondered how much she should tell him. Her condition had nothing to do with the babies.

"I'm fine and the babies are healthy."

"Are you going forth with the adoption?"

"Yes. That's why I'm calling. Please, start the paperwork or whatever you need to do."

"I'll get right on it."

Diane heard the door open and whispered, "I have to go." Quickly, she hung up the phone.

When Diane looked up, it was Lisa. They smiled at each other.

"Good morning." Lisa eyed Diane before saying, "Wow! I can't get over how terrific you look. Your color has returned but you still appear thin but overall you almost look like your old self."

"Good morning to you and thanks, I think."

"I'm sorry. You have no idea how pale you were or how dull your hair was, and yesterday you still seemed weak and lifeless. Today, you look more like yourself. It's like you were never in a coma. How do you feel?"

"Good, except for my head. I have a slight headache, but the doctor said not to worry. Considering how long I was in a coma, he said it was normal."

"I can't begin to tell you how glad I am that you came out of the coma. I was praying every day. Sam was worried too." Lisa waited for Diane to make a comment, but she said nothing.

"What do you think about the boys?"

Diane's voice was sad. "I haven't seen them yet. The nurse said they will bring them to me later on this morning."

"Wait until you see them. They are the most precious babies I've ever seen. They look like … you."

"I don't believe you."

Lisa smiled. "You're right. Both boys look like a miniature version of Sam."

"Not to change the subject, but what was Sam's reaction when you told him I was having a baby?"

"Do you want the truth?"

"Yes."

"He was confused and angry. But can you blame him?"

"I know, but I couldn't tell him."

"That's something you'll have to explain to him. But, I want you to know that from the time I called him, he came to the hospital every day and stayed by your, except for when he went to work."

"How did he react to the boys' birth?"

"Shocked, like everyone, including your doctor."

"No. I mean what was his reaction?"

"I don't know what you mean." Lisa hedged as she said, "Since the boys were healthy, our concern was about you. I know he made daily visits to the nursery and I saw him holding and feeding the boys. Does that answer your question?"

Diane was glad to see the nurse walk through the open door. This way, she did not have to continue the conversation about Sam.

CHAPTER 58

Every day, Diane made noticeable improvements. Her speech was back to normal and she was no longer using a walker. The doctors were pleased with her progress.

When Dr. Myers made his rounds, he gave Diane unexpected news. "Everything looks normal, the blood work, MRI and ex-rays were all negative. Although you were in the coma for a little over two weeks, there does not appear to be any lasting complications except for the long term memory loss. As I stated before, only time will tell if it's permanent."

Diane understood and continued to listen. Dr. Myers smiled, "With all of that said, I'll be making arrangements for your discharge."

As much as Diane wanted to leave, she also wanted to stay. When Dr. Myers left, tears fell as she thought about the boys. She wondered, "Was she making the right decision?"

Before she could feel sorry for herself, lunch arrived. Diane was eating when Sam arrived. He stood in the doorway, watching.

When Diane looked up and saw him, she wondered how long he had been standing there. She smiled in hopes to cover up her sadness. Nothing could explain what she was feeling. She prayed she would not burst into sobs.

The past several days had been surreal. For an outsider looking in, she and Sam appeared to be new parents in awe of the miracle of birth. They smiled, held, fed, and had welcomed the babies into the world with lots of love. Thinking about the truth made Diane sick.

"Hi," she said.

He hesitated and moved closer to the bed. "Hi. You're looking like your old self again."

"Thanks."

"When are you going home?"

"I'm not sure, maybe tomorrow."

"That soon."

"Yes, I talked to Dr. Myers and everything looks normal."

An awkward moment passed between the two of them. Diane opened her mouth but stopped when she heard Sam speaking.

"Is it possible to talk about the boys?"

Diane chewed her bottom lip as the tears on her eye lashes were about to spill. She cleared her throat and managed to say, "There's nothing to talk about. I'm going through with my original plan and that's to give the babies up for adoption."

Sam lowered his head to hide his surprise. But, why was he surprised? After all, he had signed the adoption papers.

"Well, I guess there's nothing to talk about."

Diane tried to explain. "This is best for the boys as well as for me." She paused for a moment and added, "And for you."

Sam had no response. He had been prepared to discuss his feelings and to offer a different alternative but once again Diane excluded him from the decision making.

Silence had entered the room and when there was conversation it was forced. When it seemed as if there was nothing else to say, Sam decided to leave. He gave Diane a peck on her cheek and left.

As Diane watched him leave, her chest heaved up and down. Her heart said to stop him but practicality made her let him go. She had made her decision and there was no turning back. Circumstances had left her no other choice. Tears ran freely down her face. She knew she was losing more than her sons. She was losing the one and only man she had ever loved.

Before Sam left the hospital, he stopped by the nursery. He held his sons and told each of them, "I'll never forget you. I'm sorry I didn't do the right thing when I had the opportunity. I hope in time you will forgive me. I love you."

CHAPTER 59

Diane was dressed, all the necessary paper work completed, the babies fed and were sleeping. She was waiting for Lisa to pick them up.

Things were not perfect but Diane was finally focusing on Donna and her happiness. She wished things could have been different but her daughter deserved a child. She could not wait to hear from Donna and her reaction to having not one but two healthy baby boys to adopt.

Before leaving the hospital, Diane made arrangements to stay at the Micro-tel Inn and Suites in Leesburg. On the way to the hotel, Diane decided to confide in Lisa.

"I'm giving the boys up for adoption."

Although Lisa was surprised, she did not react. Diane lowered her voice. "Donna is going to adopt them."

"What?" Lisa veered the car off the road.

"Keep your eyes on the road," Diane shouted.

"I'm sorry, but that was more than a surprise." Lisa chose her words carefully. "Have you thought about the consequences of your decision?"

"Yes and no ... I mean ..." Her voice drifted off.

"What happens if ... no. What happens when Donna discovers the truth?"

"I know it's a risk having Donna adopt my children, her brothers, but it solves a multitude of problems."

Lisa could not believe Diane and continued to probe. "Does Sam know about the adoption?"

"Let's say, he agreed to the adoption before I had the baby, babies. What he doesn't know is that Donna and Gary are the adoptive parents."

Lisa let out a loud sigh. What was Diane thinking when she made this decision?

"I know what you're thinking, but this is about Donna. She can't have children. That's all she's ever wanted. I'm afraid that if she doesn't adopt a baby that her marriage and her happiness will be in trouble."

"I understand and can identify with Donna and her desire to have children, but when she discovers her adopted babies are actually her brothers." Lisa shook her head. "I hate to think …"

"I can't worry about that now. The lawyer assured me that the adoption records will be sealed. No one will ever learn the truth."

Lisa realized there was no need in arguing that point. In Diane's mind, she had worked out the details and nothing was going to interfere with her plans. She did not want to upset Diane's apple cart, but in her opinion, she was not living in reality. She was in for a rude awakening. What was she thinking about?

With the Internet and cyberspace—the day of confidentiality has disappeared in space. Records that were intended to be sealed are opened every day by children wanting to learn the identity of their birth parents. Then Lisa thought about DNA. Oh, no this is definitely a new world and secrets were hard to keep in today's climate. The tension in the car was thick as icing on a cake.

"Lisa, say something."

"What if …" Lisa stopped. As much as she wanted to share her thoughts with Diane, she knew it was useless.

"I know you're concerned and you probably can't understand what I'm doing, but my heart tells me that this is something I have to do. You'll see. Everything's going to work out for the best. Donna wants a baby and now she's going to have not one but two. How exciting is that?"

"Can I ask one last question?" Lisa did not wait for Diane to respond. "Did it ever occur to you that Donna might not want two newborn babies?"

CHAPTER 60

Diane assured Lisa that Donna would not have a problem adopting two babies. Lisa said nothing.

Lisa drove to the front of the hotel and Diane got out of the car. When Diane registered, she requested a room on the first floor, in the rear, near the exit.

Once Diane was assigned a room and given the key, she walked to the rear where Lisa and the babies were waiting. Inside the room, Diane and Lisa set up the two baby carrier bassinettes they purchased earlier.

When the babies were fed and asleep, Lisa hated to leave but she had a doctor's appointment.

"I'll be back as soon as I can. The boys are sleeping and I suggest you do the same."

"Lisa thanks for everything."

Lisa nodded and smiled. "Okay. You have drinking water, fruit, the remote control, baby formula, and diapers. Is there anything else before I leave?"

"No, I'm fine. You better leave or you're going to be late."

As soon as Lisa closed the door, Diane picked up the phone and dialed her daughter's number. She hoped this was the day she worked at home. It was the third ring and before the answering machine kicked on, Donna picked up.

"Hi, mom. Did you enjoy the cruise?"

"What?"

"The 21-day cruise."

"Oh ... yes ... yes. It was great."

Donna gushed, "Well I want to hear all about it."

"Not now."

"What's wrong mom? You don't sound like yourself."

"I'm just a little tired."

"Tired … come on. You've had nothing but time to rest on the cruise and you're tired …" Donna stopped and made a face. She had forgotten her mother had been with a man. The thought almost made her choke. She agreed with her mother, she did not want to hear about the cruise nor about the man in her life. Donna changed subjects.

"Mom, I'm glad you're back. I have the most wonderful news."

"What is it?"

Donna teased. "You're not going to believe it. My persistence has paid off."

"What? Did you get a promotion?"

"Don't be silly, Mom. The lawyer called and Gary and I have the opportunity to adopt a newborn baby."

Diane exclaimed, "That's great. Congratulations."

"Before you get too excited, there is a catch. The woman had twin boys."

"Is that a problem?"

"Well, as much as we want children, we aren't sure we want two babies at once."

"What's wrong with two babies?"

"That's a lot of responsibility for someone who has never had a baby."

Diane was getting irritated, "What if you had given birth to twins?"

"But I didn't. As a result, we've asked if we can adopt one of the babies."

"What? Are you out of your mind?"

"Mom, calm down." Diane wasn't sure why her decision was upsetting her. "Gary and I think it's a wonderful idea. We're excited to think two couples will have the chance to adopt a new born."

Diane grunted. "If you ask me, and you didn't, I think it's cruel to separate the siblings. They probably have already developed a bond."

"You might be right and if that's the case then Gary and I might have to pass on this adoption. I'm not prepared to be a mother of two infants. It's going to be tough enough caring for one baby."

"I'll be there to help you."

"I know mom, but you will have to go home. Remember you live in Florida now."

Diane ignored Donna and her remark. "I think you should reconsider your decision." Diane pulled in her lower lip and added, "I think God answered your prayers. You wanted a child and now that you have been given the opportunity to adopt, you want to be picky."

Diane's intent was not to make Donna feel guilty but she had to get her to change her mind. The last thing she wanted was to have the boys separated.

CHAPTER 61

Diane glanced at the clock. She was running out of time. She had to make one last call before Lisa returned.

"Hello this is Mrs. Benson, Diane Benson. Is Mr. Wade available? It's urgent."

"Hello Mrs. Benson. Please hold."

"Mrs. Benson, how are you?"

Diane had no time for niceties. "I'm concerned that the babies will be separated and adopted separately."

"Well, yes that might happen. Do you have a problem with that?"

Diane said with conviction, "Yes I do. I can't allow that."

"Well, you don't have much of a choice."

"Why not may I ask?"

"Because that stipulation had to be in the original adoption papers and...." Diane interrupted him.

"I beg to differ. I didn't know I was having a multiple birth at the time the papers were drawn up and neither did the doctor."

After several moments, Mr. Wade responded. "You're right. An amendment will be made to the adoption, stating that the twins have to be adopted together."

Exhaustion had set in once Diane completed all the calls. Her head throbbed and the last thing she needed was a headache. In addition, she wished the tears would stop. The harder she tried to stop them, the more they streamed down her face. The only saving grace was that the twins had cried once and after she fed and changed them, they went back to sleep without a fuss.

At last, she managed to relax and fell into a light sleep until the ringing phone woke her.

"Mrs. Benson, this is Mr. Wade. I'm calling because I received a call from your daughter. She and her husband do not accept the terms of the adoption. I know you didn't ask me, but I make several other inquiries and none of the couples on the list want to adopt twins. Do you want me to search for a couple that might want to adopt them?"

Diane was not going to change her mind about separating the boys. To be truthful, she did not want another couple to adopt them. Ideally, Donna was supposed to want a child badly enough that she would be willing to adopt both boys.

❦   ❦   ❦

When Lisa returned, she wondered what had happened while she was gone. Diane's eyes were swollen red and her face was tear-streaked. She put down the bags she was carrying. She sat in the chair near the bed.

Lisa looked at Diane with concern. Dread covered Diane's face. Lisa patted her hand.

"Whatever it is, it can't be that bad. What's wrong?"

Diane sniffed. "Donna and Gary don't want to adopt the boys. They'll take one, but not both."

"And that creates a problem because?"

"I don't want the boys separated. I think it would be cruel. They're brothers."

"I understand Diane, but consider the hardship the adoption of twins might cause Donna and Gary or any couple. Being a new parent is difficult enough and then to have two babies in diapers. I can't imagine."

Lisa paused for a moment. She could tell Diane did not want to hear what she was saying, but she continued. "Maybe it's best to have the boys adopted separately. Have you ever considered that if Donna doesn't adopt the boys that no one may want them either? In addition, how will you feel if Donna doesn't get another opportunity to adopt?"

From Diane's expression, Lisa knew she had stepped on thin ice and it had begun to crack. Diane's narrowed eyes; her facial expression was murderous as she glared at Lisa.

"I hear what you're saying, but listen to me. I'll do what I have to do to keep my boys together. As far as I'm concerned Donna might have missed her opportunity to adopt."

CHAPTER 62

Diane might want to keep the babies together, but Lisa wondered if she should not discuss this with Sam. He may not be as adamant as she was about keeping them together.

Lisa tried to understand Diane's viewpoint, but in her opinion, Diane had lost her focus and goal.

"Did she want the babies adopted or not?" Lisa thought about asking her, but decided she had already crossed the line regarding her opinion on the matter. Perhaps she would bring the subject up at another time.

At the moment, Lisa was more concerned about Diane getting some rest. Lisa did not mention it but she suspected while she was gone, Diane had been busy receiving and making telephone calls.

"Diane, I'm sorry if I upset you. We can discuss this later. Right now I want you to take a nap. I'll take care of the boys."

"I'm not tired."

"I don't care how much you protest. I'm going to sit right here until you rest. Now close your eyes."

The phone rang three different times and Diane never woke up. That was a sign she was worn out mentally and physically. Lisa thought who wouldn't be after delivering two babies, being in a coma for over two weeks, and worrying about their future.

Lisa was in the bathroom when the phone started to ring. Diane picked it up as Lisa hurried into the room.

"Hi, sweetheart." It was Donna. Lisa watched Diane and listened.

"Donna, take a deep breath. I can't understand a word you're saying."
"Remember the twins?"

"Yes. Well, it looks as though we can't adopt one of the boys. The deal is that we have to adopt both babies."

"Why?"

"The mother doesn't want the twins separated and adopted by two different couples. Please don't say I told you so."

"I won't but I'm wondering if you might reconsider?"

"Absolutely not. We don't want the responsibility of two babies, even with your help. It will be too much for me to work and care for two infants."

"Had you thought about hiring a nanny? You and Gary could afford it."

"We did discuss that but we don't want a stranger living with us."

"Do you think maybe you're being a little selfish?" Diane's words were harsh. "Either you want a child or you don't. What if you had adopted a sick baby? How would you handle that?"

"Mom, what's wrong with you." Donna's voice quivered. "I can't believe you. For whatever reason, you can't support me regarding this issue."

Before Diane could respond, Donna's tone turned harsh. "Our decision is about my ability to care for two infant babies. I don't know why you can't understand that?"

"I do understand but it seems as if you've taken your eye off of the prize. You are being given the opportunity to adopt two infant boys."

"We have to agree to disagree on this point. I'm not adopting two infants. That's final."

Diane wanted to scream but what could she do. Donna was not going to change her mind. Diane murmured, "I'm sorry if I've disappointed you but you've also let down two little boys."

"Maybe but it is my decision."

CHAPTER 63

As much as Diane hated it, she had to discuss her plan with Sam. Before she even had the conversation, she knew he would not be supportive. His reaction would probably be similar to when she broke the news about the pregnancy.

Before Diane changed her mind, she started working out the details of her plan. It was not the ideal decision, but what choice did she have?

One thing for sure, she did not have much time to put everything in place. The number one item on her list was to contact a real estate agent and sale her house.

Next, she would have the agent locate a courtyard patio villa to buy. However, she had certain requirements. The house had to be located on a corner lot. That would give her additional privacy.

Before Diane dialed Sam's number, the phone rang. She could not believe it. Sam was on the line.

"Hello."

"Hi, Diane." With no hesitation, he stated his intention. "We need to talk."

"Uh … I'm at the Microtel Inn and Suites in Leesburg."

"What are you doing there?"

"I'll tell you when you get here."

"Can I bring anything?"

"Since you're coming after work, would you mind bringing a pizza?"

"No problem. Do you need anything else?"

"No. And thanks.

When Diane hung up talking to Sam, she called Lisa. "Hey. Sam's coming over. You can take a break."

"Did I hear you say that Sam was …"

"Yes. Sam is coming over."

"That means you're going to tell him everything?"

"Do I have a choice?"

Lisa was not in the mood to argue with Diane. "Thanks for calling and I'll see you tomorrow. Enjoy your evening."

Sam arrived, carrying a large pizza box. After placing the box on the table, he kissed Diane on the cheek. When he pulled away from her, he staggered and stared in disbelief.

"Why ... I mean ... I thought the babies had been adopted?"

"I was going to call you about that. The couple changed their minds."

"What happened?"

"They didn't want two infants ..." Before Diane could finish her sentence Sam cut her off.

"I can understand. That's a lot of diaper changing and not to mention the crying."

Diane shot him a ferocious look.

Sam wanted to be realistic. More importantly, he did not want to discuss his real reason for not wanting children.

"The lawyer made some other inquiries and none of the couples wanted to adopt two infants. They're willing to adopt one but not two." She paused and wanted his opinion. "How do you feel about separating the babies?"

"What is there to think about?" He rushed on. "I mean we have two healthy babies and we could give two couples the opportunity to be parents."

"I know, but the babies are brothers. I don't want them ending up as adults on one of those TV talk shows discussing how they were adopted and had been searching for each other since they were young children."

In a low tone, she added, "And I don't want them searching for their biological mother when they're adults, wanting to know why I allowed two couples adopt them."

"Whew." Sam scratched his head. He did not know what to say. He was having a difficult time understanding Diane's reasoning.

"I don't know Diane. What did the lawyer say?"

"About what?"

"You know, the legality of you changing your mind as to how the boys will be adopted?"

"Yes, you and I signed papers for the adoption but everything became null and void when I had twins. Besides, every mother has the right to change her mind about the adoption."

CHAPTER 64

The real estate agent contacted Diane immediately. "Mrs. Benson, the analysis is complete and I think we can get more than the fair market price for your home. Your house is decorated like a model and your landscaping is breathtaking."

"How soon do you want the house to go on the market?"

"I would like to do it as soon as possible."

"Great. You have some preliminary papers to sign and the *"For Sale"* sign can go up in a few days."

Diane could not believe the substantial profit she would make from the sale of the house. She would need every penny. She would have enough to pay cash for the courtyard villa as well as the interior and exterior changes she needed to make.

Despite the proceeds, she would still have to go back to doing private consulting. Her retirement income was not enough to care for her and the babies. The expense of raising a child had changed considerably from when Freddie and Donna were babies. The cost of feeding, clothing and saving for their college tuition was overwhelming.

The decisions she made were having a definite effect on her life and causing a number of unexpected problems. Her life might be complicated, but for the first time in a long time, she was in control.

❦   ❦   ❦

Several weeks had passed since Diane had talked to her daughter. After their last conversation, Diane wasn't ready to talk to her. As she thought about Donna, the phone rang.

"Mom, Angie had the baby."

"Congratulations. How's she doing?"

"She's doing great and our son is healthy and handsome like his father. Mom, he has my eyes and my coloring. It's as if I'm looking at a mirror."

Through laughter, Diane said, "I'm happy for you. Are you at the hospital?"

"No, I'm in the car."

"Did you name him yet?"

"Mom, he's named after me. Since he's the third we'll probably call him Junior Freddie, even though he's the third."

"Tell Angie I said congratulations and I'll call her later."

"By the way, Angie said to ask you, when you might be coming to help us with the baby?"

"Well, I thought I would let the new parents get acquainted with their new addition and then we can discuss when I'll come."

"Oh. She hoped you would come now."

Diane did not miss Freddie's disappointing tone. She would try and smooth things over to buy her time. Under the circumstances she could not travel even if she wanted to.

"Honey, I cannot explain how important it is for you, Angie and the baby to bond the first few weeks."

She waited for Freddie to answer. She suspected he was sulking like he did when he was a toddler.

"Aren't you taking time off from work?"

"Yes, I'm taking a two-week vacation."

"And didn't your sister say she'll take a week off to help?"

"Yes."

"Trust me, you'll have more help than you'll imagine. That's all the more reason why you don't need me there. You'll have more than enough help and you and Angie will be glad for some quiet time."

"That's not it mother. Angie's worried. She's a sound sleeper and afraid she might not hear him when he cries. In addition, she's read and heard some disturbing information about postpartum blues, especially for first time mothers."

"Freddie, do you trust me?" He didn't answer his mother because he could not understand why she was not coming. This was her first grandchild.

"Angie has been reading too many articles and watching too much television. I'm not dismissing her concerns because Postpartum Blues is something to be concerned about. I believe every woman has some degree of Postpartum Blues—crying for no reason, feeling overwhelmed and inadequate." Diane paused to let her son absorb what she was saying.

"What I suggest is that you educate yourself about Postpartum Blues. You become aware of the symptoms. Then you will know what to watch out for. All new parents have fears—there are no books to prepare you for your new role. It's scary, but manageable."

"You make it sound easier than I know it's going to be."

"Well, welcome to the exclusive club of parenthood. It's special being a parent and not everyone can be one."

CHAPTER 65

The *"For Sale"* sign in Diane's yard caught Lisa by surprise. She was hurt and confused. Diane had not mentioned anything to her about moving.

When Lisa arrived at the hotel, her words hit Diane as if she had slapped her. "You share everything else with me, but you couldn't tell me you were moving? What's going on?"

"I wanted to tell you but ..."

"But what?" I've had your back through everything but now you want to keep secrets." They exchanged looks. With hands on her hips, Lisa demanded, "Well. What are you hiding?"

Diane closed her eyes and mustered up as much strength as she could to answer her. "I'm keeping my sons."

"You're what? This is crazier than when you wanted Donna to adopt the boys. The coma must have done something to the reasoning side of your brain."

Diane was defensive. "That's why I didn't tell you. I knew you would react like this."

"I don't want to see you hurt."

"What would hurt me is to see my babies separated and I don't want strangers raising my sons." She sounded and acted similar to a little girl as she crossed her arms and pouted. "No matter what you say, I'm keeping them."

"You haven't thought this through? How are you going to keep them?"

"What do you mean?"

"You know what I mean. Don't play stupid. Where are you going to live? How are you going to manage financially?"

"Please, one question at a time. I'm going to continue living in The Villages. And to supplement my income, I'm going back to my old consulting job. It allows me to work at home and have flexible hours."

Lisa kept shaking her head. "Let me get this straight. You're going to live in The Villages with two babies? Have you forgotten you live in a retirement community that doesn't allow children?"

"I know, but I can pull it off, especially by moving to a courtyard villa. I'm going to extend the one bedroom wall and have the inside walls of the house soundproofed. With the fence separating the houses, I'll have privacy and I can take the boys out on the lanai."

Lisa stared at Diane in disbelief. The excitement in her voice matched her gleaming eyes. She was serious and to her the plan seemed logical.

"How could she respond to her?" Lisa wanted to be supportive, but at the same time she wanted to shake some sense into her. How could she convince Diane to reconsider what she was about to do? Surely, she had not thought about the consequences of her decision.

Lisa tried again. "You realize your life will be nothing but constant lies."

She shrugged. "I don't care. I'm going to do whatever it takes to keep my sons together and raise them as brothers. No one seems to understand or care about that except for me."

"But what kind of a life will they have? They will be isolated from the world."

"Who said they would be secluded?"

"Well, how can you take the babies out in public?"

"First of all, I can take them out, even in The Villages. When I take them for walks I'll tell people they're my grandchildren." Diane stopped for a minute as her eyes twinkled.

"Yes, that's what I'll say and their mother, my daughter, lives in Leesburg. On occasion I baby sit to give her a break. That will definitely work."

"Okay, what are you going to tell Donna and Freddie? You can't keep this a secret from them forever."

"I'll tell them as soon as I work out the details."

"What about Sam? What are you going to tell him? He thinks his babies are being adopted."

"Well, he knows some of the truth."

Lisa had developed a headache as she listened to Diane spin her web of lies. In her opinion, Diane no longer recognized the truth from the lies. Lies had become her survival technique.

"You mean your truth."

Diane rolled her eyes at Lisa and dismissed her flippant remark. "He knows no one wanted to adopt twins." She barked," Unlike me, he didn't mind if they were adopted by two different couples. That's because Sam doesn't want the responsibility of raising children. In fact, he's not fond of children—too loud, too needy, and too expensive."

CHAPTER 66

Diane's house sold in three days. The other good news was that the real estate agent found a corner courtyard villa.

The structural changes Diane wanted were not as easy as she had expected. The Villages did not want to approve the changes. She wanted the bedroom extended four feet and the approval was for three feet. At least the inside sounding proofing wasn't an issue.

After several meetings, The Villages approved three and a half feet.

The lies were beginning to catch up with her. To keep them straight, she began to keep a journal. Diane decided to address one lie by talking to her daughter.

She should have called Freddie and Angie first because they had continued to pressure her about coming to help them with the baby. Instead, she called Donna because she was the most critical of everything she did.

"Mother, have you lost your mind?"

"When you told me about those little babies I couldn't resist. I contacted your lawyer and she told me the babies were still up for adoption. I spoke to the mother and assured her that I would keep them together."

"How are you going to manage?"

"I'll survive. I'll make some sacrifices, but I'll be okay."

"Is this because daddy and Joanne have a baby?"

"No. Listen to me. I want my life to mean something. Don't get me wrong, I enjoyed raising you and Freddie, but I was working and I didn't get the opportunity to be a full time mom."

"Have you told Freddie yet?"

"No, but I will because he and Angie are expecting me to help them. But now I won't be able to do that."

"What about me?"

"What do you mean?"

"I was about to call you with my good news, but you spoiled it. Gary and I have a baby boy. We will be picking him up tomorrow. I didn't want to tell you until I was absolutely sure. It seemed like every time we were to adopt a baby something went wrong. So, I wanted to wait."

"Congratulations. I'm happy for you."

"Are you, mother?"

"Of course I am."

"Then, why are you doing this to us? I was counting on you, just like Freddie. We thought you wanted grandchildren and would be enjoying them instead you're going to be playing mommy to two babies that aren't even related to you."

"I'm sorry if I've disappointed you."

"I have to go. I suggest you call Freddie."

"I will."

After talking to Donna, Diane had a headache. The last thing she wanted to do was to call Freddie. Angie answered the phone.

"Diane, we've been waiting for your call. When are you coming?"

Diane did not want to be rude but she did not answer Angie's question. Instead, she asked her to put Freddie on the phone.

When Freddie heard about his mother's decision, he thought he had been run over by a semi-truck. He tried to understand but it was all too TV-like. He could not believe his mother was adopting at her age. He thought she must be having a mid-life crisis moment. The divorce had more of an impact than he realized.

The conversation was one sided as he listened to his mother explain her decision. He kept his opinions to himself. She had made up her mind and there was nothing he could say to change it.

"Freddie, you haven't said anything. Please, say something."

"Congratulations."

The phone went dead. Diane broke down into loud sobs.

CHAPTER 67

Since Diane was making telephone calls, she called Sam. She had two strikes against her and one more strike was not going to make a difference. She had to tell him about her plans.

"Hello."

"Hi, Sam. It's Diane."

"Hey. How are you doing?" He should have asked about the babies, but he didn't.

"I'm doing fine. Do you have a minute?"

"Sure. What's up?"

"I don't know where to begin, but I have something important to tell you. Are you sitting down?"

Sam didn't have to sit down. He had been waiting for this call. He knew what she was going to say. When he had fallen in love with Diane, he knew her better than she would ever know. That was one reason why he loved her. She was the most open, honest woman he had ever met. He had tried to prepare himself for this day, but at the moment his stomach was queasy and his heart was racing.

"Are you still there?"

"I'm sorry. Continue with what you were saying."

"I hope you'll believe me when I say I have given this a lot of thought and I believe this is the only thing I can do."

"I know you believe that."

She wasn't going to debate her decision. "My primary concern is the welfare of the boys. I can't allow them to be separated. We talked about it, remember?"

"I remember."

Vividly, he recalled that day. That's when he realized Diane was a loving mother and she would do everything to prevent the boys from being adopted by two couples. He understood her reasoning, but he didn't necessarily agree with it.

"Please don't hate me."

"I could never do that."

"You say that now, but when I tell you that I'm keeping our babies, what would you say?"

He was calm as he responded, "I know."

"What did you say?"

"I said, I know."

"But … how?"

"When you told me that no couple wanted to adopt two babies and you didn't want them separated, I knew."

"I didn't realize I was that transparent. I want you to know I never expected any of this to happen."

"I know."

"I do want to make something clear I'm not asking you for anything. The reason for my call was to tell you. After all, you are the babies' father and I want you to be in their lives."

"Look, I've never explained to you why I never wanted children and I'm not prepared to discuss it now because it's complicated. I guess sometimes things are taken out of our hands. As much as I never wanted children, I am now the proud father of not one but two boys. You need to understand that I will support you in any way I can. And with your help, I'll be a good father to our sons."

Diane could not talk because of the lump in her throat. Tears were flowing down her cheeks.

CHAPTER 68

❀

The contractor Diane hired had come highly recommended. He was professional and thorough. Diane had confidence that he would deliver on time and on budget. She checked on the property once. She should have visited more often but she was not prepared to meet her new neighbors.

Cee Tyson was curious about her neighbor. In an effort to meet the people who were living next door, she made an unannounced visit.

Cee rang the doorbell and waited. A man opened the door. He greeted her with a smile.

"Hello." The woman extended her hand. "My name is Cee Tyson. I'm your neighbor."

He did not shake her hand. "I'm not your neighbor. I'm the builder." He hesitated but added, "Your neighbor will be moving in when all the changes are completed."

Cee began peeking around the man. "What type of changes are you making?"

The builder hedged, "I'm making changes the owner has requested."

Cee waited for more of an explanation but he said nothing else. She left.

The second visit, Cee waited until the builder left. She was carrying a basket of brownies. She rang the doorbell.

A Hispanic man opened the door with hesitancy. He stepped outside and closed the door behind him. With broken English, the man asked, "May I help you?"

"Is the owner here today?"

"No, miss."

"Do you know the name of the owners who bought this house?"

"No speak good English." He turned, opened the door and left her standing.

Cee could not believe this man was working and could not speak English. When she turned around, the builder was pulling into the driveway.

When he got out of the car, he spoke, "Hello, Mrs. Tyson. How are you today?"

"I'm fine. I thought your men would like some brownies. I brought over a basket but the man who answered the door wouldn't take it. I hope I didn't get them into any trouble."

The builder smiled. "It's okay. They smell delicious. I'm sure they'll appreciate them. I can't wait to eat one of them."

Cee laughed. Instead of leaving, she kept standing."

"Is there, something else?"

"I'm curious. Exactly what are you doing inside?"

The builder didn't respond for a moment. Finally, he answered, "A few changes here and there. When the owner moves in, I'm sure you'll be given a tour if you ask."

"You can't give me a little hint."

"I'm sorry. I'm not at liberty to tell you or anyone else." He smiled and waited for her to leave.

Cee could not believe how tight lipped the builder was. This wasn't the norm. Usually, the contractors are anxious to show off their work in hope someone else might want something done. The neighbor down the street had some changes made on their villa and the builder not only answered her questions but showed them to her.

Since Cee had gotten nowhere with the contractor, she had only one choice. She stayed in her front her window, watching and hoping to see the new neighbor. It never happened.

CHAPTER 69

In two days, Diane would be going to settlement and moving into her new house. Everything had been completed and there had been no complications. It was hard for her to contain her emotions.

Regardless of what Lisa and Sam thought, she understood the life decision she had chosen was not going to be easy. However, with their support she could make it happen.

The most unexpected surprise had been Sam. From the day she told him she was keeping the babies, his heart softened. When he was not working, he shared in taking care of the boys. He babysat and provided financial support.

She did not know why the change in Sam and she didn't care. He had kept his promise of being in the boys' lives.

Lisa had to admit that Diane's decision might have been unconventional but she was determined to make it work. She didn't tell Diane but she couldn't believe the change in Sam. He was being a father to the boys, something Diane needed, as well as the boys.

To get everything ready for the move, Diane and Lisa had been doing a lot of shopping. Sam would babysit. When Diane and Lisa were about to leave, Lisa slapped her forehead.

"What's wrong?"

"I cannot believe it. I forgot my purse. I'll be right back." When Lisa entered the hotel room, Sam did not hear her. Lisa stood, watching.

Sam was bent over the bassinette, his voice was loud. "Listen, you need to stop crying. Why can't you be like your brother?"

Lisa waited before she let Sam know she had been watching and listening. "What are you doing?"

Startled, Sam turned around. "Oh … Lisa. I can explain."

"Don't bother." She pointed her finger at him. "You listen to me. I better never hear you raise your voice again to these precious boys. They are nothing but babies and they communicate by crying." She emphasized. "Do-you-understand?"

Sam opened his mouth and closed it. He nodded his head.

Lisa walked over to Baby Two and picked him up. She rocked him to sleep. Lisa picked up her purse, glared at Sam and left.

"What took you so long?"

Lisa lied. "With the room so filled with shopping bags and boxes, I couldn't find my purse."

"Oh."

While Lisa drove to Belk's, Diane was gushing about Sam and how good he was with the boys. Lisa listened until she finally interjected her concerns.

"I think you need to explain to Sam that babies communicate by crying. I don't think he's very tolerant with them."

Diane defended him. "He's trying."

"Are you sure? He needs to understand that Baby Two requires more attention than Baby One. Baby two can be fussy."

"I think Sam's figured that out and he's being more patient."

Lisa shrugged. "Okay but I'd watch him."

Diane appreciated Lisa's frankness but she knew Sam loved his sons and would do nothing to harm either one of them.

CHAPTER 70

The boys were nameless. Sam understood why Diane had not named them, but it was time.

"We have to think about naming the boys."

"You're right. Would you like to help me pick out their names?"

"Yes and I think we should include Lisa."

Every day, Sam continued to surprise Diane with his thoughtfulness especially since Sam sensed Lisa was not fond of him. Despite Lisa's feelings, he was willing to include her when they chose the boys' names.

Diane called Lisa and invited her over for Chinese carryout. She wanted Lisa to be surprised as to why she had been invited to dinner.

When dinner was finished, Diane shared the news. "We're going to pick a name for the boys."

Lisa's eyes were wet. She was honored to be included. To lighten the moment, she said, "I have a few rules. Let's pick names the boys will be able to pronounce and spell."

Sam wanted some information before he made any suggestions. "I assume that Freddie is a junior. Is there any significance regarding Donna's name?"

"That was my mother's and my middle name. Generations ago, the family tradition was to have the first born girl's name begin with the letter "D.""

Lisa asked, "Do you want the boys' first name to begin with the same letter?" She added, "I don't know that much about naming twins, but it seems to me that most of their names begin with the same letter."

"You might be right, but to be honest, I haven't given it much thought."

"Sam, do you want one of the boys named after you? You know, as a junior."

"I never liked that. I think the boys should have their own identity. Besides how would you decide which one to name junior. As they grow up, I would think the boys might think we must have loved one more than the other because he was named after me." He shook his head. "That's out."

"What about Donald and David?" Lisa suggested.

"Those are strong names." Sam said.

Diane agreed, "The names flow—but there are enough first names in my family beginning with the letter "*d*." Let's try something different."

Sam recommended, "Sydney David and Skye Douglas. You can continue your family tradition. The boys' middle name will begin with the letter "*d*." And the boys' first name will begin with the letter "*s*" symbolizing my first name."

Thirty minutes later, they went still going back and forth, tossing out names. Lisa would look at the boys and call them by one of the names they had chosen. If they cried, the name was eliminated. It wasn't an exact science but they used the method anyway.

They had pretty much exhausted the list of names they had come up with. Sam and Lisa proposed they continue another day. Diane was determined to name them.

Finally, they went back to Sam's original suggestion. A toast was made in honor of Sydney David and Skye Douglas.

Before the festivities ended, Diane and Sam turned to Lisa. It was Sam who said, "We want you and Patrick to be the godparents."

Lisa was overcome with emotion. Her words lodged in her throat. She gave each of them a hug.

She didn't say anything about Patrick because she had not spoken to him in days. With so much going on in Diane's life, she had not told her that they were experiencing some difficulty. Diane had been through enough and Lisa did not want her to think she had been the cause of their recent problems.

CHAPTER 71

Diane was busy getting ready for her move. To help, Lisa was at the house, waiting for Southern Lifestyles to deliver furniture Diane ordered.

As Lisa put the teakettle on the stove, the doorbell rang. Glancing at the clock, she knew it was too early for the furniture delivery.

When Lisa peered through the door's peephole, she saw a short, round woman, wearing an apron over her clothes.

Through clenched teeth, Lisa said, "Shoot. Diane's going to kill me."

She had not followed Diane's rule. She was to park the car inside the garage. Her car was in the driveway.

For a second, Lisa thought about not answering the door, but she thought that might raise suspicion. At least Diane's storm door had been installed and the woman would not be able to see inside the house.

Lisa opened the door slightly. A perky voice greeted her. The woman pulled on the storm door handle, but stopped when she realized it was locked.

"My name is CeeCee Tyson. CeeCee is not a nickname but Cee is and that's what everyone calls me. I live next door."

Lisa did not want to be rude. "It's nice to meet you, but I don't live here."

Cee cocked her head to the side and her right eyebrow was raised in a questioning manner.

"Oh. Well, is the owner home?"

"No, she isn't. I'll tell her you stopped by." Lisa was about to close the door when Cee turned back around.

She laughed. "Goodness me, I almost forgot. I baked some muffins as a welcome to the neighborhood. Will you please give them to the owner?"

Lisa unlocked the door and accepted the basket. When Lisa opened the door, Cee stood on her tiptoes, peeping to the left and to the right, trying to see around Lisa.

"Do you mind if I come in and look at the changes the owner made?"

"The owner's name is Mrs. Benson." Lisa was curious. "Why do you think she made changes?"

"I talked to the builder, but he wouldn't tell or show me the changes being made. Can I come in?"

"I don't think that's a good idea."

"Well, we wouldn't have to tell her. It would be our secret."

Quickly, Lisa locked the storm door. "I'm sorry but Mrs. Benson wouldn't like it if someone was in her house without her knowledge."

As Lisa started to close the door, she noticed Cee was not moving. Lisa sighed. "Is there something else?"

"You didn't say who you were."

"I'm sorry. My name is Lisa Henderson."

"Do you live in The Villages?"

"Yes. I live in The Village of Summerhill."

"It's nice to meet you, Lisa. Since you won't let me come in, will you tell me about the changes she made?"

"I honestly don't know." Lisa was about to explain why she was there when the Southern Lifestyles truck pulled up.

"Thanks Cee and I'll tell Mrs. Benson you dropped by to meet her."

Lisa was sure when the truck pulled up, Cee would leave. Instead, she stood planted and waited until the truck driver approached the house.

Firmly, Lisa said, "Cee, I'll be sure to tell Mrs. Benson you came over. Take care and have a nice day."

Reluctantly, Cee walked down the sidewalk. Lisa watched her until she disappeared.

She thought, "Diane is in for trouble. That's all she needs is a nosy, friendly neighbor."

While the men put the furniture in the house, Lisa made a call to Diane. "Hey girl. Where are you?"

"I'm on my way to the doctor's office? Why? What's up?"

"I wanted to warn you, don't come to the house. I had the pleasure of meeting your next-door neighbor, Cee. She's a piece of work."

"Why did she come over?"

"Why do you think? She wanted to meet her new neighbor."

"Oh, yeah. I almost forgot how friendly people are in The Villages."

CHAPTER 72

To avoid the neighbors, Diane decided to move into her house after dark. As suspected, when Sam pulled the truck up in her driveway, most of the lights were out in the surrounding houses.

What was that noise? Cee used the remote control and put the TV on mute. She listened. What's making that noise? She rose from her chair and went to the front door. She looked out.

"Les, I think our neighbors are moving in."

"What makes you say that?"

"There's a moving truck in the driveway."

Les joined his wife. "Move over Cee and let me see."

Cee wondered, "Why would they move in at night?"

"Your guess is as good as mine."

"I'll go over there tomorrow."

For several weeks, Cee tried to meet her neighbor. On numerous occasions, she visited Mrs. Benson, but when she rang the doorbell two things happened. Either no one answered or the woman named Lisa greeted her.

Cee began to wonder if Lisa might be the actual owner and there was no Diane Benson. Another theory was that Lisa and the mystery woman were in a Lesbian relationship and they did not want the neighbors to know.

Looking out the window, Cee spotted Lisa pulling into the driveway. The timing could not have been better, because Cee had baked a fresh batch of brownies. She hurried and put them in a basket.

Cee rushed next door. Before ringing the doorbell, she put her ear to the storm door. She didn't hear anything. As she continued to stand near the door, the interior door jerked open. She jumped and screamed.

Lisa watched Cee as she tried to balance the basket before losing the contents. Lisa covered her mouth to conceal a chuckle.

"Hello, Cee. How are you doing today? Can I help you?"

Cee's face turned crimson from embarrassment. Clearing her throat, she spoke. "Hi, Lisa. I thought I would bring Mrs. Benson a basket of brownies. Is she home?" Cee tried to look around Lisa, but her body blocked her vision.

Lisa did not answer. "I'm waiting for a furniture delivery."

Cee pushed the basket she was carrying toward Lisa. She unlocked the storm door, took the basket and quickly relocked it.

As Cee began to speak, Lisa shut the door.

Cee's mouth flew open. "Well, I never!"

After regaining her composure, she turned and strolled home. When she opened the door to her house, her husband yelled, "Cee, is that you?"

"Yes. I'm back."

"You weren't gone long. What's wrong?"

She huffed, "Our neighbor, that's what wrong. Something strange is going on over there."

"Why do you say that?"

"For one thing, she's never home. I've gone over there three—four times to meet her and the only person I've met is Lisa Henderson."

"Well, you know how busy you were when we first moved in. We were running to this store and that one, buying items to decorate and furnish the house."

"Yeah, but my intuition tells me it's more than that."

"You don't think maybe Lisa is holding her hostage or something?"

Her husband started laughing. "No and quit imagining things."

"Listen, people appreciate nosy neighbors. If it weren't for me being inquisitive, the police wouldn't have caught the burglars that were breaking into houses. Do you remember how you told me to mind my own business?"

"Yes and you never let me forget it."

"I'm going to be watching that house and if something's going on, I'll find out."

CHAPTER 73

When Lisa entered Diane's office, she was laughing. She placed the basket on the side table.

"Another gift basket delivered by your friendly neighbor. That woman is relentless. Cee is determined to meet you. She's not going to give up until her curiosity is satisfied."

"She is persistent."

"That's an understatement. Why don't you take a break? Go over to her house now. Catch her off guard. You know, the best offense is a good defense."

"You're probably right."

Diane sighed heavily as she shut down the computer. "I'm going to take your advice. Would you please empty that basket and get the other one?"

Diane walked next door, carrying the two empty baskets. She took a deep breath and rang the doorbell. Squaring her shoulders, she waited. When the door opened, she had a friendly smile plastered on her face.

The woman standing at the door had an odd facial expression. Diane extended her hand.

"Hi, I'm Diane Benson. You must be Cee."

Awkwardly, they stood at the door. Cee eyed Diane as a man's voice yelled out.

"Invite the woman in, Cee."

"I'm sorry, where are my manners? Please, please. Come in."

A man a little taller than the woman appeared. "Let me introduce you to my husband, Les." After Diane and Les shook hands, he disappeared.

"I can't stay long because I'm working."

"I was under the impression you weren't home. I mean Lisa said she was waiting for a furniture delivery."

"I'm sorry, but I work at home and in order for me not to be disturbed, Lisa helps me out by doing some chores for me."

Diane was not sure why she added, "I'm also expecting a telephone call from my daughter. She has a new baby boy and she calls frequently for advice."

"How old is her baby?"

"Not quite six weeks old."

"And you're not there to help her? Is this her first child?"

Before Diane could respond, Cee shared with excitement. "When my daughter had her baby I was there for over a month. Wild horses couldn't keep me from my precious bundle of joy. If I had my way I'd move back to Ohio, but Les wouldn't hear of it. He said that grown children need their own space and life."

She threw her hands up. "Les tells me all the time that I talk too much and ask too many questions. I'm sorry. What were you going to say about helping your daughter?"

"When my daughter first had the baby I spent some time with her." Diane thought, number one partial lie. "I work at home and I could only take a few weeks off from my job. I would have loved to stay longer, but that was all the vacation time I had."

Diane paused for a minute. "My company downsized and I was forced to take an early retirement. My fixed income isn't enough to live on."

"I didn't mean to pry."

Diane changed subjects. "Your muffins and brownies are scrumptious. Every time I eat one, I think I've died and gone to heaven. Listen, I really need to get back. Tell your husband it was nice meeting him. I'm sure I'll see you again soon."

Diane turned and was almost at the door when Cee's question caught her off guard. "When you finish working, why don't you come over for dinner? We would love to have you."

"I'm sorry I have plans."

"Well, maybe another time. Before you leave, I didn't think to ask about your husband."

"I no longer have a husband. I'm divorced."

"There I go again, meddling into areas I have no business going. Well, thanks for coming over and returning my baskets."

"No, thank you for the home made goodies." Diane started toward the door again when another question delayed her departure.

"Who picks up your mail and newspaper when you go out of town?"

"My friend Lisa does that for me."

"It wouldn't be any trouble for me to do it. It would save Lisa from making a daily trip. And, if you want, you can give me a spare key?"

"I appreciate your offer, but Lisa has my spare key."

Cee shrugged. When Diane began walking toward the door, she cringed. Cee asked yet another question.

"Did I understand correctly, that you don't work on Thursdays?" Cee didn't wait for an answer.

Diane was non-committal. "Why?"

"Some of the neighborhood women meet for breakfast at TooJays at Sumter Landing. Why don't you join us?" Before Diane could reply, Cee continued. "That would give you an opportunity to meet some of the neighbors."

"I don't know."

"Say, yes. We have a good time."

Diane could not think of a single reason to decline Cee's invitation. Diane agreed to the Thursday Morning Breakfast Club.

"It was nice meeting you."

Cee watched Diane until she could no longer see her. She thought, "She's hiding something."

Les appeared. "Regardless of what you think, she seems nice and harmless. I am curious to know whether she's old enough to live in The Villages."

Cee's hand went to her chest. "That's it. She's not old enough to live here and she's trying to hide it."

"Let's not jump to conclusions. You only need one person to be over fifty-five. She and her husband probably bought in The Villages before they divorced and he's probably fifty-five."

She snapped her fingers. "Darn. Yeah, that makes sense."

"Why are you suspicious?"

"I don't know. You might call it a woman's intuition. I can't explain it."

CHAPTER 74

Since the birth of the boys, Skye could cry for hours at a time. What frustrated Diane was that she didn't know how to help him. Generally, babies cried because they were hungry or wet but most times Skye cried for no apparent reason.

Sydney had been asleep for hours. Skye was still crying. Diane rocked, sang, and paced the floor, but his crying persisted. She checked his temperature and it was okay. His diaper was dry and did not need changing. When she tried to feed him, he refused to take his bottle even though he should have been hungry.

"What's wrong sweetie? I wish you could tell momma."

Skye's response was more wailing. Diane hoped he did not wake Sydney. After thirty more minutes of cuddling, he fell asleep.

Diane thought about the boys' last doctor's appointments. Despite the confidence she had in their pediatrician, she pondered over the questions she had asked and answers she had received.

"Why does Skye cry more than Sydney?"

"He might be suffering from colic. And, as you know, he'll grow out of it."

"What about his appetite?

"If he has an appetite problem, his weight hasn't been affected. In fact, the boys are progressing like other children in the same percentile and age bracket. From my exams and blood tests, they're fine."

Despite the doctor's constant reassurance, motherly instinct told Diane something was wrong with Skye. To support her suspicions, she began writing in a notebook anything she considered unusual. She recorded things such as lack of appetite, hard stools, or crying for long periods of time for no apparent reason.

After putting Skye in his crib, she made herself a cup of herbal tea. She hoped it would relax her nerves. The right temple of her head throbbed and her stomach was queasy. She finished her tea and checked on the twins.

Tiptoeing, she entered the twins' bedroom. They were sleeping. She stood between the two cribs, glancing from one to the other. They had an angelic appearance. She thought the only thing missing was a halo.

She was tired and could not wait to climb into bed. Before she left the boys' room, she decided to check their diapers. Usually, she waited until they fussed about being wet before changing them. Considering how long it took Skye to fall asleep, she wondered if she should disturb him.

Against her better judgment, she reached into Skye's crib. He was wet. Carefully, she eased his diaper down. When she had it completely off, she grabbed the side of the crib to steady her wobbly legs.

Her heart began racing. She told herself to remain calm. Closely, she examined the diaper as well as him. His skin had a yellowish hue. She finished changing him and eased to Sydney's crib.

Her hands shook as she unfastened his diaper. As she changed him, she looked at his skin coloring. Sydney's skin looked normal.

Turning back to Skye's crib, she stood biting her lower lip as she watched him. His breathing was slow and peaceful. As Diane watched him, his face had a slight smile. She wondered if he was dreaming.

She touched his forehead it was cool. Nothing indicated that he was in any discomfort.

She eased out of the bedroom and closed the door. She walked to her room.

Under the light, she examined the diaper.

CHAPTER 75

Diane glanced at the wall clock. Ten o'clock pm. She took a deep breath, hesitated, picked up the phone and dialed Lisa's number.

Lisa turned over, squinted at the illuminating clock and answered the ringing phone. "Hello."

"Lisa, I'm sorry to call you so late, but ..." The words caught in her throat.

"What's wrong?"

"I'm not sure but I need to take Skye to the hospital."

Lisa was no longer half asleep. She sat straight up in the bed. "Is he running a temperature or what?"

Trying not to cry, Diane uttered, "I don't know what's wrong but I'm afraid that it might be serious."

"Don't jump to conclusions. I'll be over as soon as I can."

Lisa broke the speed limits as she drove to Diane's. She prayed everything was going to be okay.

Lisa's mind drifted as a thought occurred to her. Why had Diane called her? Why had she not called Sam? When Lisa arrived, Diane had both boys dressed and was ready to go.

"I thought you said Skye was sick."

"I know that Sydney isn't showing any of Skye's signs but that doesn't mean he isn't sick."

"It's none of my business, but did you call Sam?"

"No."

Bitterness dripped from her mouth. "I can only deal with one problem at a time. If Sam's aware of some family genetic or inherited disease he hasn't told me about, I don't want to deal with that now. I mean if his secret jeopardizes one or both boys, I can't even think what I might say or do."

"Did it ever occur to you that Sam might not know," Lisa said in his defense. Diane glared at her.

Lisa threw up her hands. "Hey. I don't know every heredity disease in my family. Do you?"

Diane didn't answer. "We need to get to the hospital."

When Diane and Lisa walked into the emergency ward, the boys' cries sounded as if they were using microphones and the loud speakers had been turned up too loud. Without hesitation, Diane, Lisa and the boys were ushered to an examination room.

Lisa and Diane took turns holding Skye. Diane smiled at Lisa. Whatever she had whispered in Skye's ear worked. His sobs had turned into soft cooing and Sydney followed suit.

The doctor entered and smiled. "Hello, Mrs. Benson. What's going on with the boys?"

"I'm not sure. Diane handed Sydney to Lisa. She searched in the diaper bag. She withdrew a plastic bag that contained a soiled diaper. She handed it to the doctor."

He inspected it. Then he examined each boy. "I know Skye has all the symptoms, but I want to run tests on both boys."

"May I ask what you're looking for?"

"I'm ordering some blood tests but let's wait and see the results before I start guessing. In the mean time, I want to keep both boys."

"Why? You said Sydney seemed fine."

"He does but I want to keep both boys."

"Why don't you go home and get a good night sleep. I'll see you in the morning."

"Is it possible that I could spend the night?"

"I don't see why not."

CHAPTER 76

With the tests completed, Diane was anxious. She did not want to think the worse, but it was difficult not knowing about Sam's family medical history.

The doctor wasted no time explaining the tests results. "Skye has the Sickle Cell Anemia Disease trait. He hasn't formed the full disease but the probability is good."

"Please explain Sickle Cell Anemia. I don't know what that means."

"It's an inherited disease in which red blood cells, normally disc-shaped, become crescent shaped. As a result, they function abnormally and cause small blood clots. Since Skye has only the trait he may not have the episodes that are associated with Sickle Cell."

"Did you say Sickle Cell is inherited?"

"Yes. Only one parent has to have the trait in order for a child to inherit it."

She nodded her head, understanding completely that Sam was the carrier of this disease. "How is it treated?"

"Right now, there is no treatment because of Skye's age. I'll be monitoring him to watch how it progresses."

"Will he grow out of it?"

"I'm afraid not. Although Sickle Cell is incurable, it can be treated to the point that the pain crises associated with the disease can be eliminated. If Skye gets to the full blown disease, he can live a normal life with medication."

Diane was overwhelmed with the information she was told, but at least it wasn't as dreadful as it could have been. Her eyes welled up. "What about Sydney?"

"Right now, his tests were negative. He isn't showing any signs of having the trait. However, Sickle Cell may show up later as he grows older. Periodically, I will test him. In the meantime, let's take one day at a time."

The doctor waited a few minutes to give Diane time to ask questions. She said nothing.

Emotionally, Diane was drained. She could not wait to take the boys home. She was anxious about researching information about Sickle Cell Anemia. At least the mystery was solved about Sam's family's medical history.

She wished he had told her, especially when he knew her plans were to have the boys adopted. That was the only saving grace. They had not been adopted.

By the time Lisa arrived to help take the boys home from the hospital, she had calmed down, but was unable to hide her annoyance and anger. Her son had an incurable disease that would affect his life forever.

"Are you ready to go?"

"We're ready."

Lisa noticed that Diane had not shared what was wrong with Skye. Lisa and Diane rode in silence, except for the boys occasional babbling. She could tell whatever Diane had learned it was troubling her.

"What did the doctor say about Skye?"

"He definitely has an inherited disease."

"Are we going to play twenty questions or are you going to tell me what the doctor told you?"

"I'm sorry. It's disturbing to know your child has an incurable disease and there's nothing I can do to help him. He has the Sickle Cell Anemia Disease trait."

"He has what?"

"Sickle Cell Anemia and that's what's causing him to cry."

CHAPTER 77

Lisa pondered over how she could tell Diane what she knew. "Do you know anything about Sickle Cell?"

"Only what the doctor told me. Why?" When Diane glanced at Lisa, her face was frowning.

Diane became concerned. "What do you know that the doctor didn't tell me?"

Lisa answered Diane with a question. "Did the doctor say anything about Sickle Cell being more prevalent in certain ethnic groups?"

"No, should he have?" Diane was becoming annoyed and firmly she said, "For God's sake Lisa, tell me what you know."

Lisa exhaled nosily and thought, "Why me, Lord?"

After a long pause, Lisa answered. "Sickle Cell is commonly known to affect mostly black Americans."

Diane cocked her head to the side. Lisa must be confused, she thought. Sam is not black.

Neither woman said anything the rest of the ride to Diane's house. Once the boys were fed, changed, and put in their cribs, Diane and Lisa sat at the kitchen table, drinking sweet ice tea.

"I've been thinking about what you said and I'm confused. I would know if Sam was black."

"I don't know what Sam is. I only know that Sickle Cell is usually associated with black people."

"And you know this because?"

"Remember Diane, I'm black."

"I'm sorry Lisa. I keep forgetting."

"It's okay."

"No, it's not. I need to be more sensitive." Before Diane continued, a realization hit her.

She covered her mouth with her hand and whispered, "My sons are technically black."

Lisa smiled. "Yeah and probably so is their daddy."

A slight chuckle escaped Diane.

"What's so funny about that?"

"I'm not laughing about Sam or the boys being black. It occurred to me that every time I think nothing else can surprise me, something else happens to top the last life change. And, I'm never prepared."

Lisa started laughing.

"Why are you laughing?"

"I used to think your life was like a soap opera, but now I'm thinking you would be better suited to be a guest on the Jerry Springer Show."

"Thanks a lot." They laughed.

"On a serious note, I'm sorry about Skye. What about Sydney?"

"So far, his tests indicate he doesn't have the trait."

"When are you going to tell Sam?"

"I don't know. I can only deal with one thing at a time and Sam is the least of my worries."

"I hear what you're saying, but eventually you're going to have to discuss this with him."

"First I want to research the disease and understand what my son has and what I need to do. Then I'll talk to Sam."

CHAPTER 78

Although Les was satisfied that everything was normal next door, Cee had doubts. She was curious and wanted to know more about her neighbor.

"Cee, what's wrong with you? You seem a little jittery."

"I probably shouldn't have had two cups of regular coffee."

"Well, it's time for me to leave. I'll be back in about two hours. Remember, I'm golfing at Saddlebrook." He gave her a kiss.

"Have a good time golfing. Hit the ball straight."

Sometimes, Les had a habit of returning to the house because he had forgotten something. Cee waited ten minutes before going into the garage.

She pulled and tugged. The ladder wouldn't budge. It was heavier than she had expected.

Frustrated, she went back inside the house and plopped down in the over-stuffed chair. Just as she felt defeated, she straightened up. She had an idea.

She dragged a chair outside and placed it as close as possible to the fence that divided the two houses. With care, she climbed up on it. She stood on her tiptoes.

"I can't see a darn thing." She stepped down and carried the chair back inside.

If Cee was to find out what her neighbor was up to, she needed to get inside the back yard. She glanced at her watch. She did not have much time before Les would return.

Before leaving the house, she scribbled a quick note to him, explaining where she was. It was a lie. Not to draw attention to herself, she walked as if she was out for her daily exercise.

At the edge of Diane's driveway, she slowed her steps. She looked to the right and to the left. When she saw no one, she hurried up the sidewalk. Standing at the storm door, she placed her ear up to it. She heard nothing.

Before walking to the fence, she glanced over her shoulder. No one was in sight.

Again, she looked toward the street no one was still in sight. Her steps were quick as she approached the fence. Her hand trembled as she touched the door handle. Her eyes widened. It was unlocked. At least by police standards, she could not be arrested for breaking and entering. The only crime she was committing was trespassing.

Her legs wobbled and the hairs on her neck stood edge as she pushed the door open. She crept up to the window nearest her, cupping her hands on each side of her face, she peeped in.

Next, she eased up to the sliding glass doors, put her face close when she finished her inspection of the last window, she walked back home.

As she punched in the code to open her garage door, she turned around. She watched Les pull into the driveway.

Cee waved. She waited until he parked the golf cart. As he took off his golf shoes, he eyed her suspiciously.

"You're acting like a teenager who was caught breaking curfew. What were you up to while I was gone?"

Lowering her eyes and in a low murmur, she said, "Nothing."

They went inside the house. Les' voice accused, "I don't believe you, Cee. What have you been up to?"

Cee's lower lip quivered. "Don't be mad at me." She closed her eyes and whispered, "I went next door and managed to get into the back yard."

"You did what? Have you lost your mind?"

The corners of her mouth turned down as she replied. "No one was home."

"That's no excuse for acting like a Peeping Tom. What would have happened if one of the neighbors called the police?"

"I was careful." Pouting, she said, "I wanted to see inside her house, but I didn't find out anything."

"Why was that?"

Cee put her hands on her hip and mocked, "I thought you weren't interested?"

"I'm not but since you took such a risk, you might as well tell me what you found out?"

"I saw nothing. All the windows and the sliding glass doors are covered with a dark tint. From the outside, you can't see inside. Nothing, nada."

"Maybe she's telling you how much she values her privacy."

"Or maybe, she's doing something illegal or immoral." Cee squinted and pursed her lips. "I'm going to find out what's going on next door if it kills me."

CHAPTER 79

Several days passed and Sam had not talked to or seen Diane. He tried calling her and had left several messages but she had not returned his calls. He decided to stop by her house unannounced.

He smiled as he recalled what happened when he pulled into Diane's driveway. Before he could get out his car, a robust woman, probably in her early to mid-seventies, was hurrying across the lawn. For some reason, Mrs. Santa Claus came to mind when he climbed out of the car as she stood in front of him.

"Hello." She stuck her pudgy hand out and said, "My name is Cee Tyson. Who might you be?"

To avoid laughing, Sam coughed to clear his throat. Sam shook her hand and returned the greeting.

"Hello. My name is Sam Childers."

"Are you here to see Mrs. Benson?"

"Yes."

"Well, she's not home."

"Excuse me."

"I've been over to her house several times today and she didn't answer the door. I also noticed last night that none of her inside lights came on after dark."

The woman had thrown Sam off guard. He didn't know what to say. The woman stared at him and before he could respond, she began asking him an array of questions. "How do you know Mrs. Benson? Do you live in The Villages? Are you related to her?"

When she paused to catch her breath and waited to hear his answers, Sam dodged her questions by climbing inside the car.

"It has been a pleasure meeting you, but I'm late for an appointment. If you see Mrs. Benson, you can tell her I stopped by."

Cee's mouth was open as she watched Mr. Childers back out the driveway.

He could laugh now but then it wasn't funny. He was still trying to locate Diane. If anyone knew where she was, Lisa would. Sam called her several times, but got the answering machine. He left messages for Lisa but she had not returned his calls.

The only other person he could call was Patrick. He didn't have his telephone number.

Sam was frustrated from not hearing from Diane. Taking matters into his hands, he decided to pay her another unexpected visit.

When he parked his car, he waited, glanced around to see if Diane's friendly neighbor was anywhere nearby before getting out of his car. When he emerged from the car, he hurried up the sidewalk.

He rang the doorbell several times and was about to leave when the door opened. He smiled, but Diane's greeting was less than cordial and somewhat formal.

"Hello Mr. Childers. Please come in." When he walked inside, she told him to have a seat.

She walked to the kitchen and asked, "Would you like something to drink?"

"No thank you."

Diane had a glass in her hand when she joined him. Instead of sitting on the sofa, she sat in a chair facing him. After sipping her drink, she put the glass down and glared at him.

Sam wondered why Diane had such a scowl on her face. He was the one who should have been angry. When Sam began to talk, he didn't want to match Diane's expression.

In a non-confrontational voice, he said, "I've been worried about you and the boys. Why didn't you return my calls?"

"I've been at the hospital."

"Are you okay? Or is something wrong with one of the boys?" Sam's voice became loud. "Why didn't you call me?"

"I can explain."

Sam shook his head. "I can't believe you didn't call me. What possible explanation can you justify for not calling me?"

"Please calm down, before you wake up the boys."

"I'm sorry but you can understand why I'm upset?"

"Yes, but let me explain." Diane sipped her drink before she started. "As I said, several days ago, Skye was sick." She hedged the truth. "He didn't seem to be getting better and I made the decision to take him to the hospital. I didn't call you because it was late and I know how early you have to get up to go to work. I didn't want to bother you."

Sam looked at Diane in disbelief. "That's no excuse. Even if I get up early, you could have called." He shook his head. "This is what you always do."

"Please lower your voice. The boys will hear you."

Sam lowered his voice. "Fine but it's hard to remain calm when you continue to make decisions about our children."

Diane's voice rose. "Maybe I was wrong but I find it difficult to depend on someone who can't be truthful."

CHAPTER 80

Sam ran his fingers through his hair and shrugged. "I have no idea what you're talking about?"

Diane threw up her hands. "How can you sit there, look me in my face and lie."

"What am I supposed to be lying about?"

"Come on Sam."

For several minutes, they sat in awkward silence. Sam was the first to speak. "You're turning this all around. Regardless of what you think I'm hiding, there's no excuse for you not calling me about Skye."

"Let's not argue about something that doesn't matter. It's over. Maybe I should have called you but I didn't." Diane persisted. "I want you to tell me about your family's medical history."

"I have no idea what you're talking about?"

"The heck you don't. Our child has the inherited disease called Sickle Cell Anemia. Does that help you understand what I'm talking about?"

Sam lowered his head and avoided Diane's probing stare. "Maybe he inherited it from your side of the family."

"I don't think so."

To be truthful, Sam had no idea whether someone in his family had Sickle Cell, but it's possible.

"Why are you sure that it's my family and not mine?"

"I've researched my family tree and as far as I know the disease is not a part of our DNA."

Sam thought, "She knows about Sickle Cell's origin. He had no idea where to begin. Trying to explain his family to Diane was not going to be easy. He ran his hand over his face.

"I'm waiting, Sam."

"You're accusing me of something I know nothing about." Sam exhaled. "Listen, I bet you don't know everything about your family medical history."

Diane could not believe how clever Sam was at avoiding her questions. "You're right but I think I would know if my family had a hereditary disease."

Sam wanted to disagree but he saw no reason to counter what Diane had said. As far as he was concerned she had not answered his question about why she did not call him about Skye.

Diane inhaled and exhaled. "Skye has Sickle Cell Anemia. What do you know about the disease?"

"Not much. Why?"

Diane responded through clenched teeth. "Do you know that it only affects certain ethnic groups and that it's inherited?"

"I guess I knew it was an inherited disease."

Diane thought, "Maybe Sam doesn't know whether anyone in his family has Sickle Cell. Perhaps a distant relative, like a great-great-great-great grandfather or grandmother was black and no one knew it. It's been a secret until know."

She tried another approach. "I'm sorry."

"About what?"

"I accused you of lying. I thought you were trying to hide information about your family, especially your family's medical history. You're right, it's impossible for a person to know everything about their family. However, something isn't right and I think you are hiding something about your family."

Sam closed his eyes. Should he continue the lie? With the birth of the boys, Diane deserves the truth but where would he start? How much should he tell her?

Diane watched him. His facial expression was one of someone who looked as if they were in pain.

She reached out and touched his hand. "Are you okay?"

He opened his eyes. "I'm fine." He leaned forward and said, "I want to tell you about my family but it's complicated."

"It might seem that way to you but every family has things they don't like to discuss. You know what I mean—the uncle who's in prison, the cousin who's homosexual or the aunt who has three children by three different men."

Sam smiled. He wished what he had to tell her was that simple.

CHAPTER 81

Sam wondered if Diane would be as understanding once she discovered the truth. His experience was that people could seldom handle the truth.

"Let me start from the beginning. My family has deep roots in Southern Maryland."

Diane was perplexed and interrupted him. "What does that have to do with …"

"Please let me tell it my way."

"I'm sorry."

"To understand my family, you need all the background history. Starting back to slavery, part of my family's bloodline began when the plantation owner had a child by my great-great-great grandmother. The child's skin was as white as the owner's other children." He paused, and glanced at Diane whose expression was still one of confusion.

"It didn't take long for my family to understand that lighter skinned slaves were treated better and were given the better jobs on the plantation. I guess that's when my family began to make decisions about keeping the color in the family."

Diane rolled her eyes. She did not want an education on slavery. She wanted Sam to get to the bottom line but she kept her mouth shut.

"You have to understand that with the end of slavery, things weren't that much better. However, if your skin was light or you looked white, things were easier. I mean, most white people didn't bother to question what you were when you looked like they did."

Sam paused and asked for a glass of water. When Diane returned, he took a sip and continued. "Years ago and even today, it isn't always easy for a black man to be hired, obtain better housing or an education. Skin color, with no questions asked was a ticket into the white man's world."

Diane's eyes widened. Sam had confirmed what Lisa told her. "Sam is black."

"In case you haven't been following my explanation, I'm saying that by America's law, I have one-fifth drop of black blood which classifies me as a black man."

Diane swallowed the lump in her throat. "That means that our sons are black."

"That's correct."

Diane huffed. "It would have been nice to have known all of this when we started dating."

"Why, was it important?"

"I feel as if I was tricked."

"Into what—dating a black man?"

"I'm not saying that, but it would have been nice to know the truth. Obviously, your family …"

"Leave my family out of this. I'm talking about you. Under normal circumstances you wouldn't have given me the time of day if my color had been a deeper brown."

"I didn't say that. I said it would have been nice to have known."

"Known what? You would have liked to have known about my race? I can apologize for not telling you, but it still remains that you're angry because I'm black and now you have black sons."

Tension hung in the air. Diane was uncomfortable. Why was she angry about learning about his race? She had taught her children not to judge a person by the color of their skin. Why was she having this reaction?

Slowly, Diane began. "I'm going to be as honest as possible. Until now, I never thought about dating outside my race." She raised her hand to stop him from interrupting her.

"For one thing, I was never asked out by a man of color." She paused for a moment, choosing her words carefully. "I'm not sure if a black man had asked me out, if I would have said yes."

Sam eyes narrowed. He folded his hands in a tent and leaned close to her. His voice was harsh. "Thanks for being honest. Lots of people say they're liberal about race until they're faced with the acid test."

"What does that mean?"

"In other words, black people are okay as friends, co-workers, or neighbors, but you don't want them in your family, especially when it comes to marriage and fathering children."

Diane fumed at his remark. Her voice had taken on a high-pitched tone. "That's not fair. Okay, I haven't dated someone from a different race, but I have two children and they dated people from other races, including blacks. I would have welcomed anyone they might have chosen as a mate."

Sam chuckled. "Somehow that makes everything okay. Listen to yourself. You sound like a lot of white people when they say, *"When I was growing up, I played with black children."*

Diane threw up her hands. She didn't know what he wanted from her.

CHAPTER 82

For several hours, Diane and Sam continued their conversation about race. At times, the dialogue heated.

"Diane, we can go round and round about this, but we need to agree to disagree. Race is still one of those subjects that evoke feelings most people can't even begin to explain. We may never reach a common ground about this."

"Where does this leave us?" Diane defended. "I'm not prejudice."

Sam hissed, "You have no idea what that sounds like when people say they aren't prejudice. The fact you have to say it puts doubt in my mind. It's like people who proclaim to be a Christian. Actions speak louder than words."

Diane hung her head down. She didn't want to agree with him but he was right. She was embarrassed as she recalled how she first reacted to learning that he was black.

"Sam, I hear you but you have to understand this is not easy. I'm the mother of two black children and I have no idea what that means. My world has changed forever. I can't even begin to understand what situations they might encounter as they grow up."

Sam ran his hand over his face. "What I suggest is that we let them grow up knowing who they are and where they come from. I don't want them to ignore either side of their heritage. I also don't want them to have race as a constant issue."

"Does that mean they will lie like you have all these years?" The minute the words escaped Diane, she wanted to take them back.

"Maybe I deserve that. However, I lived the way I was raised. I'm not trying to make an excuse but what your calling lies was the only truth I knew."

"How will our sons live?"

"Like human beings. Besides, I think today's climate is better. There are more children who are bi-racial then when I was growing up. I see no reason for the boys to tell people. People can believe what they want."

"I guess you're right. Maybe, there is far too much emphasis on color."

"You think."

"I have another question." Diane paused. What she wanted to ask was not easy but she had to know.

"What is it? You appear scared."

"If Skye had not been diagnosed with Sickle Cell, would you have told me you were black?"

Sam blew out air and ran his fingers through his hair. Before he answered, he thought about his deceased wife, Wendie. In all the years they were married he never told her about his race. For one thing, it never came up. Another reason for not telling her was because he learned after they were married that she had little tolerance for people who were of another race as well as those opposing her views regarding religion and politics.

He leaned forward and whispered, "Honestly, I don't know." He explained that he never allowed himself to concentrate on any particular race. He told himself he was of the human race. That's the only way he was able to live without feeling as if his life was a lie."

Diane's eyes began to well up. "It must be hard for you and I can't begin to understand your plight. But, I do know the boys are going to need you."

Sam gave Diane a slight smile. "It's been more difficult than you think. Since we're putting everything on the table, is there anything else you want to know?"

"I …"

"What is it?"

Diane did not want to upset Sam but she needed to find out everything. "Is there anything else I should know about your family that you haven't told me?"

CHAPTER 83

The Childers' family was not a subject Sam liked to discuss. His family's morals, conduct, and way of life was survival. Most people could not understand what his family has done and continue to do.

Sam's family was no longer a part of his life. Except for his sister and a few cousins, Sam had no contact with his family.

At birth, marriages were arranged. The parents selected who they thought would make the best match. For the most part, the children honored the marriages without question. He had been expected to marry his second cousin. His sister was destined to marry their third cousin.

When Sam's parents died, he and his sister decided not to be pressured into following family tradition. They were not going to honor the arranged marriages. Their decisions made them outcasts and were no longer welcomed in the family.

Sam asked for another glass of water. He needed more time to think. He was not sure how much he needed to share with her.

When Diane returned with a glass of water, she handed it to him. He took his time sipping it. He put the glass down and tried to find the right words.

"You have to understand, we're talking generations and generations of hiding the truth about being black. This is not discussed with people outside our family."

She sneered at his remark. "As far as I'm concerned, I became a part of your family when I had your sons."

"You might think so, but you're not one of us. What you don't realize is that my family's color survived by not marrying outsiders. It would be difficult to explain to someone who was not in the family. Most people wouldn't under-stand."

Sam hesitated and thought about stopping there, but he had come this far why not continue. "The passing on of white skin, straight hair, and other features was protected by our family marrying within the family."

"What are you talking about?" Diane's eyes widened. "Are you talking about incest?"

Sam focused his eyes on his hands and whispered. "My family doesn't consider it to be that. I mean fathers and daughters, mothers and sons, or sisters and brothers don't marry but it is common practice for cousins to marry. The elders of the family say it's no different than Biblical times."

Diane fought the bile from rising from her stomach. How could his family refer to the Bible to justify what they have been doing?

Sam thought Diane's face had turned a little green and might throw up. "Are you okay?"

Diane nodded her head. She could not speak.

Sam wanted to say, "*You wanted the truth and now you're having difficulty accepting it.*"

"The consequences of the intermarriages have resulted in some health problems among the children."

He stopped and waited to see if Diane had anything to ask or add to what he had explained. Sam wondered if Diane realized her mouth was hanging open.

"I have to say that was the real basis for me not wanting children. I worried about what disease or disability I might have in my gene pool and possibly pass on to my offspring."

"Excuse me. Then, you knew about Sickle Cell being in your family?"

"No. I'm aware of other diseases but I didn't know about Sickle Cell."

Awkwardly, Sam and Diane sat, avoiding each other's stares, lost in their own thoughts.

Sam knew from Diane's reaction he had told her too much. He wished there was something he could say to make her feel better but sometimes the truth is not always pretty.

Diane wanted to say something to let Sam know she was okay, a little shocked but she was okay. He had confided in her about his family and she was trying to process it all.

Sam changed subjects. "Before I forget, you didn't say anything about Sydney? Does he have Sickle Cell too?"

"Right now, Sydney's not showing any signs of it, but he'll have to be monitored."

CHAPTER 84

As Diane dressed, she admonished herself. What had she been thinking when she accepted Cee's invitation to the neighborhood breakfast? She should have canceled, but she did not want to raise any more suspicion regarding her life. Lisa agreed to keep the boys while she attended the gathering.

Before Thursday arrived, Cee surveyed the neighborhood. She wanted to know what they had seen or heard about Diane.

Cee's first visit was to Joyce Billows. She lived across the street from Diane.

"Good morning, Joyce."

"Are you going to the breakfast?"

"Yes. Why?"

"I'm curious. Have you met your new neighbor, Diane Benson?"

"No, I haven't."

"That's interesting. I would have thought that with her coming and going you would have met her."

Joyce knew Cee wanted to gossip. If she knew something about Diane she wouldn't have told her.

"I try to mind my own business."

Cee's hand flew to her chest. "Oh, I was just curious. She seems to be a loner but there's a hint of mystery about her. You can't be too careful. I read the police watch all the time regarding pedophiles and where they live. I was shocked to discover how many live in The Villages."

"Are you saying she's a pedophile?"

"Oh my goodness no. I was merely making a point."

Joyce rolled her eyes and chuckled. "What has she done illegally to make you concerned about her? Or, is she on the America's most wanted list?"

"Oh, you can laugh now but remember when I found the neighborhood thieves?"

Joyce said nothing but thought, *"You'll never let anyone forget it."*

"Does she go out much?"

"I don't know. I mean I see her coming and going but that's about it."

"You do?"

"Yes. Why are you surprised?"

"I guess because, I seldom see her car passing my house."

"What do you mean? She parks her car in the driveway."

"Oh. That's not Diane Benson's car. That's her friend, Lisa Henderson's car."

"Well, you know more than I do."

Cee talked about what was going on around The Villages and then she left disappointed. She had learned nothing.

Cee continued her quest to find out what she could about Diane as she went from house to house. The conversation was about the same. Most of the neighbors did not even realize Diane had moved in. One neighbor stated if she had known Diane had moved in, she would have invited her to the Friday night cocktail party. Others wondered why she had not attended the Friday night neighborhood cocktail social or the driveway party.

Cee had no answers for them. After talking with the neighbors, it only confirmed that Diane was a mystery to everyone and for some reason, she wanted to keep it that way.

Cee had another theory—maybe she was in the witness protection program. Anyway, Diane accepted the invitation to join the women on Thursday and she could not wait to have the opportunity to question her.

CHAPTER 85

Most of the neighborhood women rode together to the breakfast outing. Cee offered Diane a ride, but she declined, stating she might have to leave early.

All the women arrived about the same time. While they stood in line, waiting for the tables to be arranged, Cee introduced everyone to Diane. As one of the women started to ask Diane a question, the hostess interrupted the conversations and laughter.

"Ladies, excuse me. Your table is ready."

As much as Cee had tried, she was unsuccessful in sitting next to Diane. They were sitting at opposite ends of the table. Because of the distance between them, she could not ask her a single question.

Cee watched Diane and Joyce Billows. Their conversation seemed lively. Cee noticed that whatever they were discussing it was causing them to laugh often.

To Diane's surprise, she was enjoying herself. She learned that her neighbor, Joyce, did not like Cee any better than she did. Diane hoped their voices were not carrying because Joyce was saying some unkind things about Cee.

Joyce leaned into Diane and whispered, "When I first moved in, Cee was a regular visitor. She was like ants. They invade your house unnoticed and to get rid of them was next to impossible." They laughed before Joyce continued.

"Cee is nice, helpful, and of course she has an unbelievable talent for baking, but that does not make up for her nosiest. And she likes to be bossy."

Diane did not want to be known as a neighbor who gossiped, therefore she listened more than she added to the conversation. A tinge of guilt did cause Diane some discomfort because she laughed at some of Joyce's cruel remarks about Cee.

When the breakfast ended, Diane was invited back. She thanked Cee for asking her and told the women she would join them again.

Cee was in her car and was waiting for Diane. When Diane got in her car and pulled out of the parking lot, Cee followed her. The reason Diane told Cee they could not ride together was because she had an appointment. Another lie, Diane was on her way home.

When Diane turned the corner to their street, Cee blew the car horn. Cee watched Diane glance in the rear view mirror. Cee waved and was saying something. Diane did not have a clue as to what she wanted.

When Diane reached her driveway, Cee blew the horn and was waving again. Diane parked the car and got out. She exhaled as she waited for Cee.

Cee drove into her driveway, parked, got out her car and walked over to Diane.

"I'm glad you came this morning. You looked like you had a good time."

"I did have a good time. Thanks for inviting me. I was glad I was able to meet some of the neighborhood women."

"On Fridays, we take turns having a cocktail party. To see who is hosting the party, look for the color balloons hanging from the lamp post. This Friday, Roger and I are the hosts. I hope you'll come."

"Uh … I would like to, but I don't drink Cee."

"Oh, that's no problem. We might call it a cocktail party but we serve all sorts of alcoholic and non-alcoholic drinks. We usually have just about anything you want to drink or you can bring your own." Cee stared at Diane, waiting for an answer.

"I'll think about it. Right now, I need to go."

CHAPTER 86

The conversation Sam had with Diane had been uplifting, almost a cleansing. But, he knew it was overwhelming for Diane. In addition, Sam knew they had more to discuss.

He had not seen Diane since their last conversation. He wanted to see her but he was not looking forward to the discussion they had to have.

When Sam rang the doorbell, he was taken back. He was lost for words as he admired the clingy red dress that draped her shapely curves.

After dinner, Sam played with the boys while Diane cleaned the kitchen. She had already given the boys their bath. After they played with the boys together, they put them in bed.

"I don't know about you but I'm tired."

"I can understand why. You have your hands full."

"Thank God, I have Lisa. I don't know what I would do without her."

"How are Freddie and Donna doing with their babies?"

Diane's eyes were misty. "They're doing fine. I talk to Donna almost daily but I feel guilty from time to time because I couldn't help them the way they wanted me to."

"How much longer are you going to keep the boys a secret?"

"I don't know."

"What about …" Sam stopped. He wanted to ask her about her family but he didn't want to spoil the evening.

"What were you going to ask me?"

"It can wait for another time."

"Are you sure?"

"Yeah."

"But I can tell something's on your mind. Why don't we discuss whatever it is before it festers?"

"Well, do you have any secrets you want to share with me about your family?"

Responding, Diane's tone was snippy. "I'm not aware of my family having any secrets. If I knew I would be more than happy to discuss them."

Sam taunted, "You're trying to say you don't have any secrets. Maybe, I've asked the wrong question. Is there anything you care to share with me about you?"

Indignantly, Diane answered, "I told you, I have no secrets. I have no idea what you're talking about."

He continued to apply pressure. "Really, think about it."

Diane inclined her head slightly. She shook her head. "This is getting to be ridiculous."

"Fine but you have no idea what I'm talking about?"

"No. Why don't you tell me instead of asking me a thousand questions?"

"Okay, I'm talking about your ex-husband."

"What about him?" Diane scoffed. "I don't talk about him because he's no longer a part of my life. What else do you want to know about him?"

"What about his wife?"

Diane tried to remain calm and not show any emotion. She glanced at Sam.

He shrugged. "I now think you know what I'm referring to."

"Sam, please believe me when I say I had no idea your sister was married to my ex-husband. I didn't realize it until I saw the picture on the coffee table at your apartment."

Curious, she asked, "How did you find out?"

"When you told me your last name was Benson and you were from Baltimore. I put two and two together. But I wasn't sure. You confirmed my suspicions when I saw how you reacted to my sister's picture."

"Why didn't you say something?"

"I didn't want it to be true. Besides, I wanted you to tell me, but you never did."

"Since you knew, why did you continue seeing me, especially knowing how it would affect our families?"

"I wanted to quit seeing you, but …" He scratched his head. "To be honest, I should have broken off the relationship, but by that time I had fallen in love with you and you were pregnant."

"What are we going to do?" Shaking her head, Diane kept saying, "This is a mess." Why hadn't he been more responsible? He knew before Diane. The minute he suspected the truth he should have broken off the relationship. Now they have sons.

Diane asked, "What are we going to do?"

"I don't know. One thing for sure, we can't solve this today or even tomorrow. We're going to have to take one day at a time and address the problems as they arise."

Diane wanted a better answer than that, but like Sam, she had no solution to their problems.

"I think our first priority is our sons. Everything else is secondary."

"I agree with you."

Sam picked up Diane's hand. He loved her and wanted them to have a future, but he knew this was not the right time to discuss it. Can we make a pact?"

"What do you have in mind?"

"No more secrets."

Diane let out a slight laugh. "I agree."

CHAPTER 87

✿

Whatever was going on next door, Cee failed to find out. She hated defeat. To relax her mind, she decided to read a book. She fixed herself a glass of sweet tea and retreated to the lanai.

Cee sat in the lounge chair, picked up her book and started reading. As she turned the page, a familiar noise caught her attention. It was faint but the sound was from the direction of Diane's house. She closed the book and placed it on the nearby table.

In an effort to hear the sound better, she stood up, listened, and walked over to the dividing fence. Leaning close to it, she heard it again. Cee smiled and rushed into the house.

"Les," she screamed, "Come quick. Les."

Les ran out of the den. "What's wrong?"

She grabbed his hand. "Follow me."

"What's going on?" She led him to the fence.

Cee put her finger up to her lips and whispered, "Be quiet." They eased to the fence. She lowered her voice. "Do you hear it?"

"Hear what?"

"Shhh. Lower your voice."

Les heard nothing. He shrugged and threw up his hands. He turned away from the fence. As he started to walk toward the house, he halted. He cocked his head to the side and smiled.

He whispered, "How many cats do you think she has?"

"Cats." Cee groaned, "Is that what you think you're hearing?" She nagged, "Listen again."

Their heads were almost touching as they listened. Keeping his voice low, Les asked, "What do you think is making that noise?"

"I think it's a baby crying."

Les started to laugh and covered his mouth to stifle it. He shook his head and this time he did not hesitate. He left Cee standing alone. She rushed after him.

Once inside, Cee quizzed him. "Did you really think it was the cry of a cat or cats?"

"Cats meowing can sound similar to a baby crying. That's what it sounded like to me."

"Fine, my gut tells me it was a baby crying. I'm calling someone who will investigate my suspicions."

"Who are you going to call?"

"Neighborhood Watch of course."

❈   ❈   ❈

Neighborhood Watch had responded to a lot of complaints, but this was a first. The man rang the doorbell. When Diane answered the door, she made no effort to hide the boys.

"Hello, Mrs. Benson. May I come in?"

"May I ask why?"

"I have a complaint from one of your neighbors." He did not have to ask about a baby. Two of them were in plain sight.

"May I ask about the babies?"

"What about them?"

"Uh …" The man did not want this inquiry to be hostile. He changed tactics. "Are you aware of The Villages' rule concerning grandchildren?"

Diane could not believe it. Without her having to lie, he assumed the babies were her grandchildren.

"Yes and these are my grandchildren. I'm babysitting for my daughter. They're her sons, my grandchildren." She paused. She was repeating herself. She thought, "The sign of a nervous person."

With indignation, she asked, "I am allowed to have my grandchildren visit me?"

"Yes ma'am. However, I do have to remind you that you can't have your grandsons visit more than two consecutive weeks at a time and not more than 30 days."

"Thank you for the reminder."

Diane was about to close the door when she had a suggestion. "If you tell me which neighbor made the complaint, I would like to apologize if the boys' crying disturbed them."

"To be honest, the complaint was not only about the noise and I'll leave it to that. Anyway, I can't tell you the neighbor's name. However, I'll extend your apology to them. I'm sorry if I bothered you. Thanks, and I hope you have a nice day."

CHAPTER 88

After having the conversation with Diane, Sam made an appointment with the doctor. Even though he and Diane had not been intimate since the birth of the boys, he wanted to be prepared and make sure there would be no other slip ups.

Before going to the doctor, he called Diane. The conversation did not go as well as he expected.

"I didn't want to tell you until after the procedure had been performed."

"I appreciate you calling me, but don't you think it's a little too late?" Her attitude caught Sam off guard.

"I mean you could have called me when you were thinking about having it done. You know to discuss the options."

"I can understand how you might feel, but have you ever discussed your birth control methods with me?"

"Touché, I'm sorry."

When Sam hung up, he should have felt guilt but he did not. Despite Diane's feelings, he knew what he was about to do was a personal choice. He called Diane only as a courtesy and to keep his promise of not keeping secrets.

Sam sat in the examining room, waiting for the doctor to perform the simple procedure. The doctor could say that, but to him it was a delicate operation. One slip of the knife and there goes his manhood. Regardless of his fears, the vasectomy had to be done.

When the procedure was over, he had to wait thirty minutes before he could leave. Everything went well, and he could no longer father children. Children were something he never wanted, but yet he had been granted two beautiful sons. He loved them and would do anything for them.

While he waited to be released, he thought about Diane. Their lives started off with such ease and then it was as if they collided. The result had been a terrible accident with lasting after effects.

What he wanted more than anything was to have a life with her and the boys. He was not sure if she wanted a relationship with him. She had not been discouraging but yet she had not been encouraging.

Before any reconciliation, Sam believed Diane had to tell her children the truth about the twins and not some made-up story about adopting them. To give her courage, he would test the water by volunteering to tell his sister.

He and Diane had to face the truth and all its consequences if they were to have a future together.

When Sam arrived home, he called Diane. "My procedure is over and I'm doing fine. I have a few restrictions for a couple of days, but that's about it. How are you and the boys?"

"We're all fine. We had a pretty uneventful day." Diane noted something else in his voice. "What's wrong?"

"I think we should tell our families," he said, and waited for Diane's reaction.

"I'm not sure that's a good idea."

"What's your biggest fear?"

"That Donna and Freddie will never speak to me again."

"They wouldn't do that."

"You have to remember they're still upset with me about adopting the twins."

"Listen, your children are grown adults and they'll understand."

"No, you don't understand. Until now, you never had children. Just like I didn't want to lose the twins, I don't want to lose them either."

"Okay. Maybe I don't understand, but I do know they love you and with time, they will forgive you." He took a risk. "Besides, if we are to have a life together, we need to start telling the truth."

Either his comment went over her head or she chose not to address it because she asked, "What about your sister?"

"What about her?"

"I can't believe she's not going to have some sort of negative reaction. She's all the family you have."

"I'm not saying she won't react. What you don't understand is that this is minor compared to most of our family situations. What may cause a problem is your ex-husband. My sister might have to tell him things she would rather keep a secret."

CHAPTER 89

For almost an hour, Diane and Sam discussed the best way to tell their families. The one thing they agreed on was that it was not going to be easy for either one of them. Sam would tell his sister first.

Diane prayed she would not have to say anything to her children. She believed that after Sam told his sister and she told Fred, he would tell Donna and Freddie.

Despite what Sam told Diane, he was not as confident about telling his sister as he had led her to believe. After several days of practicing how he would tell her, he made the call.

When they left the family, they vowed not to take on their family traits and habits. A nervous laugh escaped him as he dialed her number. Before he heard his sister's voice, he asked for God's help.

"Hey big sis, how are you?"

"I'm fine. Something must be wrong? I hope it's not bad news."

"If I had some bad news I would not deliver it over the phone. Besides, I'm insulted. I can't call my favorite sister."

Joanne laughed, "I'm your only sister. What's up?"

"Nothing, I just wanted to talk."

"Right. I can't ever remember you calling me during the day to chit-chat."

"Whatever."

"Fine, I'm not going to argue with you but you did call at the right time. I just finished talking to Jim and he gave me all the latest family gossip."

When Joanne finished, Sam exhaled. "Whew. I see nothing has changed in the family."

"Yeah, things are crazier than ever. Now, why did you really call me?"

"You're right. I did call for a reason." He paused and asked God for courage. Then he let out a laugh. "It's kind of a family matter."

"I don't like the sound of this."

Sam inhaled and blew out a puff of air. "Do you remember the woman I told you about? The one I've been dating."

"Sure, but you haven't talked about her lately. Are you still dating her?"

"Yes, we're still dating. That's why I'm calling."

"You're not getting married, are you?"

He tensed at her flippant remark. In fact, he wished that was the reason he was calling. It would have been easier.

"If it will relieve your mind, I'm not getting married." He paused before continuing. "Did I ever tell you that she lived in Baltimore before she moved to Florida?"

"No."

"Well, she did and you know her."

"Why didn't you ever mention this before?"

"Well, because it's complicated."

Sam, you're scaring me. "What does that mean?"

"I never told you because her name is Diane Benson."

CHAPTER 90

Sam held the phone from his ear as his sister screeched like she had seen a mouse running across the floor.

"Sam, how could you? I thought you loved me."

"I do love you. When I first started dating Diane I had no idea who she was. I know it's complicated but it shouldn't affect our relationship."

"The hell it doesn't."

"Look, I don't want to argue but you're the one who had an affair with her husband."

"It wasn't like that."

"Then, what do you call it? You got involved with a married man."

"Okay, a minor point but this is cruel. I mean I knew Diane was bitter and vindictive but to date my brother. How low could she go?"

"It's not like that."

"You're telling me."

After going back and forth about the merits of what's right and wrong, Joanne started laughing.

"I don't see how you can find this funny?"

"The two of us is what's funny. We made it a point to break away from our family and look what's happened. I would say family traditions are hard to break."

Sam chuckled. "Yeah, it is kind of ironic, isn't it?"

"Seriously, Sam, you can break the cycle. You can stop it here and now. For everyone's sake, don't continue this relationship."

Joanne hoped her brother could understand that continuing to date Diane would do nothing but cause pain for everyone. What she did was wrong but what he and Diane are doing is more than wrong. It will be damaging. It could ruin her family. She and Sam were used to this kind of family intermingling. She had to convince him to stop dating Diane.

"Sam, I have never asked anything of you but I'm pleading with you. Stop dating Diane."

"I can't."

Joanne screamed, "You can't or you won't?"

"I can't because our relationship has gone too far."

"For God's sake, quit talking in riddles. What have you done that won't let you end this relationship?"

"Okay, there is no easy way to tell you.

"Diane and I are the proud parents of twin boys, my sons."

"Wait a minute." Joanne screamed again. "You mean to tell me that the babies she supposedly adopted are actually yours and hers?"

"Yes."

"Oh-my-God. I don't believe it. This is messed up."

Joanne became fearful. "Wait a minute. You didn't tell Diane anything about our family did you?"

"I'm sorry."

He heard Joanne sigh heavily.

Sam explained, "I had no choice. One of our sons, Skye, has Sickle Cell Anemia. I had to tell her."

He was curious, "How much does Fred know?"

"Not much. There was no reason to tell him about our mixed-up family. He thinks besides you and our two cousins that's all the family I have and I'm going to keep it that way."

"You can tell him as much or as little as you want. That's your cross to carry."

Joanne had to ask, "What about Diane? Will she keep our secret?"

"The only way she'll say anything is if the boys are threatened in any way."

CHAPTER 91

❀

The doorbell chimed. "Lisa, hold on for a minute. Someone's at the door." When Diane opened it, Cee stood at the door, smiling and carrying a basket.

"Good morning, Diane."

"Hi, Cee."

"Can I come in?"

"I'm afraid not. In fact, I was on a conference call. I really need to get back to it."

"Oh. Well, I can come back later. I brought a peace offering." She looked down and lowered her voice.

"I was the one who called Neighborhood Watch. You didn't show up for the cocktail party and I thought it was because you needed a babysitter for the babies you have living with you."

"Look, I really have to go." Annoyed, Diane explained. "I didn't come to the party because I was busy painting my bathroom." Diane closed the door.

"Lisa, are you still there?"

"I was about to hang up. Who was at the door?"

"Guess?"

"Cee."

"Bingo. The woman is unrelenting. She called Neighborhood Watch to report that I have babies living with me."

"Well, you do." Lisa chuckled and then turned serious. "Do you think she knows or is she guessing?"

"I don't know, but in another life I can guarantee she used to be a private investigator or a FBI agent."

They laughed.

"Where was I before the doorbell interrupted us?"

"You were telling me about Sam calling Joanne."

"Oh yeah. At first she was upset, but her concern is more about Fred. She doesn't want him to know about their family."

"You mean about them being black?"

"Right."

"Well, she might be able to keep it a secret for a while, but as you know, it will eventually rear its ugly head."

"You should know. I'm sorry Lisa. I didn't mean …"

"It's okay because you're right. My past caught up with me and it will do the same to Joanne. Let's change the subject. When are you going to call Donna and Freddie?"

"I don't know. Soon, very soon. Sam's putting pressure on me to make the call. I've told more lies than I want to admit as a result I think this lie might damage our relationship. I know they think I've let them down. After this, I don't think they'll ever trust me again."

"I think you're being too hard on yourself. When you explain everything to them, I think they'll understand."

"I wish I was as optimistic as you are."

❦   ❦   ❦

After Diane realized Fred had not said anything to the children she found the courage to call Donna. Since she and Gary adopted their son, she had taken six months leave from her job. When Diane dialed the number, she almost wished she would be out.

In a cheery voice, Diane said, "Hi, Donna. How's Gary II?"

"Hello, mother." Donna's greeting was chilly. "Everyone's fine." Under her breath, Diane heard her say. "As if you care."

Diane ignored the comment. "Are you busy?"

"I will be. It's time for Gary II to wake up from his nap."

"I won't be long. There's something I need to tell you."

"Don't you always. What's up now?"

Diane sighed. "I hope you can forgive me. Please try and understand that what I did was out of love for you and your desire to have children."

Donna was concerned. She did not miss the catch in her mother's voice. "What's wrong?"

The lump in Diane's throat grew as she talked. "I have two things to tell you and I'm nervous."

Donna's tone softened. "At times, I know I can be despicable and selfish, but I love you. You're my mother."

Diane's eyes were misty. She would do anything to have this conversation in person. She wanted to hug her daughter and tell her how much she loved her.

Donna was anxious. "Mother, please tell me what's wrong?"

"I'm trying." Diane exhaled and released the air she had been holding.

"Mom, you're scaring me. Please tell me what's wrong? It can't be that bad."

"Okay. Here is goes. Joanne's brother and I have been dating."

"You mean daddy's Joanne? The woman he's married to."

Diane whispered, "Yes."

"What?" Donna screamed, "Are you sick?"

"I didn't know it when I met him. By the time I found out, it was too late to do anything about it."

"What does that mean? What would prevent you from ending the relationship?"

"It's complicated."

"Why?"

"Do you remember the twin boys you didn't want to adopt and then I adopted them?"

"Yeah."

"Well, I didn't have to adopt the twins. They're my babies and Sam's the father."

Dead silence filled the phone, followed by the dial tone.

CHAPTER 92

❀

When Diane hung up the phone, she called Freddie. She hated calling him at work, but she wanted to get this over with. In addition, she did not want Donna telling him before she had the opportunity.

"Hello. Mr. Benson. May I help you?"

"Hi baby. It's mom."

"Hey." Freddie thought she sounded as if she had been crying. "Mom, what's wrong. Is everything okay?"

"Not really. I just finished talking to your sister."

"What's wrong with her?"

"I'm sorry. I didn't mean to imply that something was wrong with Donna." She paused.

"Are you on your way to lunch?"

"No. I have a project I need to complete. I'm working through my lunch."

"I hope you'll have time to eat."

"Mom I don't want to rush you, but I don't have much time. What's going on?"

"I want you to know I love you very much. I hope you can understand that sometimes when certain decisions are made its life altering and if I could turn back the clock, I would."

"Mom, if this is about you adopting the twins, I know I wasn't very understanding, but ..." Before he could finish his sentence, he heard his mother say.

"In a way it does have something to do with the boys." She rushed on before she lost her nerve. "They're my babies and your brothers."

"What?" Freddie almost fell out of his chair. "How did that happen?"

Diane chuckled. "The way babies usually happen."

Freddie's voice was sharp. "You know what I mean. I didn't even know you were dating."

"That's another problem. The man I've been dating is also your step-mother's brother?"

"Tell me I'm not hearing you correct. Please."

"I'm sorry honey but your father's wife, Joanne and the father of my twins are brother and sister. His name is Sam. I met him when I moved to The Villages. I didn't know until recently, he was Joanne's brother."

"What a mess. Does dad know?"

"I don't know, but Joanne knows because Sam called and told her."

Freddie exhaled nosily. "I can only imagine what his reaction is going to be."

"I don't care about your dad. I'm only concerned about you and Donna."

"What did Donna say?"

"She was surprised of course. To be truthful, I don't know how she feels because she hung up on me."

"I hope you're not too shocked. It's overwhelming for me too. I'm still trying to understand it all." Diane did not interrupt him as he vented his anger.

"I can't believe this. I mean you and dad divorce and now, you both have children. I have three brothers who are about the same age as my son. And to add to it, my father's wife and my mother's boyfriend are related. I can't begin to understand the relationship of everyone."

Bitterly, he said, "If you get married, your ex-husband will be your brother-in-law and you will be their child's aunt and dad will be your children's uncle."

He smirked. "You've given new meaning to the family tree."

CHAPTER 93

After Neighborhood Watch paid Diane a visit, she thought it was time for the boys to meet Cee. After their feeding and changing, she put them in the stroller and pushed it next door. When the door opened, Cee's eyes were as big as quarters.

"Oh, my. Who do we have here?" Cee was in awe. "They are the cutest little boys. Are they identical?"

When Cee stopped, Diane chimed in. "Hi Cee. These are my grandsons and they are identical twins. May we come in?"

"Please. Please, come in."

"Les, Les. We have guests."

When Les entered the room, he walked immediately to the stroller. He stooped down to the boys' eye level. "Hi there." He shook each of their hands.

When he stood up, he told Diane. "They're adorable. How old are they?"

Rather than answer his question, she explained. "These are my daughter's sons. She lives in Ocala."

Cee was curious. "I thought she lived in Leesburg." What Cee really wanted to ask, when did her daughter move, from Maryland?

"She does. It's only been a couple of weeks since she moved to Leesburg. You know what they say I was having a Village moment." She waved her hand. "Anyway, these are her babies."

"Do you keep them often?"

"Not really. Sometimes her babysitter has something to do and I fill the void. And from time to time, I keep them on the weekends to give her a break. They're a hand full."

"So, you only had to work this morning?"

"I didn't work today."

Cee was perplexed. "This morning when I stopped by, you said you were on a conference call."

"Oh that. I was." Perspiration rolled down Diane's back. "I was on a conference call, but I didn't have to work today. The call was scheduled and there wasn't anything I could do about it. Thank God, it was an early call meeting because I had agreed to babysit the boys."

She had to change the subject. She was rambling. "When you came over earlier you had a basket full of goodies." Diane's eyes sparkled. "Were there any left?"

"My goodness, where are my manners? What can I get you? Would you like a cup of hot tea or coffee or maybe a glass of sweet tea?"

"Whatever you fix will be fine." Cee rushed off to the kitchen. Diane focused her attention on Roger.

"How long have you and Cee lived in The Villages?"

"It will be one year next month. What about you?"

She regretted the query, but she started it. "Three years." She stopped. "You probably think I have a lot of senior moments. Let me start over. I've been in Florida for three years, but I've only been in The Villages for six months."

Cee's arrival was just in time as she placed the tray of brownies and cookies on the table. "Do you want tea or coffee?"

"A cup of hot tea would be nice. Thank you. Cee, your baking is to die for. Everything you've given me has been mouth-watering delicious. There's no way I could eat these every day or my hips would suffer." Diane smiled brightly.

Les patted his stomach. "Tell me about it. But wait until you taste her cooking. She makes the best meatloaf, mashed potatoes and gravy."

Les touched Cee's knee tenderly. His face expressed pride and affection when he looked at her. It made Diane wonder if that could be she and Sam one day.

"Exactly, what kind of work do you do?" Cee asked, as she eyed Diane.

"I do consulting."

"That covers a lot. What type of consulting?"

"I develop training materials for companies. The training is geared for supervisors and managers."

"How do you work at home and baby sit for your daughter?"

"As I said, I don't watch the boys every day. Besides, I have a lot of flexibility when I work."

"I'm sorry. You did tell me that."

Diane frowned. Cee did not forget and her curiosity was growing by the minute. Cee's mouth was open, prepared to ask another question, but Skye's crying interrupted her. Diane picked him up. He quieted down. Then Sydney began whimpering.

"What can I do to help?"

"Do you mind picking him up?"

Before Cee lifted the baby out of the stroller, she hesitated. Why did his features look familiar?

CHAPTER 94

✿

As Diane pushed the stroller down the sidewalk, Cee watched her. Curiosity caused her to wonder, "Who is the real mother of those babies?"

When Cee joined Les at the kitchen table, she shook her head. "That woman wouldn't know the truth if it smacked her in the face."

"I hate to admit it, but there is something a little fishy about the answers to the questions we asked her. She wouldn't make a good poker player. In addition, her body language was a constant give away."

"It's the tiny lies that usually trip people up. Les, I'm telling you, she's the mother of those babies. And, guess what? I know who the father is."

"You do."

"Yes. Remember when I told you I met a man who stopped by to see Diane. Well, I think that was her boyfriend."

"Wait a minute. How did you jump to that conclusion?"

"Well, if you saw the man, you would know what I mean. Those boys are his mirror image."

"Are you sure?"

"Les, I'm telling you. He's the father of those babies. I'd bet your next social security check on it."

"Why does it have to be my check?" They laughed.

Cee turned serious again. "Why would she be living in The Villages? More importantly how did she think she could get away with it? I'm going to turn her in."

"Wait a minute. You called Neighborhood Watch once and they believed her explanation. Without proof, they are going to think you're nosy and contrary."

Roger paused. "Did it ever occur to you that the man might be her son-in-law? Didn't you say the man was fairly young?"

"Oh shoot. I forgot about that. Poop."

"Well, one thing for sure, she did lie about a number of things. The question is why? What could she be hiding?"

"There could be a number of reasons for her actions—she might have kidnapped the boys, she's in the witness protection program, or she could be on the list for America's most wanted. Maybe, we should call the police."

"Quit letting your imagination run wild. How about if you believe her? The boys are really her grandsons."

Cee shook her head. "No. I don't buy it. "I'm going to find out, but this time I'll get the proof I need."

"How are you going to do that?"

In a low murmur, she said, "I don't know yet."

Cee busied her days by making telephone calls to friends who volunteered at The Villages' Hospital. She was waiting for one of them to call her back. In the meantime, she was spending time on the Internet, trying to find out what she could. Her search had turned up nothing. The telephone rang, but Cee let Les answer it.

"Cee, the phone's for you."

"Hey, Cee. This is Roxie."

"Hi. How are you?"

"Fine."

"I hope you have the information I've been seeking."

"I'm sorry, but I couldn't find anyone with that name giving birth to twins. I went back as far as a year, and no babies have been born at The Villages' Hospital. Have you tried the Leesburg's Hospital?"

"That's a possibility, but I don't know anyone who volunteers there. Do you?"

"No, I don't. I'm really sorry I couldn't help you."

"It's okay. Thanks anyway. I'll talk to you soon."

CHAPTER 95

The visit with Les and Cee had been more stressful than if the police had interrogated her. At times, it would have been easier if she would tell the truth. Diane begun to realize that lies sounded like lies. Her life was spiraling out of control and she did not know what to do to get it back in line with the universe.

She was waiting for Lisa. The boys had a doctor's appointment. Usually, Sam went with her, but he couldn't get time off from work.

Someone was approaching the door. It was probably Lisa. When she opened the door, it was a man carrying a box.

"I have flowers for Diane Benson."

"That's me."

"Please sign here."

Diane took the box from the man and was about to close the door when she saw Lisa pulling up to the curb. She left the storm door unlocked. When Lisa walked inside, her eyes were wide.

She whistled. "It's not your birthday. What's the occasion and who sent the long stem roses?"

"I'm not sure who sent them or why."

"Maybe they're from Donna and Freddie, congratulating you on the birth of their brothers."

"Right!"

"You might not be curious, but I am." Lisa ordered. "Stop putting those flowers in the vase and read the card."

Diane picked up the card and read it out loud. "Beautiful flowers to match your beauty. Love always, Sam."

"I didn't know you and Sam were back together again. I mean as a couple."

"We're not as far as I know." Diane blushed as she noticed Lisa's gleaming eyes. "Don't go there."

Lisa spread her hands out to her sides. "I didn't say a word."

"You didn't have to. I saw the twinkle in your eyes."

Lisa glanced at her watch. "We better get going or we'll be late for the appointment."

Later that evening, Sam called Diane. He really wanted to see her, but he was trying not to rush her. Since the birth of the boys, he wanted nothing more than to talk about their future. Nothing had changed how he felt about her, but he was not sure about her.

Most of the time they spent together was caring for the boys. When the boys were put to bed, Diane often invited him to stay and chat. At times, Sam had to remember that they were not in a relationship. He was in her life because they were parents.

Sam was confused about Diane's feelings because of the mixed signals. Sometimes she flirted with him and even made sexual overtones. Every moment they spent together made it more and more difficult for him to control his emotions. At times, he wanted to gather her in his arms and devour her with kisses and make love to her.

Despite her subtle hints, he was waiting for her to make the first move. He did not want to assume anything, nor did he want rejection.

"Did you receive your flowers?"

"Yes and they're beautiful." Diane gushed, "Thank you for thinking about me."

"You deserved them." He wanted to say more, but he didn't. "You've been through so much lately that I wanted to do something to let you know how special you are." He bit his lip to stop the words he wanted to add at the end, "*to me.*"

"You'll never know how much the gesture meant to me. When a man sends a woman roses usually it's because of a special occasion, the man's in the dog house about something or he wants to show his love."

Sam did not know how to take the latter part of Diane's comment. He changed the subject. "How did the boys make out at the doctor's today?"

"Everything went fine. I wished you had been there. When you're with us, they're calmer when they get their shots and they don't cry as much."

Sam grinned from ear to ear as he listened to Diane giving him compliments. Maybe there was hope for them after all. He hated to bring it up, but he did.

"How did Donna and Freddie take the news?"

"Donna hung up on me and Freddie wasn't necessarily accepting, but he was cordial. Without them saying it, they believe I've been irresponsible."

"In time, they'll come around. You'll see." Sam changed the subject. "How's my favorite neighbor?"

"She's nosy as ever. I thought that if I took the boys to meet her, she wouldn't be as curious, but that was a mistake. The minute Cee let us inside her house, she and Les bombarded me with questions."

"You probably did better than you think. I wouldn't worry too much."

"Are you kidding me? Cee reminds me of a hunting dog, she'll keep her nose to the ground until she sniffs out her prey."

CHAPTER 96

Cee was frustrated and disappointed. Usually, she was much more cunning in obtaining information. She was at a lost about what to do next.

Les was convinced that Diane had told the truth about the boys being her grandchildren, but he had doubts about other aspects of her life. He believed that if Diane were hiding something, sooner or later the truth would come out.

He kept saying, "If Diane's concealing something, she'll eventually make a mistake. Give her time. If she's like most criminals she'll become too comfortable and let her guard down or she'll begin to think she's above the law."

Cee agreed with Les, but she lacked patience. She wanted answers now. As Cee and Les continued to discuss Diane, several ideas came to her. She could force Diane's hand and help her make a mistake.

As Cee surfed the Internet, she came across a service that could possibly assist her. She would sign up for the seven-day trial subscription service that would give her unlimited access to search for people.

Primarily, the service was used by genealogists looking for relatives, adopted children searching for biological parents, and women searching for deadbeat fathers who were delinquent in child support payments.

Seven days should be enough time to discover the information she wanted. Intently, she scrolled through the various subject areas. She could not believe it. Nothing was sacred or safe in cyberspace. Anyone could obtain all types of private information about people such as birth, death, or divorce information.

She clicked on an area marked birth certificates and began to read. According to the instructions, she could order the boys' birth certificates by completing a form and paying the fee.

She rubbed her hands together and exclaimed, "I'm cooking with hot sauce now."

As she filled in the various boxes and reached the question about the boys' names, she stopped and scratched her head. Their names escaped her. Think, Cee. What were their names?

She yelled, "Les. Les."

"What?"

"Do you remember the names of Diane's grandsons?"

"Uh ... let me think. She never told us their names."

"Yes, she did."

Annoyance laced Les' response. "Well, if she did, I don't remember. Why? What are you doing?"

"Nothing." She hurried. "I was just curious." The last thing she wanted was Les coming to see what she was doing.

Cee had to find out their names. This was a major roadblock. She stared at the computer for several minutes. Frustrated, she shut it off.

Les was watching television when she interrupted him with a kiss. "I'll be right back."

"Where are you going?"

"Next door."

"For what?"

"I'm going on a searching expedition."

"What are you up to now?"

"Nothing that you should concern yourself with. I came up with an idea, but I need those boys' names."

"I thought you were going to wait for Diane to make a mistake?"

"I never said that." Walking to the kitchen, she asked, "Did you eat all the chocolate chip cookies?"

"Yes. Why?"

"I don't want to go next door empty handed. Since Diane enjoys my baking, I thought I would take a basket with me."

Cee opened and closed the kitchen cabinet doors, searching for a morsel of something sweet. No luck.

The banging noise was so loud Les got up from his chair and went to the kitchen to see what was going on. He stood in the doorway, watching.

"Why don't you wait and visit Diane tomorrow. It's not going to make a difference whether you go now or later."

Weakly, Cee smiled and agreed, but in reality, the clock was ticking.

CHAPTER 97

Since Diane gave birth to the babies and was working again, she had not been able to take time to go to her favorite place. She loved the beach and the ocean. Something about the water, waves, and sand that made her relax and seemed to energize her.

Before she took time off from work, she discussed her plans with Lisa, who had a suggestion. Although Diane had reservations, she gave it a lot of thought before making the call.

"Hi, Sam."

"Hi, Diane. How are you and the boys doing?"

"We're fine." For several minutes Diane talked about the weather, Sam's job, and Cee.

Sam was clueless as to why Diane was babbling. "I hate to rush you, but I was about to go to Wal-mart."

"I'm sorry. I should have asked if you were busy." She cleared her throat. "Before you go, I was wondering … I mean I know its short notice and I know you have a job, but I was wondering …" She was making a mess of this.

"What's wrong?"

"Nothing's wrong. It's difficult to ask you this question."

"Just ask."

She took a deep breath and exhaled. "Do you want to go to the beach with me and the boys?" I have a timeshare at Daytona."

She rushed on, "It won't cost you anything and there will be two bedrooms. You can sleep in one and the boys and I will have the other one."

Silence descended abruptly. Diane waited and thought, "That's why she did not want to ask Sam. Her biggest fear had been his rejection."

An uncomfortable quiet was all Diane could hear. As she considered what to say, Sam began speaking.

"I'm sorry for the long silence, but I was booting up my computer to look at my calendar. I don't see any meetings or commitments for the week. Guess what? I don't see any reason why I can't go with you."

"Great!" Sam could not see her, but when Diane heard his answer, her face lit up like a glowing candle.

❧   ❧   ❧

She knew Sam did not know what to expect traveling with two small babies and neither did she. The boys surprised them. They had been angels during the car ride.

The trip proved to be an enjoyable experience. If Diane was giving out gold stars, Sam certainly deserved one. He was patient and sensitive by making frequent stops and giving her time to feed and change the boys.

When they arrived at the condo, it was the boys' bedtime. Sam unpacked the car while she tended to the boys' needs. Once the boys were settled, Sam joined Diane on the sofa and leaned his head back against the pillows.

"I don't know about you, but I'm beat."

"Would you like a glass of wine?"

"That would be nice."

Diane poured wine into two glasses and walked to the lanai where Sam had gone. Before she joined him, she watched from the doorway. When she stepped outside, he reached out and took the glass.

"Thanks."

She sat down in the chair beside him. As they sipped their wine, they were both lost in their own thoughts. Sam placed his glass on the table.

"The sky is full of stars tonight."

"It's beautiful." She fell silent, unable to think of anything else to say.

Sam turned to Diane. "Have you thought about the future?"

CHAPTER 98

❀

Quietness invaded the small space while Diane pondered over Sam's question. Rather than answer, she asked, "In what terms?"

"I'm talking about you, the boys, and your living situation."

He paused and did not know whether to continue, but he did. "I guess I should have been more specific. I'm talking about our sons, me, and you or should I say—us." She kept looking straight ahead and he could not read her expression.

Diane avoided eye contact with Sam. She stared into the darkness. She was at a loss. How did she answer him?

To be honest, she had been too busy juggling work, the boys, and trying to hide the truth to concentrate on anything else. Her focus was getting through one day at a time without creating new problems.

She touched his hand that was on his thigh. Softly, she answered. "Sam, I've dealt with changes I was not prepared to deal with since my divorce and retirement. It's been overwhelming."

No tears, she warned. A lump formed in her throat, but she managed to continue. "If I had not had Lisa I don't know what I would have done. At times, I've felt nothing but loneliness as I struggled to make decisions that would impact my life forever. At times, I wasn't sure I wanted to live. To answer your question, I haven't thought about anything but taking care of and protecting the boys."

It was hard to tell with the dim lighting but Sam thought he saw tears falling from her eyes. The last thing he wanted was to make her sad. That was not the intent of his questions.

He took her hand and leaned close to her. He smelled her familiar sweet, citrus scent. He dropped her hand and gathered her face in his hands and kissed her tenderly.

Sam was surprised when Diane responded with eagerness to his kisses. He deepened the kiss. As she began to relax in his embrace, he pulled away.

Breathlessly, she asked, "Is something wrong?"

Sam's response was slow, sexy, and deep. "No, nothing's wrong. Let's go inside."

He stood up and grabbed her hand. He led her inside. Before proceeding to the second bedroom, they stopped and checked on the boys. They were sleeping peacefully.

They continued to the bedroom. Once inside, Sam pulled her close to him. He kissed her throat as her head tipped back. Warmth and shimmering energy flickered throughout her body. His mouth closed in over hers. He made the kiss linger for a long time. He did not want to rush her.

A slow increasing hunger began to creep throughout her lower body. Diane slid her palms under Sam's shirt. The smooth, muscled contours of his back felt amazing beneath her hands. She continued to explore his body as she glided her hands to the front of his chest.

As they kissed, his hands moved smoothly down the curve of her hips. Diane's body was covered with a rush of pure, intense sensation.

Expertly, he touched her as she sensed a deep, clawing need for him. She was dazed and panting as Sam did magical things with his hands and lips.

She groaned as he scooped her up and placed her tenderly on the bed. Leisurely and deliberately, Sam removed her clothes while kissing each exposed body part. It was all she could do to keep herself from screaming.

When he finished taking off all her clothes, he began stripping off his shirt and pants. Her eyes fixated on the fascinating sight of his body. He joined her in bed.

As he made love to her, the climax glided through her, as deep and unstoppable as a tornado. Tears cascaded down her face. Her emotions were in complete, mystifying chaos. The only thing that mattered was that she was in Sam's arms.

CHAPTER 99

The next day, Cee was ready to make her visit. She had a basket full of oatmeal cookies, but no plan. How was she going to ask about the boys' name? She practiced several different strategies, but everything sounded like she was snooping.

She could hear the doorbell ringing, but no one seemed to be at home. Before she turned around, she heard a familiar voice.

"Hi, Cee."

"Hi, Lisa. How are you doing?"

"I'm fine, and you?"

"It's a beautiful day in The Villages. I'm doing great."

Lisa did not have time to make small talk with Cee. Not to mention, she did not want to have to answer Cee's game of a thousand questions.

"Are you looking for Diane?"

"Yes I am." Cee raised the basket. "As usual, I baked too much and I thought she might enjoy eating some of my oatmeal cookies."

"I'm sure she would have enjoyed them, but she's not home."

"When will she be back?"

"I'm sorry. I should have made myself clearer. She's out-of-town. I'm here to pick up her newspaper and mail."

"I could do that and save you a trip."

"I appreciate the offer, but it's no bother."

Cee frowned. "I guess I should be going. When did you say she was coming back?"

"I didn't, but she'll be back no later than Friday. I'm not sure of her exact plans, but when I talk to her, I'll be sure to tell her you stopped by to see her." Politely, they smiled at each other.

"Please do." They stood for a few minutes, avoiding each other's probing stare. "By the way, doesn't she have the cutest babies?"

"You mean her grandbabies."

Nervously, Cee chuckled. "I don't know what made me say that."

Lisa eyed her and thought, "That wasn't a slip of the tongue."

"She brought the boys over to meet me and Les. We really enjoyed the little fellows."

With pride, Lisa agreed. "They are precious."

"Well, I hope Diane will bring them over again soon." Cee exclaimed. "I just love babies."

"I can understand why."

"Do you have children?"

"No. I don't. My husband and I were never that lucky."

"I'm sorry. Since you and Diane are close, are you the godmother?"

Lisa was taken back with her question. "Why would you ask that?"

"I just thought … never mind. I guess you're Diane's daughter's god-mother."

Lisa didn't answer her. "I have to go Cee. It was nice seeing you."

"Would you like the cookies?"

"I couldn't."

"Sure you can."

Lisa took the basket from Cee. As she began to walk down the sidewalk, she turned and said, "Twins are an exceptional blessing. I thought it was clever how Diane named the boys."

"What do you mean?"

"You know, how she picked similar names for the boys. I mean her daughter. I don't know why I keep making that mistake."

Again, Lisa knew Cee had not made a mistake. "I'm sorry, but I have to go. I have a doctor's appointment. I'll be sure to tell Diane you stopped by."

Head hanging low, Cee strolled down the sidewalk. She thought, "Girl, you've lost your touch. Any other time, you would have gotten the information you wanted and more."

CHAPTER 100

Friday night and Diane had not returned home. Lisa could not believe she would miss Arlene's birthday party. Lisa doubted Arlene would remember whether Diane was there or not, but it was the principle.

The old neighborhood was not the same. Diane, Arlene, and Kellie had all moved. Lisa was the only one still living on the same street. They had been a motley group, but they had developed more than a friendship. They were like sisters.

When Arlene's dementia worsened, her daughter, Missy moved to The Villages to care for her. She bought a bigger house and it was located around the corner from Diane's villa.

The party was bitter sweet. Missy had Arlene beautifully dressed and she appeared younger than seventy-five. Unlike other days, Arlene was lucid, talking, laughing, and enjoying her guests.

"Where's Diane?"

"She went to the beach. I expected her back today, but something must have happened."

"What about Kellie?"

"I've talked to her but I haven't seen her since Rogers' death."

Arlene did not seem to be bothered, but Lisa could tell she was disappointed that her friends had not shown up for her party. Regardless, Arlene and Lisa reminisced about some of their adventures and laughed until they were in tears.

Lisa enjoyed the party, but missed the old gang. That was one reason Lisa believed she drank one glass of wine too many and instead of trusting herself to drive home, she walked the short distance to Diane's house. She would pick her car up in the morning.

Sleep came easy to Lisa but the wine induced dream was causing her to hallucinate. Was someone trying to wake her? Regardless of what was going on, she was having difficulty coming out of the deep slumber.

Instead of fighting it, she laid still on her back, trying to separate reality from the wine induced grogginess. She remained quiet and listened.

Was she hearing chimes? Or was the doorbell ringing? The sound would start and then stop. She turned on her side.

Bang. Bang. Bang. The sound was loud. She eased up on her elbow. Someone was at the front door. The loud knocking continued and someone was yelling. "Mrs. Benson." The knocking and yelling increased.

The smell of smoke invaded Lisa's nostrils. She threw her legs over the side of the bed and sat up. With her head throbbing, she steadied herself. She grabbed her robe and put it on.

"Mrs. Benson."

She put her bedroom slippers on. She yelled, "I'm coming."

When Lisa unlocked the door, a firefighter stood before her. "Mrs. Benson, we need you to get out of the house." She unlocked the storm door.

"Is anyone else in the house with you?"

No. No one is in the house but me. Lisa followed the command and hurried outside.

What's going on? Where's the fire?"

"It's in the back of the house."

"What? What's burning?"

"Please, Mrs. Benson, step across the street."

When Lisa crossed the street, a small crowd of neighbors had gathered. Cee was the first person she spotted. Cee rushed up to her.

"Are you okay?"

"Yes."

"Where's Diane?"

"What do you mean?"

"Where are Diane and the babies?"

"I told you, Diane is out-of-town."

"But I thought she would be returning today?"

Before Lisa could respond, the firefighter approached her. "Mrs. Benson."

"I'm sorry, but I'm not Mrs. Benson. My name is Lisa Henderson. I'm a friend of Mrs. Benson. She's out-of-town."

"Oh. Well, you can go back inside the house. Everything's under control and we were able to put the fire out. Thank God, it had no time to spread."

"What was on fire and what caused it?"

"The gas grill in the back was on fire."

"How did that happen?"

"I'm not sure. An investigation will be conducted."

The firefighter was not addressing his comments to anyone in particular as he said, "Folks, everything is under control. You can return to your homes."

CHAPTER 101

The bright sunshine peeping through the blinds woke Diane. When she reached over in the bed, it was empty. She glanced at the clock and could not believe the time. She leaped out of bed.

She hurried to the bedroom to check on the boys. The room was empty as well as the condo. Rather than panic, she showered and dressed.

As she walked out of the bedroom, she heard the front door open. "Diane. Diane, we're back."

"Good morning." The boys and Sam brought a smile to her face.

"Where have you been? Why didn't you wake me?"

"Good morning. When the boys woke up crying, you didn't hear them. I got up, changed them, gave them a bath, dressed and fed them. I took them for a walk, allowing you time to sleep as long as you wanted."

"I don't know what to say."

Sam smiled as he teased. "Obviously, you received something last night that made you get the rest you needed."

Diane blushed and quickly changed subjects. "Did you eat?"

"No, but I bought some bagels, cream cheese, fruit and coffee."

They ate their breakfast on the lanai while the boys took a nap. Diane would be forever grateful to Lisa. She was right about inviting Sam. The trip turned out better than she had expected.

Maybe she and Sam could put everything behind them and have a new beginning. After all, no one's perfect and every day she tried to forget about the devastating and horrendous pain he had caused her. She knew God had given her a forgiving heart and that was what she had to do, forgive Sam.

After last night, she knew her love for him had not changed. If she loved him as much as she proclaimed, then it was time for her to release her anger, resentment, and hurt. What she had to remember was that forgiving him did not mean she accepted what he did.

As Lisa always says, everything happens for a reason. She did not want to give Sam a lifetime punishment because she had a difficult time forgiving herself for the decisions she had made.

"Diane. Are you okay? You've been quiet for such a long time."

"I'm fine. I was thinking about us and the boys."

"You must have been reading my mind. Before the boys wake up, I need to say something."

He rose from the chair and stood in front of her. Then, he got down on one knee and picked up her hand.

"I know I have been the world's worse example for handling crisis situations and reacting to relationship issues, but I love you and our sons." He fell silent.

Diane listened. She noticed he was taking great care in what he was saying.

"I can never make up for my past behavior, but I can promise I will love you and take full responsibility for our family. From the moment I saw you carrying that casserole, I knew you were special. You have enriched, balanced and given me a healthy perspective on life. Like many couples, we have experienced some difficulties, but I know that the quality of our relationship will determine the quality of our life. Our boys know they are loved, but they need both parents, as a family. I love you and I want you to be my wife."

CHAPTER 102

The week ended too soon. Diane could not have asked for a more exciting, relaxing, and refreshing week. She was about to embark on a new life, and she was looking forward to it.

Lisa was going to be upset with her. She had promised to call every day. Instead, she called the first night to say they had arrived safely. Diane's thought was—no news was good news. Besides, Lisa would have called if something had gone wrong.

After dropping Sam off at his apartment Diane drove home. They made plans to see each other later.

When Diane pulled into the garage, something nagged at her, but she could not put her finger on it. She took care of the boys, and once she put them down for a nap, she began unpacking the car.

After she finished, she would call Lisa and tell her about the week as well as the news. As she picked up the phone, the doorbell rang.

"Hey, Lisa. It's so good to see you." They hugged. "I have the most amazing news. The trip was amazing. Thanks for telling me to ask Sam.

"Your neighbor, she's a piece of work."

"Why, what's wrong?"

"Let's say, I'm glad you're back. You're not going to believe what I've been through since you've been gone."

"Let me fix us a cup of hot tea and then we can talk." While Diane busied herself in the kitchen, Lisa sat at the table.

"How are the boys?"

"They're angels. They traveled like pros. Lisa, I'm blessed." Diane carried the cups and joined Lisa at the table.

"Now, what's going on?"

"No. You go first."

Diane gushed. "Sam asked me to marry him?"

Lisa blinked away the tears. "I'm happy for you. I mean you did say yes?"

"Yes, I did. If you could see how Sam is with the boys. I know he acted like a teenager when I told him about the pregnancy, but I can't keep holding that against him. I love him Lisa."

"I know you do and he definitely loves you. I saw that when you were in the hospital and we didn't know whether you were going to come back to us."

"When are you planning on getting married?"

"I think we'll get married soon."

"Whatever you need me to do, I will."

Diane had an idea. "Why don't we have a double wedding?"

Lisa started laughing. "That would be different." Lisa turned serious. "Before we get carried away with wedding plans, I have an important matter to discuss with you."

"What is it?"

"As I stated earlier, your neighbor, Cee is getting out of hand."

"What happened?"

"I can never prove it, but I think she started a fire in your back yard."

"What? You mean deliberately."

"Yeah. I think she hoped the fire would prove to everyone that you have babies living with you."

"You're kidding?"

"I wish I was. Remember Arlene's birthday party?"

"Oh, my gosh. I forgot about the party. Did she know I wasn't there?"

"Yes. In fact, she asked about you and Kellie. Arlene was like her old self. We had a great time and I drank a little too much. That's why I spent the night at your house. Sometime after I fell asleep, a fire broke out in the back yard. Thank God, the fire did not spread but I had to leave until it was put out."

Diane shook her head. "This woman puts a new meaning to being a nosy neighbor. She's fanatical."

"I know, and that's why you need to be careful."

"I will, but under the circumstances, I won't have to put up with her too much longer."

CHAPTER 103

Cee stood in her driveway before she picked up the morning newspaper. She was surprised and curious.

"Les, where are you?"

"I'm in the bathroom." He made a face and thought, "I can't even go to the bathroom in peace. He finished and joined Cee.

"It's early. Why all the ruckus this morning?"

"There's a *"For Sale"* sign in Diane's front yard."

Les stood up and walked outside to see for himself because he knew Cee's mind had been working over time, trying to find answers to all her questions about Diane.

"I wonder why she's moving. She hasn't lived here that long."

"As a single woman, maybe she's scared. I mean that fire is enough to upset anyone."

Cee shook her head. "That's not it. I stand beside my first theory—she's the mother of those baby boys. She's afraid someone's going to find out."

"Well, if she's afraid, I can certainly understand. I don't feel safe knowing that someone might be starting fires."

Cee rolled her eyes. Les was not listening to her. "I'm not talking about the fire. I'm talking about those babies."

"I know, but I am. I'm curious about how the fire started in the first place."

"We've discussed this before. Maybe some of our neighbors' teenage grandchildren were visiting and they were up to no good."

"That's one explanation, but I'm not buying it. Things may not add up for you about Diane, but for me I'm more concerned about the fire and how it started and who did it. The fire department hasn't finished their investigation and I'll be glad when they do. If the fire was set deliberately, then maybe we need to move. The last thing we need is an arsonist living in The Villages."

Nervously, Cee added, "Is that what you think?"

"I don't know what to think, but I hope they catch the person or persons responsible. It was too close for my comfort."

Cee changed the subject. "I think I'll go next door to find out why and where Diane's moving?"

"You're not taking her any goodies?"

"No." Indignant, Cee said, "I'm tired of trying to be her friend."

Cee walked next door. As she strolled up the sidewalk, Diane's garage door opened up. She waited while Diane backed the car out. Cee waved and approached the car. Diane stopped and lowered the window.

"Hi, Cee. How are you and Les doing?" Diane was glad she did not have the boys with her.

"We're fine." Cee was not in the mood for small talk and got right to the point. "I haven't seen you since you returned from your out-of-town trip. Did you have a good time?"

"Yes I did and thanks for asking." Something made Diane say, "Oh and thank you for calling the fire department."

"Uh ... what?"

"Lisa told me you were the first to see the fire and called the fire department. I was lucky the fire didn't have a chance to spread or my house could have caught on fire. According to the fire department, the fire was set deliberately."

"What?" Cee's hand went to her chest. "I hadn't heard."

"Well, whoever did this, I hope they catch the person and throw away the key."

Cee gulped the huge lump that was in her throat. "Well, I'm glad Les and I was home. I'm glad I could be a good neighbor. After all, that's what neighbors do, take care of each another."

"You're right." Diane looked directly at Cee and added, "I've been fortunate to have you as a neighbor."

"That's why I'm surprised to see you're selling your house?"

Diane smiled mischievously. "Well, I'm going to share a secret with you." Diane watched Cee. Her eyes were bright, eager to hear the secret.

"I'm moving because I'm getting married."

"Married?"

"Yes, but I'm staying in the area. I'll be living in Leesburg."

"Who's the lucky man?"

"No one you would know."

Diane dismissed Cee when she put the window up, but not before she said, "I would love to continue talking to you, but I have to go. Take care and tell Les I said hello."

Cee stood with her mouth agape, as she watched Diane back her car out of the driveway and leave.

CHAPTER 104

Patrick had been angry with Lisa. He could not understand why she had to be involved with every aspect of Diane's life. Perhaps, he was being selfish in his old age? The last thing he wanted to do was to lose her. He also did not want to turn their differences into a situation where she had to choose between him and her friend. If he stopped to think about it, he would be the loser.

He was anxious about having dinner with Lisa. Something they had not done in a long time. Although he offered to take her out, she wanted to stay at home. As she explained it, "She wanted them to have the ability to talk in privacy." Her explanation made him nervous.

When Patrick arrived, Lisa greeted him with a hug and brushed a quick kiss across his lips. He tried to grab her but she dodged his embrace.

"What's for dinner? Is smells delicious."

"I've made scallops, mashed potatoes, broccoli and apple pie for dessert."

"Wow. This is better than anything I could get at a restaurant. Thank you for inviting me."

Dinner conversation was strained. He tried talking about the latest gossip and construction going on in The Villages but his attempts were met with a shrug or no response.

He cleaned off the table while Lisa put away the leftovers. He also put the dishes in the dishwasher and made coffee. He carried the cups into the living room as Lisa followed. They sat on the sofa.

Patrick talked while Lisa sipped her coffee. "This was nice. We haven't done this in long time. I could get used to this."

"I bet you could," she teased.

"I …" Patrick paused, ran his fingers through his hair and looked at Lisa. "I guess I haven't been very understanding."

Lisa stared but said nothing. He thought, "She's not going to make this easy."

"I love you with all my heart. I didn't know how much until you called the night of the fire. I don't know what I would have done if something had happened to you."

"I love you too." Lisa was near tears.

He shook his head. "I guess I don't do well when it comes to sharing you with others. Life is short and you were spending what seemed all your time at the hospital. Unlike you and Sam I did not believe Diane was coming out of the coma. I felt left out."

Calmly, Lisa said, "That was your decision. You're the one who stopped coming to the hospital with me."

He held up his hands. "You're right but then Diane was discharged from the hospital and things did not get any better. Everything was about Diane and the babies." Before Lisa could say anything, he rushed on. "I admit I handled this completely wrong. I should have communicated how I was feeling." He looked at her but she said nothing.

"Will you promise me something?"

"It depends."

"Will you tell me when I'm being unreasonable regarding you and your friendships?"

Lisa smiled. "Listen, I'm not going to let you take all the blame. I neglected you but I thought you understood. Diane was fighting for her life, Sam wouldn't make a decision about the babies, and there were Diane's children to think about."

"I know. You had a big responsibility, especially if Diane had died." He shook his head. "You needed me and I let you down. I should have been there for you. Will you forgive me?"

"Yes." She gave him a kiss. He returned the affection. She pulled away from their embrace. "Before I forget, I have some incredible news about Diane and Sam. They're getting married."

"When were you going to tell me?"

"To be honest, I don't know I was so mad at you that …" She didn't finish her sentence. Sam looked hurt. "You weren't thinking of breaking our engagement were you?"

Lisa did not response. It didn't matter now but in the future she would remember Patrick's fragile ego. "It's not important. Every couple has their ups and downs and this was ours. Anyway, the wedding will be in one month. There's a lot to do. I will be busy and my time is going to be full of wedding preparations."

He nodded his head as if he understood.

"I promise to talk to you every day. If I don't call, then you call me. Do we have a deal?"

"We have a deal."

"Before I forget, I suspect Sam might call you about being his Best Man."

"Are you kidding?"

"I think he wants you because I'm the Maid of Honor."

CHAPTER 105

When Sam heard about the fire, he insisted that Diane and the boys move into his apartment. It would be crowded, but he did not want to worry about their safety and he was not about to move in with Diane.

It was Sam who suggested they get married in a month. Diane thought she would not have enough time to plan the wedding and make all the arrangements.

"We don't need to have a big wedding. As far as I'm concerned, we could go to the courthouse." Sam said.

"Absolutely not. We can have the wedding at The Villages United Methodist Chapel."

"What about the boys?"

"What about them?"

"When we get married, people will be curious."

"I know, but I don't have a problem telling them the truth. The reason I couldn't tell anyone before was because I was living in The Villages."

"I know." He did not want to dwell on it, but if he had taken responsibility from the beginning, she would not have had to live a life of lies. He changed the subject.

"Are we inviting Cee?"

Diane started laughing. "You bet I am."

"Before I forget, do you think Patrick would be my Best Man since Lisa is your Maid of Honor?"

Diane's eyes widened with surprise. "He might but you'll have to ask him."

"Are you having Arlene in the wedding?"

"That's my plan but we'll have to play it by ear." With sadness in her voice she added, "I wish I knew how to get in touch with Kellie. I would love to include her too."

❦   ❦   ❦

While Diane and Lisa were shopping at Macy's for Lisa's dress, Diane asked, "Is Patrick going to be the Best Man?"

"He said yes. He was honored and looking forward to it."

Diane noticed a reflection in Lisa's voice that she didn't quite understand. "Is something wrong?"

"Not really. Patrick and I were having some problems that we had to work out."

"Why didn't you tell me?"

"You had enough problems of your own."

"That may be but I'm your friend. Do you want to talk about it?"

"Not really. We've worked everything out. We're okay."

"Are you sure?"

Firmly, Lisa said, "Yes."

Good because you two were made for each other. I'm looking forward to your wedding day."

"Speaking of which, have you heard from Donna or Freddie?"

"Yes, they can't make it. I didn't expect them to come. But, guess who is coming?"

Lisa's shrugged. "No, don't tell me."

"Yes. Fred and Joanne accepted our invitation. To be honest, I only sent them one because of Sam. After all, she is his only sister."

Lisa kept shaking her head. "This should be interesting."

"Before I forget, I heard from the church and the Orange Blossom Country Club. We're on the books. Guess what?" Diane gushed, "We're having a wedding."

CHAPTER 106

While shopping in Albertson's grocery store, Diane stood in the snack food aisle when a glimpse of a woman caught her attention. Quickly, she stopped what she was looking for and pushed her shopping cart in the woman's direction.

"Kellie." Diane yelled louder. "Kellie."

The woman kept walking. Diane hurried her steps and was within inches of the woman's heels.

"Kellie."

Slowly, the woman turned around. They stared at each other and ran to each other's opened arms. They eased their embrace and stepped away.

Kellie spoke first. "You look fabulous. Motherhood agrees with you."

Diane cocked her head to the side and looked inquisitively. "How did you know I kept my baby or should I say babies?"

"I have my sources." She smiled, "Lisa told me. I've also kept up with Arlene's progress. Every week since I left The Villages, I've called to check on her. I mostly talk to Missy. On Arlene's good days, I have talked to her."

"It's nice to know you've kept up with your old friends."

"You know me. I'm always full of surprises."

"You certainly are. Listen, I'm glad I ran into you. With all the niceties I almost forgot, I'm getting married."

They started screaming like teenage girls, jumping up and down and hugging each other. "When is the blessed event going to happen?"

"In a month. Will you be one of the Bridesmaids? Lisa is the Maid-of-Honor and if all goes well, Arlene and you will be the Bridesmaids."

Kellie hugged Diane and with tears said, "I would be honored." She used the back of her hand to swipe at the falling tear.

"Why are you crying?"

Kellie cleared her throat. "This will be the first social event I've attended since Chris …" She stopped and turned her head.

Diane rubbed her back. "What's wrong?"

In a low murmur, she said, "Chris died. That's why I moved back to The Villages. I wouldn't want to be single living anywhere but in The Villages. Besides, with no family, I wanted to be near my friends."

Diane didn't know what to say. Hearing that Chris died stunned her. She wondered what caused his death. She waited for Kellie to offer an explanation, but she said nothing further.

"How's Lisa? I called her when you had the babies but I haven't spoken to her since. Did she get married yet?"

"She's fine." Before Diane continued, she pulled out her cell phone and dialed Lisa's number.

"Hey girl. Are you busy?"

"Hey to you. I was sitting on the lanai, reading a book. Why, what's up?"

"Guess who I'm talking to?"

"I haven't a clue. I know, Cee."

Diane laughed. "No, Kellie."

Lisa sat up straight in the lounge chair. "You're kidding."

"No, she's right here." Diane handed Kellie the phone.

"Hi, Lisa. What a shock, huh? I'm back, living in The Villages."

"Well, welcome back." Lisa was lost for words and finally said, "At least you're back in time for the wedding.

"Hey, I've got an idea. Why don't we have a Bachelorette Party?"

CHAPTER 107

The weeks leading up to the wedding were as if someone turned the page of the calendar and before they could flip it back, the wedding date had arrived. Lisa was glad to have Kellie back because her artistic talent and flair for details made everything go better than either she or Diane could have expected. Not to mention, Kellie's assistance allowed Lisa to spend time with Patrick.

The day before the wedding, Kellie made all the arrangements for the Bachelorette Party. At first Diane said no.

Lisa was clear. "There will be nothing risqué. No male strippers or drinking hard liquor. After all, you're getting married and we want you to be beautiful." Everyone agreed.

Everything was on schedule. All the arrangements had been finalized and there was nothing else to do. Not that Diane was a superstitious person but Sam had been living with Patrick until after the wedding. Lisa told her that Patrick was having a Bachelor Party with some of Sam's co-workers and the men who were in the wedding.

"Don't look so worry. Patrick knows that he is responsible for some very fragile cargo and he won't let anything happen to him."

"Okay and I'm holding you just as responsible."

It was like old times, the four of them—Diane, Lisa, Kellie, and Arlene. Since everyone was to meet at Diane's in the morning, she suggested they have a slumber party.

Missy did not think it was a good idea. She believed the evening and the wedding would be too much for her mom. Missy agreed that Arlene could have dinner with them but she would have to skip the sleep over.

With that in mind, the women started their evening early. To everyone's surprise, Kellie hired a woman to give each of them a pedicure and manicure. After everyone had been pampered, they ordered Chinese carryout and the chatter and laughter began. Several times, Diane had to remind the women to lower their voices before they woke up the boys.

The women waited until Arlene left before Diane offered them a glass of wine. Diane checked on the boys to make sure they were doing okay. When she returned, Kellie was crying.

"What did I miss? Before I left to check on the boys, there was nothing but laughter. I wasn't' gone that long."

"I'm sorry. I can't help but think about Chris."

Lisa was curious. "If you don't mind, exactly, what happened?"

"He had a stroke. Since I liked the Regal Care Assisted Living Complex I placed him there. Within several weeks, he died in his sleep."

"Oh-my-goodness," Lisa paused. "Well, if it were me, I wouldn't put a love one in Regal Care if they paid for it. It reminds me of a scary movie with all the mysterious deaths."

"That's not true. An autopsy was conducted and Patrick died of natural causes. Besides, you don't know what you would do under the circumstances."

"I know I wouldn't use Regal Care."

"Well, I would use them again."

"If you want someone to die, chose Regal Care. That's what I think."

Ladies. Ladies, this conversation has taken all the fun out of the evening. Let's talk about something more pleasant."

Both Lisa and Kellie apologized.

"Let's have some more wine," Kellie suggested.

Lisa did not want to spoil the evening and agreed that this was neither the time nor the place to discuss Regal Care. Perhaps Kellie was right and the deaths were just that or maybe Lisa was feeling guilty because Roger pleaded for her to help him and before she could do anything, he died. Either way, if there was a problem with Regal Care, she prayed someone would get to the truth.

CHAPTER 108

On the day of the wedding, Diane was no different than other brides, beautiful, but nervous. Lisa tried to calm her down.

"What's wrong? This is what you want?"

"Without a doubt, I want to marry Sam. I don't know why I'm jittery." She looked in the mirror and put finishing touches to her make-up.

"Oh my goodness. Who has the boys?"

"They're fine." Lisa hedged.

"Okay, but where are they and who's watching them"

"Do you promise not to get mad?"

"Lisa, I'm already edgy who has the boys?"

Lisa let out a nervous chuckle, "They're with their Aunt Joanne."

Diane rolled her eyes and shook her head. "Oh well. She is their aunt. I'm going to have to learn how to deal with this and it's not easy."

"Don't worry about that right now." Before they could discuss it any further, a woman stuck her head in the room.

"We're ready."

"Thanks." Lisa gave Diane a hug before she left the room. She managed not to cry, yet. She whispered, "I wish you the best, be happy."

Cee could not contain herself when she received the wedding invitation. She showed it to the women at the Thursday Morning Breakfast Club. Everyone was all ears as Cee shared what she knew about Diane's move and the upcoming wedding.

When Cee and Les arrived at the chapel, they were greeted by an usher. "Welcome, you may sit anywhere."

"Thank you." Cee directed Les to one of the middle pews, up front. This would give her the advantage to see everything up close and it would be easier to take pictures.

When they sat down, Cee began to survey the chapel. Leaning close to Les, she whispered, "The woman upfront, I wonder who she is? She looks too old to be Diane's daughter but she's holding one of twin boys?"

Before Cee could explore the rest of the people, Les pointed at the men entering and walking to the altar. "Which man is the groom?"

Cee's eyes widened. "It's the man from Diane's driveway." Triumphantly, she said, "I told you he was the father of those boys."

"But you don't know that."

"Believe me. He's the groom and the father of those boys."

The music began and two women walked down the aisle, Cee did not recognize them. Behind them was Lisa. Cee snapped her picture. Shortly after, Diane began her walk down the aisle.

Cee dabbed at the corners of her eyes. "She looks beautiful." When Diane stood at the altar, Sam joined her and took her hand.

Cee whispered, "I told you he was the groom."

At the wedding reception, Cee could not believe it. She watched Diane and Sam as they each held one of the boys and introduced them to the guests.

When Diane and Sam approached Les and Cee, she was all smiles. Diane made the introductions. "Les and Cee, this is my husband, Sam and you all have met our sons."

Normally, Cee is talkative but for some reason, she wasn't able to speak. Les responded by shaking Sam's hand. "We are glad to meet you." Les shook each of the boys' hands, "Good to see you again."

As Diane and Sam left their table and moved to the next, Les was concerned about Cee.

"Are you okay?"

"Yes, I don't know why I was loss for words. That's not like me. Anyway, I'm happy for her. At the rate that I'm going, maybe I should hang a shingle out in front of our house—Investigator for Hire." She and Les laughed.

"I'm serious. I knew from the beginning Diane was hiding something and I was right."

"But you didn't piece it all together until today."

"You're right but that was because I didn't have enough time." Cee threw up her hands and smiled. "Besides, no one would believe me if I told them the truth." Her eyes twinkled as she leaned into Les and uttered, "I think this would make a good novel."

978-0-595-48378-5
0-595-48378-X